LARGE
PRINT
EDITION

RANDOM
HOUSE

Also available
in Random House Large Print

ANYTHING CONSIDERED

CHASING
CÉZANNE

—

Peter Mayle

Published by Random House Large Print
in association with Alfred A. Knopf, Inc.
New York 1997

Library of Congress Cataloging-in-Publication Data

Mayle, Peter.
Chasing Cézanne : a novel / Peter Mayle.
p.   cm.
ISBN 0-679-77432-7
1. Cézanne, Paul, 1839–1906—Fiction. 2. Large
type books. I. Title.
[PR6063.A8875C48 1997]
823'.914—dc21   96-48620
CIP

Random House Web Address: http://www.randomhouse.com/
Printed in the United States of America
FIRST LARGE PRINT EDITION

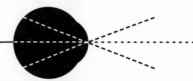

This Large Print Book carries the
Seal of Approval of N.A.V.H.

For Ernest

1

THE receptionist echoed the decor, a human accessory precisely in tune with the restrained, almost severe chic of her surroundings. Glossy and cool in beige and black, she murmured into the phone, ignoring the rumpled young man standing in front of her. A slight frown threatened the smooth mask of her makeup as she glanced at the scarred leather shoulder bag that the young man had put on her otherwise immaculately bare desk of polished sycamore. She put down the phone, pushing back a wing of blonde hair to replace the gold earring that had been removed to facilitate conversation. Her eyebrows, plucked to perfection, rose in two questioning arcs.

The young man smiled. "Good morning. I have an appointment with Camilla."

The eyebrows stayed up. "You are?"

"Andre Kelly. Are you new here?"

The receptionist declined to answer, as she unhitched her earring and took up the phone. Andre wondered why Camilla kept on hiring girls like this.

They rarely lasted more than a couple of months before being replaced by another polished clone—decorative, faintly unwelcoming, relentlessly blasé. And where did they go once they had left? The cosmetics department at Barney's? The front office of a smart funeral home? Or were they swept off their feet by one of Camilla's many friends in the lower levels of European aristocracy?

"Her meeting's running late." A finger flicked toward the far corner of the reception area. "You can wait over there."

Andre smiled at her again as he picked up his bag. "Were you always this unpleasant, or did you have to take classes?"

But it was wasted. The phone was already tucked beneath the burnished wing of hair, the murmuring already resumed. Andre settled into a chair and prepared himself for an extended wait.

Camilla was known—and, by some, admired—for her deliberate unpunctuality, for double-booking appointments, for manufacturing situations that emphasized her editorial charisma and her social importance. It was she who had broken new ground in the world of power lunches by booking two tables at the Royalton on the same day, shuttling from one table to the other—a nibble of arugula and endive here, a sip of Evian there—while she simultaneously entertained an important advertiser and a promising South American architect. It was a tribute to her reputation that neither of them was offended, and the two-table lunch then became an occasional part of Camilla's sociocorporate repertoire.

In the end, of course, she was allowed to get away with such displays because she had achieved success, for which, in New York, all manner of bad behavior is forgiven. She had rescued an elderly magazine from its lingering death and modernized it, changing its name, retiring its venerable contributors, instituting a zippy but socially concerned "Letter from the Editor," updating its covers, its typography, its photography, and, indeed, its receptionist and reception area. The circulation had tripled, advertising pages were increasing steadily, and the magazine's owners, while still losing money, were bathed in the reflected glow coming from a suddenly hot property. The magazine was being talked about, and Camilla Jameson Porter, for the moment, could do no wrong.

The magazine's rapid rise, while certainly helped by the cosmetic changes in its appearance, was in fact due almost entirely to something more fundamental: Camilla's editorial philosophy.

This had evolved in a curious way. During her earlier years, as an ambitious but unknown journalist working on the R and L (rumors and libel) page of a London tabloid with social pretensions, she had managed to acquire a wealthy upper-class husband—the tall, dark, and inconsequential Jeremy

Jameson Porter. Camilla had embraced his name (which sounded *so* much smarter than the one she'd been born with, which was Camilla Boot) and also his well-connected friends. Alas, she had embraced one of them too enthusiastically and had been caught doing it. Divorce had followed, but by then Camilla had mingled with the wealthy long enough to learn the lesson that was to serve her so well in New York.

It was very simple. The rich are acquisitive, and with a few notable exceptions, they like other people to know about their acquisitions. After all, half the satisfaction of a privileged life is the envy it engenders; and what is the point of having rare and costly possessions unless others know you have them?

This fairly obvious insight kept returning to Camilla's thoughts as she pondered her future as an unattached woman in need of a job. And then one day she found the catalyst that turned her insight into a career.

She was in her dentist's waiting room and had picked up a copy of a brightly colored gossip magazine, intrigued by the cover photograph. It showed an aristocratic and internationally known art collector, posing in front of his latest Titian with his latest wife. Why, Camilla wondered, would such a couple agree to appear in such a magazine? Her question was answered by the story inside. It had been written on bended knee, shameless in its flattering descriptions of the collector, his pneumatic young bride, and their art-filled, fifty-seven-room love nest perched on the most select hillside overlooking Lake Como. Many photographs—artfully lit and equally flattering—accompanied the gush of prose. Every word, every image, attested to the fact that this was an absolutely wonderful couple living a wonderful life in a wonderful home. It was a seven-page massage.

Camilla looked through the rest of the magazine, an illustrated chronicle of the doings of the underemployed section of European society—charity balls, perfume launches, gallery openings, the frothy distractions that provide excuses for the same group of people to keep bumping into each other—*quelle surprise!*—in Paris and London and Geneva and Rome. Page after page of smiling faces, vapid captions, bogus events. Nevertheless, as Camilla left the dentist she took the magazine with her, and she spent that evening brooding over the cover story. Gradually, an idea began to take shape.

Success is rarely achieved without a little luck, and in Camilla's case this came in the form of a phone call from a journalist friend in New York. All of media Manhattan, it seemed, was talking about the Garabedian brothers and their unexpected move into publishing. Having made several fortunes in nursing homes, invoice factoring, and waste disposal, they had recently acquired a group of companies that included a minor book publisher, a Long Island newspaper, and several specialist magazines in varying stages of decrepitude or collapse. The assumption was that the Garabedians had taken over the group for its main asset, which was a building on Madison Avenue, but there were rumors that one or two of the magazines might be kept alive and, in the words of Garabedian the younger, "goosed." Financial analysts interpreted this as an indication of significant injections of capital. And one of the magazines considered suitable for goosing was *Decorating Quarterly.*

It was the kind of publication you might expect to find, its pages curled and yellowing, in the salon of a long-deserted Newport mansion. It was staid in tone, dowdy in appearance. The advertisements, few and far between, were mostly devoted to curtain fabrics and faux-baronial lighting fixtures. Articles discussed the joys of ormolu and the proper care of eighteenth-century porcelain. The magazine kept its editorial face firmly turned away from anything remotely contemporary. And yet it had managed to retain a core of readers as it limped along making a marginal, shrinking profit.

Garabedian the elder looked at the numbers and was all for killing the magazine. But his brother was married to a young woman who described herself as a homemaker and who had read thrilling things about Philippe Starck. She persuaded her husband to consider a rescue operation, and the demise of

Decorating Quarterly was postponed. If the right editorial formula could be found, it might even have a future.

The word went out; the grapevine throbbed. Camilla, briefed by her friend, came over to New York with a detailed proposal, which she presented, in her shortest skirt, to Garabedian the younger. The presentation lasted from ten until four, with a two-hour break for a mildly flirtatious lunch. Garabedian, it has to be said, was impressed as much by her ideas as by her legs, and Camilla was hired. As her first editorial act, she announced a change in the magazine's name: henceforth, *Decorating Quarterly* would be known as *DQ*. New York watched and waited.

In the way of new editors making their mark, Camilla promptly invested a considerable amount of Garabedian's money in self-promotion. She was seen—appropriately and expensively dressed, of course—at all the right occasions, beaming at all the right people, the magic moments being photographed by her personal *paparazzo*. Well before her first issue of *DQ* appeared, she had managed to establish a certain level of celebrity based on nothing more substantial than social stamina.

But those countless evenings of seeing and being seen and cultivating, those dozens of follow-up lunches, were to pay off. Camilla quickly came to know everybody she needed to know—that is, the rich and the bored, the social mountaineers and, perhaps most important, their decorators. Camilla paid particularly close attention to the decorators, knowing that their influence over clients often extended far beyond advice about fabrics and furniture; knowing also the fondness that decorators have for publicity.

And so, on those rare occasions when one of the magazine's chosen victims showed any reluctance to have her home invaded by photographers, writers, florists, stylists, and numerous black-clad attendants with cellular phones, Camilla called the decorator. The decorator twisted his client's arm. The doors were opened.

In this way, Camilla managed to go where no other glossy magazine had gone before. In fact, her very first issue contained a scoop, a double triumph —the Park Avenue triplex (an Impressionist in every bathroom) and the Mustique cottage (three servants per guest) belonging to Richard Clement of the Wall Street Clements. A normally private, almost reclusive bachelor, he had surrendered to a pincers movement mounted by his young Italian companion (a neophyte decorator himself) and Camilla. The resulting article, twenty pages of honeyed description and luscious photography, had been widely noticed and much admired. *DQ* was off to a fine start.

Three years had passed, and by keeping rigidly to its credo—"Never, *ever,* a nasty word about anybody"—the magazine had flourished. Next year, even allowing for Camilla's expenses, it would make a noticeable amount of money.

Andre picked up the latest issue and turned to the pages featuring the photographs he had taken of Buonaguidi's apartment in Milan. He smiled at the memory of the little industrialist and his bodyguard being directed by Camilla to rehang the Canaletto in a more photogenic spot. As it happened, she'd been right. He enjoyed working with her. She was amusing, she had a good eye, and she was generous with Garabedian's money. Another year of regular assignments from her, and he would have enough to get away and do his book.

He wondered what she had for him today and hoped it would take him to the sun. The New York winter had been so cold that when the city's sanitation department had gone on one of its strikes, very few people had noticed. The whiff of rotting garbage, usually a potent negotiating tool, had been neutralized by ice. Union men were counting the days until spring, and a pungent thaw.

The sound of high heels on the polished slate floor made Andre look up in time to see Camilla clicking by, her hand tucked under the elbow of a young, bearded man who appeared to be dressed in a black tent. As they stopped in front of the elevator, Andre recognized Olivier Tourrenc, a fashionable

Parisian designer renowned for his minimalist furniture and currently at work transforming a SoHo meat-packing plant into a boutique hotel.

The elevator arrived. A flurry of air kisses—one for each cheek and one for luck—was exchanged. As the elevator doors slid shut, Camilla turned to Andre.

"Sweetie! How *are* you? How boring of me to keep you waiting." She took him firmly by the elbow and started to propel him past the receptionist's desk. "You've met Dominique, of course."

The receptionist looked up and offered a token rictus, which barely stretched her lipstick.

"Yes," said Andre. "I'm afraid so."

Camilla sighed as she steered Andre down the corridor. "Staff are *so* difficult. She's a bit po-faced, I know, but she does have a rather useful father." Camilla looked at Andre over the top of her dark glasses. "Sotheby's."

They were followed into Camilla's office by the senior secretary, a willowy middle-aged man armed with a notepad and wearing a deep, out-of-season tan. He smiled at Andre. "Still taking those heavenly snaps, are we?"

"We're doing our best, Noel. Where have you been?"

"Palm Beach. Don't even *think* of asking who I was staying with."

"I wouldn't dream of it."

Noel looked disappointed and turned to Camilla.

"Mr. G. would like a word with you. All the other calls can wait."

Camilla paced to and fro behind her desk, the phone cradled on her shoulder, her voice a low and intimate purr. Andre recognized it as her Garabedian voice, and he wondered, not for the first time, if their relationship was confined to business. Camilla was a little too overpowering for his taste, too much like a corporate missile, but she was undoubtedly an attractive woman, successfully resisting the passage of time with every available artifice. She was slender, just the acceptable side of skinny, her neck still smooth and unwattled, the backs of her arms, her thighs, and her buttocks lean and taut as a result of her daily six a.m. workouts. Only one part of Camilla was remotely thickset: her hair. Camilla's hair, dark brown, helmet-cut, so straight, so clean, so shiny, so fabulously bouncy, was a legend at Bergdorf's, where it was serviced three times a week. Andre watched it fall across her cheek as she leaned forward, cooing goodbye to Garabedian before hanging up.

She looked at Andre and made a face. "God, the things I have to do. He's giving an Armenian dinner party. Can you imagine?"

"You'll love it. Give you a chance to wear the national costume."

"What's that?"

"Ask Noel. He'll probably lend you his."

"Not funny, sweetie. Not funny at all." Camilla made a note on her pad and looked at the oversized Rolex nugget on her wrist. "God, I must fly."

"Camilla? You asked me to come in and see you. Remember?"

"I'm late for lunch. It's Gianni. I daren't keep him waiting. Not again." She stood up. "Listen—it's icons, sweetie. Icons on the Riviera, maybe a little Fabergé as well. You'll have to root around. The owner's an old Russian dowager. Noel has all the details." Camilla scooped her bag off the desk. "Noel! Is the car down there? Where's my coat? Call Gianni at the Royalton and tell him I'm stuck in traffic. Say I'm on my way back from a deeply upsetting funeral."

Camilla blew Andre a kiss before clicking off to the elevator, her hair performing its fabulous bounce, the junior secretary trotting alongside with her coat and a fistful of messages. Andre shook his head and went over to perch on the edge of Noel's desk.

"Well," Andre said, "it's icons, sweetie. On the Riviera. That's all I know."

"Aren't you the lucky one." Noel referred to his notepad. "Let's see, now. The house is about twenty miles from Nice, just below Saint-Paul-de-Vence. Ospaloff is the old dear's name, and she says she's a princess." Noel looked up and winked. "But don't we all these days? Anyway, you're booked in for three nights at the Colombe d'Or. Camilla's coming through to do the interview on her way to Paris. She'll be staying the night, so the two of you will be able to have a cozy little dinner. Just don't do anything I wouldn't do."

"Don't worry about it, Noel. I'll say I have a headache."

"You do that. Here." Noel pushed a folder across the desk. "Tickets, car and hotel confirmations, and Mother Russia's address and phone number. Don't miss the plane. She's expecting you the day after tomorrow."

Andre slipped the folder in his bag and stood up. "Anything I can bring back for you? Espadrilles? Cellulite cream?"

Noel raised his eyes to the ceiling and shuddered. "Since you ask, a little lavender essence would be very nice." The phone rang. Noel picked it up, waggling his fingers in farewell as Andre turned to leave.

The Riviera. Andre wrapped the thought around himself like a blanket before going out to face the frozen grime of Madison Avenue. A bitter wind, cold enough to split skin, made pedestrians flinch and lower their heads. The nicotine fraternity—those huddled masses yearning to inhale who gather in small, guilty groups outside the entrance doors of Manhattan's office buildings—looked more furtive and uncomfortable than ever, their faces pinched in a vise of frigid air, sucking on their cigarettes and shivering. Andre always thought it was ironic that smokers were denied equal-opportunity privileges and banished to the street, while their colleagues with a weakness for cocaine could indulge themselves in the warmth and relative comfort of the office rest rooms.

He stood on the corner of Fifty-first and Fifth, hoping for a cab to take him downtown. *The Riviera.* By now the mimosa should be in bloom, and the more hardy inhabitants would be having lunch out of doors. The operators who ran the beaches would be adjusting their prices upward and wondering how little they could manage to pay this summer's batch of *plagistes.* Boats would be having their bottoms scraped, their paintwork touched up, their charter brochures printed. The owners of restaurants, boutiques, and nightclubs would be flexing their wallets at the prospect of the annual payout, the May-to-September grind that allowed them to spend the rest of the year in prosperous indolence.

Andre had always liked the Riviera, the effortless, usually charming way in which it plucked money from his pocket while somehow making him feel that he had been rendered a favor. He was quite happy to endure the overpopulated beaches, the occasional rudeness, the frequently grotesque prices, the infamous summer traffic—all these and worse he could forgive in return for an injection of south of France magic. Ever since Lord Brougham reinvented Cannes in the 1830s, the coastal strip had been

attracting aristocrats and artists, writers and billion-
aires, fortune hunters, merry widows, pretty girls on
the make, and young men on the take. Decadent it
might be, expensive and crowded it certainly was,
but never dull. And, thought Andre, as the arrival of
a cab saved him from frostbite, it would be warm.

He was still closing the door when the cab took
off, cut across the nose of a bus, and ran a red light.
Andre recognized that he was in the hands of a
sportsman, a cut-and-thruster who saw the streets of
Manhattan as a testing ground for man and machine.
He braced his knees against the partition and prepared to assume the fetal position recommended by
airlines in the event of a crash, as the driver swooped
down Fifth Avenue in a series of high-octane lunges
and sudden-death swerves, cursing the traffic in a
guttural, mysterious tongue.

At last the cab lurched into West Broadway, and
the driver tried his hand at a form of English.

"OK. Where number?"

Andre, feeling his luck couldn't last forever,
decided to travel the last two blocks on foot. "This
will be fine."

"Fine?"

"Here. Right here."

"You got it." The brakes were applied with gusto,
causing the car behind to lock its wheels and slide,
very gently, into the back of the cab. The cabdriver
jumped out, clutching his neck, and reverted to his

mother tongue to deliver an agonized tirade in which the only two familiar words were "whiplash" and "sonofabitch." Andre paid him and made a hasty escape.

The building he reached after a brisk two-minute walk had started life as a garment factory. Now, as with so much SoHo real estate, its humble origins had been thoroughly concealed by several coats of gentrification. The high-ceilinged, light rooms had been subdivided, partitioned, repainted, rewired, replumbed, rezoned, and, needless to say, repriced. The tenants were mostly small businesses in the fields of arts and communications, and it was here that Image Plus, the agency representing Andre's work, had its headquarters.

Image Plus had been founded by Stephen Moss, a young man with intelligence, taste, and a liking for warm weather. His clients were photographers and illustrators who specialized in nonfashion subjects— Moss, quite rightly, being wary of the temperaments and complications involved in anything to do with clothing and androgynous models. After the early years of struggle, he now had a tight, profitable little business, taking fifteen or twenty percent of his clients' income in return for representation, which covered everything from career counseling to tax advice and fee negotiation. He had extensive contacts, a doting girlfriend, perfect blood pressure, and a full head of hair. His only problem was the winter in New York, which he detested.

It was this fear of freezing, as much as a desire to expand his business, that had caused him to take on Lucy Walcott as a junior partner. Nine months later, he had felt sufficiently confident in his choice to leave the office in Lucy's hands during that first, suicidally unpleasant part of the year, from January to March. She was pleased to have the responsibility. He was pleased to have the sunshine in Key West. And Andre was pleased to be working with a pretty girl. As he came to know Lucy, he found himself looking for chances to extend the relationship, but he traveled too much, and she seemed to attract a new and dauntingly muscular young man every week. So far, they had yet to see each other outside the office.

Andre was buzzed through a steel door, which led into an airy open space. Apart from a couch and a low table in one corner, the only furniture was a large, square production desk built for four. Three of the chairs were empty. Lucy, head down over a computer keyboard, was in the fourth.

"Lulu, it's your lucky day." Andre dropped his bag on the couch and went over to the desk. "Lunch, Lulu, a real lunch—Chez Felix, Bouley, you name it. I've just picked up a job, and I feel an overpowering urge to celebrate. How about it?"

Lucy grinned as she pushed back her chair and stood up to stretch.

Slim and straight, with a mop of black, curly hair that made her seem taller than her official five feet six, she looked far too healthy for a New Yorker in winter. Her skin color was halfway between chocolate and honey, a glowing dark caramel that seemed to retain some of the sunlight from her native Barbados. When asked about her background, it sometimes amused her to describe herself as a purebred quadroon and to watch the polite nods of incomprehension that usually followed. She thought that getting to know Andre might be interesting, if he ever stayed in town long enough.

"Well?" He was looking at her, half smiling, hopeful.

She shrugged, waving a hand at the unattended desk. "Both the girls are out today. Mary's got the flu, Dana's got jury duty. I'm stuck here." Even after her dozen years in New York, Lucy's voice retained the sweet lilt of the West Indies. "Another time?"

"Another time."

Lucy moved a stack of portfolios off the couch, making room for the two of them to sit. "Tell me about the job. It wouldn't involve my favorite editor, would it?"

A mutual antipathy had grown up between Lucy and Camilla. It had started when Camilla had been overheard describing Lucy as "that quaint little girl with ruched hair," and had grown steadily worse with further acquaintance. Camilla found Lucy distinctly lacking in respect and far too demanding on behalf of her clients. Lucy found Camilla arrogant and pretentious. For the sake of business, they managed to maintain a precarious, icy politeness.

Andre sat next to Lucy on the couch, close enough to catch the scent of her: warm, spiced with citrus. "Lulu, I cannot tell a lie. Camilla wants me to shoot some icons in the south of France. Two or three days. I'm leaving tomorrow."

Lucy nodded. "And you didn't talk about money?" Two very large brown eyes looked at him intently.

Andre held up both hands, a look of horror on his face. "Me? Never. You're always telling me not to."

"That's because you're lousy at it." She made a note on her pad, sat back, and smiled. "Good. It's time you had a raise. They're paying you like a staff photographer, and they're using you on almost every issue."

Andre shrugged. "Keeps me out of mischief."

"I doubt it."

There was a short, awkward silence. Lucy pushed back her hair, exposing the clean, delicate line of her jaw. She turned to smile at him. "I'll work something out with them. You concentrate on the shots. Is she going to be there?"

Andre nodded. "Dinner at the Colombe d'Or,

sweetie. It's one of her officially approved restaurants."

"Just you and Camilla and her hairdresser. How nice."

Andre winced. Before he had a chance to reply, the phone rang. Lucy picked it up, listened, frowned, and put her hand over the mouthpiece. "This is going to be a marathon." She blew him a kiss. "Have a good trip."

———

As the driver pulled away from the Royalton, Camilla reached for the phone, careful of her nails as she punched in the number. It had been a long but constructive lunch, and dear Gianni had been so helpful. She made a mental note to have a box of cigars sent to his hotel.

"Yes?" The voice on the other end of the phone sounded preoccupied.

"Sweetie, it's me. It's all set for Paris. Gianni's arranged everything. One of the servants is going to show me round the apartment. I can have all day if I want."

The voice became more interested. "The paintings will be there? Nothing in storage for the winter? None of them out on loan?"

"Everything's there. Gianni checked before he left Paris."

"Excellent. You've done very well, my dear. Very well. I'll see you later."

In the richly furnished twilight gloom of his study, Rudolph Holtz replaced the phone carefully, took a sip of green tea from a Meissen cup, and went back to the article he had been reading. It was from the *Chicago Tribune,* datelined London, and described the recovery by Scotland Yard's Art and Antiques Squad of Norway's most famous painting: *The Scream*, by Edvard Munch, valued at forty-five million dollars. It had been stolen in 1994 and found two years later in a cellar in southern Norway, wrapped in a sheet. Holtz shook his head.

He read on. A "conservative" estimate of the value of stolen or missing art around the world was well in excess of three billion dollars, according to the journalist, a statistic that brought a contented smile to Holtz's face. How fortunate he had been to meet Camilla two years before.

Their relationship had begun socially, when they had met at one of the gallery shows Holtz routinely attended in his legitimate capacity of dealer in fine arts. While he had been bored by the paintings, Camilla had intrigued him. He sensed that they might have something in common, and this was confirmed during an exploratory lunch the following week. Beneath the banalities of polite conversation ran an undercurrent, the first signs of a meeting of minds and ambitions. Dinners had followed, the verbal fencing had given way to something approaching honesty, and by the time Camilla had taken to sharing Holtz's four-poster bed, surrounded by the splendors of Holtz's Park Avenue apartment, it was clear to both of them that they were made for each other, soul mates in greed.

Dear Camilla. Holtz finished his tea and stood up to look through the window at the sleet slanting down. It was past four o'clock, and in the icy murk of Park Avenue, fifteen stories below, people battled for cabs. On Lexington, they would be waiting in sodden lines for buses. How agreeable it was to be warm and rich.

2

"DID you pack these bags yourself?"

"Yes."

"Have they been out of your sight since you packed them?"

"No."

"Are you carrying any gifts or other items on behalf of someone else?"

"No."

The girl at Delta's business class desk flicked through the passport. *Name: Andre Kelly. Place of birth: Paris, France. Date of birth: June 14, 1965.* She glanced up for the first time, to check that flesh and blood resembled the photograph, and saw a pleasant, square-jawed face under cropped black hair, a face made striking by the green eyes that were looking back at her. She had never seen truly green eyes before and found herself staring into them, fascinated.

Andre grinned. "My father's Irish. Green eyes run in the family."

The girl colored slightly. "That obvious, was it?

Sorry. I guess it happens a lot." She busied herself with the ticket and luggage tags, while Andre looked around at his fellow passengers on the night flight to Nice. They were French businessmen for the most part, weariness on their faces after their having to deal with the New York weather, the New York noise and energy, the machine-gun rhythms of New York English, so different from the measured enunciations that Berlitz had taught them.

"You're all set, Mr. Kelly." The girl returned his passport and ticket. "Can I ask you something? If you're Irish, how come you were born in Paris?"

"My mother was there at the time." Andre stuck his boarding card in his top pocket. "She's French. I'm a mongrel."

"Oh, really? Great. Well, have a nice flight."

He joined the line shuffling onto the plane, hoping that he would have an empty seat next to him, or a pretty girl, or, a poor but acceptable third, an executive too exhausted to talk.

He had just settled into his seat when he felt a presence hovering over him; looking up, he saw the encumbered body and tense, thin face of a young woman dressed in the standard corporate uniform of dark power suit and attaché case, a bulging black bag slung over one shoulder. Andre got up to let her through to the window seat.

The young woman stood her ground. "They promised me aisle. I always have aisle."

Andre checked his boarding card against the seat number, and saw that he was sitting in his allotted seat. He showed the stub to the young woman.

"You don't understand," she said. "I'm window sensitive."

Andre had never encountered this particular affliction and certainly didn't want to hear about it for the next seven hours. For the sake of a peaceful flight, he offered his aisle seat to the young woman, whose mood brightened visibly. He moved across to the window seat, watching as she arranged documents and a laptop computer in front of her to create the necessary business environment. Not for the first time, the thought crossed his mind that modern travel was a vastly overrated pastime: crowded, tedious, often uncomfortable, and almost always irritating.

"Don't you love travel?" said the young woman, her good humor now fully restored by her having had her own way. "I mean, getting to go to the south of France. It's so . . ."

"French?"

She looked sideways at Andre, unsure of how to respond. He nodded at her and opened his book. She returned to the contents of her laptop.

The airline passenger seeking a few hours of undisturbed silence is most vulnerable during the serving of meals, when feigning sleep is out of the question and hiding behind a book while eating is physically impossible. As the trolley laden with gourmet-in-the-sky dinners approached, Andre was aware of occasional glances from his neighbor, who had abandoned her communion with the laptop and seemed poised for another attempt at conversation. And so, when the inevitable piece of frequent flier chicken landed in front of him, he slipped on his headset, bent over his tray, and tried to distract himself from the cooking by reflecting on his future.

He had to stop traveling so much. His social life, his love life, and his digestion were all suffering. He camped, nothing more, in his studio in Manhattan; cartons of books and clothes were still unopened, eight months after he'd moved in. His New York friends, tired of speaking to a machine, had virtually given up calling him. His French friends from university days in Paris all seemed to be having children and settling down. Their wives accepted Andre, but with reservations and some suspicion. He was known to chase girls. He stayed up too late. He liked a drink. In other words, he was matrimonially threatening and was regarded as a bad influence on young husbands not yet completely come to terms with the pleasures and constraints of domesticity.

He might have been lonely, but he didn't have the time even for that. His life was work. Fortunately, he loved it; most of it, at any rate. Camilla, it was true, was becoming more eccentric and dictatorial with every issue of *DQ*. She had also developed a tiresome habit of insisting that Andre take close-ups of paintings, which, he had noticed, seldom appeared with the published article. But the money was good, and he was building a reputation for himself as one of the top interior photographers in the business. A couple of publishers had already approached him about doing a book. Next year, he promised himself, he'd do it: work at his own speed, pick his own subjects, be his own boss.

He gave up his halfhearted attempts to conquer the chicken, switched off his light, and leaned back. Tomorrow there would be real food. He closed his eyes and slept.

The familiar smell of France welcomed him as he passed through Immigration and into the main concourse of Nice airport, a smell whose components he had often tried to analyze. Part strong black coffee, part tobacco, a soupçon of diesel fuel, a waft of eau de cologne, the golden scent of pastry made with butter—it was as distinctive as the national flag and, for Andre, the first pleasure of being back in the country where he had spent so much of his youth. Other airports smelled bland and international. Nice smelled French.

The girl in the power suit was standing in the baggage claim area, checking her watch and chewing her lip while the black rubber caterpillar of the carousel made its unhurried, unburdened loop through the passengers before returning to its hole in the wall. Her expression was straight out of New

York—frowning, impatient, fraught. Andre wondered if she ever allowed herself to relax. He took pity on her.

She flinched as he tapped her on the shoulder. "You look as though you're late," he said. "Anything I can do?"

"How long do these guys need to get the bags out of the plane?"

Andre shrugged. "This is the south of France. Nothing happens fast."

The girl consulted her watch again. "I have a meeting in Sophia Antipolis. Do you know where that is? How long will the cab take?"

The business center of Sophia Antipolis, or the *Parc International d'Activités,* as the French had christened it, was back in the hills between Antibes and Cannes. "Depends on the traffic," said Andre. "Forty-five minutes should do it."

The girl looked relieved. "That's great. Thanks." She almost smiled. "You know, on the plane? I thought you were a wiseass."

Andre sighed. "Not me. My good nature gets in the way." He saw his bag creeping toward him on the carousel. "Have your meeting and get out of that place as quick as you can."

Her eyes widened. "Dangerous?"

Andre shook his head as he picked up his bag. "The food's terrible."

He left the coast road at Cagnes-sur-Mer and

aimed the rented Renault along the D6 that twists above the river Loup toward Saint-Paul-de-Vence. There was a snap to the air, an early morning chill that would soon disappear. The sun was already warm through the windscreen, the peaks of distant hills glittered white against the blue sky, the countryside looked newly washed. Manhattan and winter had been left behind on a different planet. Andre opened the window and felt his head begin to clear after a night of rationed oxygen.

He arrived in Saint-Paul in time to see, emerging from the café, the village police force, a corpulent gendarme with the reputation of giving the fastest parking tickets in France. The gendarme paused in the café doorway, wiping his mouth with the back of his hand as he surveyed the little *place,* an eye out for the first offender of the day. He looked on as Andre backed into one of the very few permitted parking places. He studied his watch. He walked over to the car, his boots creaking, his pace measured and slow, befitting his position of authority.

Andre nodded at him as he locked the car. *"Bonjour."*

The gendarme nodded back. "You have one hour. After that"—he tapped his watch—"*contravention.*" He adjusted his sunglasses and moved off, alert for any hint of wrongdoing, pleased with this first small triumph of the morning. How he looked forward to July and August! They were his favorite months, when he could stand grim-faced at the entrance to the village, turning away a continuous procession of cars. On a good day, he could infuriate several hundred motorists. It was one of the perks of the job.

In the café, Andre ordered a croissant and a coffee and looked out at the center of the *place,* where, weather permitting, vicious games of *boules* took place throughout the year. He remembered his first visit to Saint-Paul as a child, in the days when Yves Montand, dressed in waiter's black and white, used to play against the old men of the village while Simone Signoret smoked and watched, and when James Baldwin drank in the hotel bar. Andre's mother had told him that these were famous people, and he had stared at them for hours, drinking Orangina through a straw.

On his second visit, ten years later, he had fallen in love with a Swedish girl. Greedy kisses behind the post office, heartbreak on the train back to Paris, an exchange of letters that faltered and finally stopped. Then the Sorbonne, and other girls. Then the years of apprenticeship as a photographer's assistant in London. And then, drawn by the thought of exotic assignments and American-sized fees, New York.

He finished his croissant and spread his map on the table. The Russian dowager and her icons lived below Saint-Jeannet, no more than ten minutes away. He decided to go and introduce himself before checking into the hotel.

Saint-Paul was coming to life as he pulled out of his parking spot, the gendarme on the prowl, a waiter from the Colombe d'Or hosing down the entrance to the hotel courtyard, drops of water bouncing off the stone like diamonds in the sunlight. Andre drove slowly up toward Saint-Jeannet, comparing the views on either side of the road. To his right, *jolies villas* huddled together as far as the eye could see, a jumble of concrete and tile that covered the terraced land and extended all the way down to the Mediterranean. To his left, the slopes of the Col de Vence rose up above the treetops, bleached and barren and building-free. It was the kind of contrast found often along the south coast, with intensive development abruptly giving way to emptiness, as though a line had been drawn beyond which no villas were allowed. Andre hoped the line would endure. Modern architecture was not one of France's great accomplishments.

He turned off the narrow road, following instructions that led him down a gravel track into a fold of the valley, and found himself in a pocket of land that had escaped the developers. A range of old stone buildings sprawled along the banks of a small stream, swags of geraniums drooping from the walls, a breath of smoke coming from one of the chimneys.

Andre parked the car and went up a flight of shallow, uneven steps to the front door of the largest of the buildings. Two stout cats sitting on a wall watched him through half-closed, supercilious eyes, and he was reminded of one of his father's favorite quotes: "Cats look down on you. Dogs look up to you. But pigs look you straight in the eye." He was smiling as he knocked on the door.

There was a rasp as iron bolts were drawn. A round, ruddy face with brown button eyes under a frizz of gray hair peered around the side of the door. Andre felt the cats push past his legs to go inside.

"Madame, *bonjour.* I'm the photographer from America. From the magazine. I hope you were expecting me."

The face frowned. "I was told a woman."

"She'll be here later today. If it would be more convenient, I could come back then."

The old woman rubbed her nose with a bent, arthritic finger. "Where is your camera?"

"In the car."

"*Ah bon.*" This seemed to help the old woman come to a decision. "Tomorrow will be better. The girl comes today to clean." She nodded at Andre, closing the door firmly in his face.

He took his camera from the car to shoot some exteriors of the house while the light was still coming from the east. Through the lens, he saw the pale blur of the old woman's head as she watched him through a window. How would she cope with Camilla? He finished a roll of film and, squinting at the sun, decided to leave the other exteriors until the evening.

He drove back to the hotel and checked in, swinging the heavy key in his hand as he went down the corridor to his room. He liked it here. It was rambling and informal, more like a simple country house than a hotel—until you started to look at the paintings on the walls and the sculptures in the gardens.

The Colombe d'Or had been founded after World War I by Paul Roux, an ex-farmer with a sympathy for hungry artists. They came to eat at his restaurant and, in the way of artists, sometimes found themselves a little short of funds. Monsieur Roux obligingly allowed them to pay for their food with their work, accepting paintings from and by Chagall, Braque, Picasso, Léger, Bonnard, and many others. With his acquisitive instincts awakened, Roux then began to buy—at friend's prices, one hopes—and after forty years, he had assembled one of the finest private collections of twentieth-century art in France. He died leaving a few hundred dollars in the bank and a fortune on the walls.

Andre dropped his bag by the bed, and was pushing open the shutters when the phone rang. There was a fax for monsieur. He told the girl he'd pick it up on the way out. From previous trips, he knew exactly what it would be.

Camilla was incapable of going anywhere simply and quietly. Her travels were always preceded by a fusillade of notes and reminders that supplemented her standing instructions (a litany commencing with "Never put me in a pink room" and going on to describe her every whim, from the size of the bubbles in the mineral water to the color of the fresh flowers). Additional bulletins, such as the one Andre was reading in the sunlit courtyard, covered Camilla's imminent movements and appointments. Behind her back, these communications were known as Court Circulars, after the *London Times* column that lists the engagements of the Queen and the royal family.

Wednesday. Concorde a.m. to Paris, connecting with Air France to Nice. LimoAzur to pick up at Nice airport, drive to Colombe d'Or, dinner with Andre.

Thursday. The day with Princess Ospaloff. Air Inter 5 p.m. to Paris. LimoEiffel to pick up at Orly, drive to Ritz. Dinner with Vicomtesse d'Andouillette.

Friday. The day chez Beaumont, Avenue Foch. Lunch with Gilles at L'Ambroisie. Drinks at the Crillon with . . .

So it went on, a breathless catalogue of self-importance, each minute of Camilla's trip accounted for, each drink and each meal itemized. As Noel had once said, merely reading the schedule was enough to exhaust any normal person. Glancing down the page, Andre could almost hear the thud of names being dropped. There were times when it was quite an effort to find Camilla amusing. He shook his head and stuffed the fax in his pocket.

He spent an enjoyable day, dividing his time between pleasure and work: visits to the Fondation Maeght and the Matisse chapel, a late outdoor lunch in Vence, a return to the dowager's house for more exteriors, this time with a western light. Back at the hotel, he showered and changed and sat in the bar with his old and often-read copy of M. F. K. Fisher's *Two Towns in Provence.*

Business that night was slow. A couple doing their best not to look guilty drank champagne in the corner, their hands and knees touching under the table. A man at the bar delivered a stern monologue to the bartender about the spreading influence in France of Jean-Marie Le Pen, the right-wing ideologue, and was rewarded by the intermittent, perfunctory nods of the bored professional listener. From the restaurant came the sound of a cork being drawn from its bottle. Outside, darkness fell swiftly and the courtyard lights came on.

The throb of an idling engine made Andre look up from his book, and he saw that a Mercedes had eased across the courtyard entrance and stopped. The chauffeur opened the back door to reveal Camilla, in head-to-toe Chanel. She issued instructions to the night air as she clicked over the flagstones.

"Luggage to my room, please, Jean-Louis, and be sure to *hang* the garment bag. I'll see you here tomorrow afternoon at four on the dot. *Comprenez?*" She caught sight of Andre, who had come out of the bar. "Ah, there you are, sweetie. Be an angel and tip Jean-Louis, would you? I'm just going to check my messages."

The chauffeur dealt with the bags. Andre dealt with the chauffeur. Camilla's incredulous voice echoed down the hall. "But that's impossible. *C'est impossible.* Are you sure there isn't anything?" Other staff were summoned and interrogated. The hotel played hunt the message.

Andre picked up two menus from the restaurant and retreated to the bar. It was remarkable how quickly a single determined individual could disrupt the calm of an entire establishment. He ordered another *kir* for himself and, hoping he remembered Camilla's water of the moment, some Badoit.

She joined him, sitting down with a prolonged sigh, and took a pack of cigarettes from her bag. "What a day. I must look a complete hag." She crossed her legs and leaned back, waiting for Andre to contradict her.

"Nothing that dinner won't put right." Andre

smiled and passed her a menu. "The lamb here is very good. Nice and pink."

"Oh, *please.* Do you know how long meat stays in the colon? For *days.* Now, tell me all. How was the princess?"

Andre went over his brief meeting, while Camilla sipped her water and, careful not to inhale, puffed at her cigarette. She seemed unaffected by a long day of travel, bright and attentive, asking questions, planning the next day's work. Her energy continued over the salad Niçoise that was her dinner, while Andre, sedated by roast lamb and red wine, felt himself becoming more and more drowsy.

"You're fading, sweetie," she said, as the bill was placed on the table. "Do you want to go to bed?" The waiter, whose English covered the essentials, raised his eyebrows and pursed his lips.

Andre looked at her. She looked back, with a half-smile that didn't reach her eyes. He had an uncomfortable feeling that an invitation had been extended. Office gossip had it that Camilla maintained a liaison with a wealthy lover and possibly enjoyed discreet matinees now and then with Garabedian. Why not the occasional photographer? Editor's comforts while on location.

"I haven't had an offer like that for weeks." And then he laughed, and the moment passed. "Some more coffee?"

Camilla tossed her napkin on the table and stood up. "Eight o'clock tomorrow. In the lobby."

Andre watched her leave the restaurant, a woman declined. He wondered if he'd just jeopardized his meal ticket.

3

PUNCTUAL to the minute, Andre stood at the hotel entrance and inspected the morning. Apart from a few sparse licks of high cloud drifting above the hills, the great blue sweep of the sky was clear. It promised to be a day like yesterday. He walked across the terrace and looked down at the pool, guarded along one side by a closely planted, military-straight row of cypress trees, watched over at one end by a gaunt Calder mobile. The couple he had seen last night in the bar were in the heated water, laughing and splashing each other like children. Andre thought how pleasant it would be if he had someone to share a glorious day like this with him. Which, of course, he did have.

"Ah, there you are, sweetie. I hope you've got your Instamatic loaded. Where's the car?" Camilla stood posed in the courtyard, one hand lightly holding the brim of the straw hat that everyone would be wearing by summer. She was dressed in what she liked to call her working clothes—medium heels and a rugged little Armani suit—and appeared to be in a mood that matched the weather. Andre thought, with some relief, that he must have misread her signals the previous night.

On their way to Saint-Jeannet, she told him how she absolutely *adored* icons and, indeed, all things Russian. If they had been going to a Bavarian schloss or a Venetian palazzo, she would have adored all things German or all things Italian. It was her way of limbering up, of preparing to charm her subject.

And this she did throughout the morning. She exclaimed with delight at everything, from the elegant but slightly shabby simplicity of the ancient house—"The allure of the unspoiled, sweetie. Wonderful architectural bones. Make sure you capture the essence of it all"—to the icons themselves, which, although few, were magnificent. While Camilla enthused and interviewed, Andre shot, and by midday he felt he had covered the job. With the afternoon's photographs, he could afford to experiment.

The old woman had prepared a kitchen lunch for them, and here Camilla's relentless good humor and flattery were put to a severe test. It was the kind of simple meal Andre would have been happy to eat every day: fat, shiny black olives, radishes with white butter, country bread that stood up to chewing, a jug of red wine, and, sliced with great care and ceremony, a wonderfully dense, rosy *saucisson.*

Andre held out his plate for the old woman to serve him. "What a treat," he said. "This is impossible to find in America. Actually, I think it's illegal over there."

The old woman smiled. "They tell me some French cheeses are, too. What a very strange country it must be." She turned to Camilla. "Do you have enough, madame? It comes from Arles, this *saucisson*. A little beef, a little pork, a little donkey. They say the donkey gives it that particular taste."

Camilla's smile froze. Lunch was already an ordeal, with no Badoit—no water at all, except for the highly suspect liquid that came from the kitchen tap—no salad, and one of the cats sitting on the table next to the wine jug. And now donkey. Despite the risk of traumatizing her intestinal tract, she had been willing herself to choke down a slice of sausage for the sake of politeness and the greater good of the magazine. But *donkey*. Donkey was beyond her.

André glanced up, took in her rigid face and the glazed desperation of her stare, and saw that she was lost for words. He'd never known this to happen before, and it had the effect of making her seem very close to human. He leaned across to the old woman.

"I'm so sorry," he said. "I completely forgot to tell you—madame my colleague is vegetarian." He couldn't resist adding, "She has an extremely sensitive colon."

"*Ah bon?*"

"I'm afraid so. Her doctor has forbidden her red

meat of any description. Particularly the donkey, which is most aggravating to delicate tissues."

The old woman nodded gravely. They both looked at Camilla, who assumed an expression of deep regret. "Silly old colon," she said. "Such a bore."

An offer of cold noodles and salt cod was quickly made and just as quickly waved away—Camilla declaring herself more than satisfied with olives and radishes—and lunch was soon over. Only the cat lingered at the table, hoping to make off with the remains of the sausage as the others pushed back their chairs to resume work. In fact, there was little more to be done. Andre repositioned the icons, photographing them against a variety of backgrounds—stone, faded plasterwork, a wooden shutter—and coaxed an unexpectedly youthful smile out of the old woman when he took a portrait of her sitting on a low stone wall next to one of the cats. Camilla made notes and murmured into a small tape recorder. By three, they were finished.

As the car pulled away up the hill, Camilla lit a cigarette, blowing smoke out of the window with a long, thankful sigh. "God," she said, "donkey. How could you possibly eat it?"

"It was very tasty." Andre slowed down as a mud-colored dog sidled across the road and paused to sneer at the car before hopping into an overgrown ditch. "You should try eating tripe. Now, there's a challenge."

Camilla shuddered. She sometimes found the French—or at least the rural French, not her dear, civilized chums in Paris—offensively earthy in their eating habits. And what was worse, they took as much delight in talking about those frightful ingredients as they did in eating them: the gizzards and underbellies, the rabbits' heads and sheep's feet, the nameless jellied morsels, the various and unlovely permutations of offal. She shuddered again.

"Now, sweetie," she said, "when are you going back to New York?"

It was Andre's turn to shudder. He had no desire to leave early spring for the bitter tail end of a Manhattan winter. "Over the weekend, I guess. I thought I'd go into Nice tomorrow and do a few shots of Alziari and Auer."

"Doesn't ring a bell. Are they people I should know?"

"They're shops." Andre turned in to Saint-Paul and pulled up outside the hotel. "Marvelous-looking shops. One sells olives and olive oil, the other one has terrific jams."

This was of no interest to Camilla, who could see nothing of any social consequence in olives or jam. Getting out of the car, she looked around, then beckoned imperiously at a Mercedes parked on the far side of the *place.* "There's dear Jean-Louis. Tell him to come in and get my bags, would you? I'm just going to check my messages."

The hectic ritual of Camilla's departure for the airport occupied the next fifteen minutes: Under the attentive eye of the gendarme, bags were ferried to the Mercedes and stowed; the services of a chambermaid were enlisted to search beneath Camilla's bed for a missing earring; a last-minute fax was sent to New York; the airport was called to confirm that the flight was on time; tips and compliments were distributed. Finally, with a collective sigh of farewell, the hotel staff watched Camilla cross the courtyard and settle in the back of the car. Through the open window, she looked up at Andre.

"You *will* have the transparencies in my office on Tuesday, sweetie, won't you? I'm putting the issue to bed next week." And then, without waiting for an answer, *"Ciao."*

With that, the window slid up, and Camilla set off to take Paris by storm. Hoping that the concierge at the Ritz was braced for the coming assault, Andre watched the Mercedes move cautiously up the narrow street and out of the village.

Now there was the luxury of a free evening and an entire day to himself. After a shower, he went down to the bar with his map, the creased, worn, yellow Michelin 245 that he'd had since university, and spread it on the table next to his *kir*. The 245 was his favorite map, a souvenir of sentimental journeys, a map of memories. Most of his long summer vacations had been spent in the area it covered, from

Nîmes and the Camargue in the west to the Italian border in the east. Fine times they had been, too, despite a chronic shortage of money and frequent romantic complications. He thought back to those days, days when it seemed the sun had always shone, the five-franc wine had tasted like Latour, the cheap backstreet hotels had been clean and welcoming, and there had always been a tanned body next to his, dark against the white sheets. Did it never rain? Had it really been like that? Probably not. If he were honest, he could barely remember the names of some of the girls.

He picked up his *kir,* and condensation from the base of the glass dripped onto the Mediterranean just south of Nice. It stained the dotted lines that marked the routes of the ferries to Corsica, and as the stain spread across to the tip of Cap Ferrat it triggered another memory, this one more recent. At the end of the previous summer, he had spent two days shooting on the Cap, in the elaborate villa—Camilla's whispered description was *"bourgeois-sur-mer,* sweetie"—belonging to the Denoyers, the old-money Denoyers, a family that had been quietly wealthy since the days of Bonaparte. A contract to make uniforms for the many Napoleonic armies had, over the generations, developed into a giant enterprise, successfully providing a variety of textiles to a variety of governments. The current head of the family, Bernard Denoyer, had inherited a well-run company that demanded little of his time, a privilege he enjoyed to the full. Andre remembered liking him. He also remembered liking his daughter.

Photographs of Marie-Laure Denoyer appeared regularly in the smarter French magazines. Depending on the season, she could be seen at Longchamps chatting with one of daddy's jockeys, on the slopes at Courcheval, at the Red Cross Ball in Monte Carlo, beautifully turned out, smiling prettily, invariably surrounded by a knot of hopeful young men. A graceful wisp of a blonde in her very early twenties, with the permanent light-golden tan of someone who is never too long away from the sun, she was surprisingly normal for a rich man's daughter: vivacious, friendly, and, so it appeared, unattached. Camilla had disliked her on sight.

Andre decided to change his plans. Instead of going to Nice in the morning, he'd drive over to Cap Ferrat and pay his respects to the Denoyers. With luck, Marie-Laure might be free for lunch. He finished his *kir* and went through to the restaurant, his appetite sharpened by anticipation of what tomorrow might bring.

———

Cap Ferrat, elegantly wooded with palm and pine trees, impeccably maintained, furiously expensive, has long been one of the most fashionable addresses on the Côte d'Azur. It juts into the Mediterranean to the east of Nice, villas of the famous and notorious screened by high walls and thick hedges, guarded by iron gates, insulated from the common herd by a buffer of money. Past residents include King Leopold II of Belgium, Somerset Maugham, and the coiffure-conscious Baroness Beatrice de Rothschild, who never, ever, ventured abroad without a trunk containing fifty wigs.

Most of the current residents in these more democratic and dangerous times prefer to be unlisted, unknown, and undisturbed, and Cap Ferrat is one of the few places along the coast where they are able to avoid the jostle and clamor of tourism. Indeed, one of the first things the visitor coming from Nice notices is the absence of hubbub. Even the lawn mowers—heard but not seen behind the walls and hedges—sound muted and deferential, as though fitted with silencers. There are few cars, and they move slowly, almost sedately, with no signs of the normal competitive urgency of the French driver. A sense of calm prevails. People who live here, one feels, never have to rush.

Andre followed the Boulevard General de Gaulle past the lighthouse, turning off down a narrow private road, a cul-de-sac that led to the very tip of the cape. The end of the road was the beginning of the Denoyer estate, marked by ten-feet-high stone walls and massive double gates of heavy iron, decorated with the Denoyer coat of arms. Beyond the gates, the land dropped away steeply, terraced lawns divided by a drive more than a hundred yards long, lined with palm trees, ending with a turning circle, an ornate fountain, and a rather pompous front door. The slope of the land made it possible to see, above the roof of the house, a silvery strip of the Mediterranean. Andre remembered being taken through the tunnel that led from the garden to the boathouse and private beach, Denoyer remarking on the problems of erosion and the high cost of shipping in extra sand every spring for the enjoyment of his guests.

Andre got out of the car, tried the gate, found it locked. He peered through the iron bars at the house below. Those windows he could see were shuttered, and he had to accept the obvious: The Denoyers were not at home. It was too early in the year; they were doubtless still perched on an alp or prone on a beach, with Marie-Laure refreshing her tan.

With a pang of disappointment, he was turning to get back in the car, when he saw the front door opening. The figure of a man appeared, holding something in front of him. It looked like a square, a vividly colored square, and the man was holding it slightly away from his body with extreme care as he turned his head to look toward the side of the house.

Curious, Andre narrowed his eyes against the glare of the sun, unable to make out any details. And then he remembered his camera. He had put it on the passenger seat, fitted with the long lens on the off chance of his coming across an interesting shot on the road, a habit he had developed years before. Taking the camera from the car, he adjusted the focus until the figure at the front door was sharp and clear. And, now, familiar.

Andre recognized him as Old Claude (so called to distinguish him from Young Claude, who was the head gardener). For twenty years, Old Claude had been Denoyer's *homme à tout faire,* his handyman, caretaker, runner of errands, driver of guests to and from the airport, supervisor of the indoor staff, guardian of the speedboat, an essential member of the domestic establishment. On the shoot, he had been good-natured and useful, helping to move furniture and adjust lights. Andre had joked about hiring him as an assistant. But what the hell was he doing with the painting?

That, too, was familiar: a Cézanne—the family Cézanne, a very fine study that had once belonged to Renoir. Andre remembered exactly where it had hung, above the ornamental fireplace in the main salon. Camilla had insisted on a series of close-ups, to catch the ravishing brushwork, so she said, although she had never used a single close-up in the article.

Acting on photographer's instinct as much as considered thought, Andre took several shots of Claude on the doorstep before his body was hidden from view by a small van that pulled around from the side of the house and stopped in front of him. It was a conventional, dirty blue Renault of the kind found by the hundred in every town in France. A small panel on the side identified it as belonging to *Zucarelli Plomberie Chauffage,* and as Andre watched through the lens, the driver got out, opened the back doors of the van, and removed a large cardboard carton and a roll of bubble wrap. He was joined by Claude.

The two men wrapped the painting carefully and placed it in the carton. The carton went back in the van. The doors were closed. The men disappeared inside the house. All of this recorded on film.

Andre lowered the camera. What was that all about? It couldn't possibly be a burglary, not in broad daylight in the presence of Claude, the infinitely trustworthy Claude with his twenty years of faithful service. Was the painting being sent away for cleaning? Reframing? If so, why was it leaving the house in the back of a plumber's van? It was odd. It was very odd.

But as Andre had to admit, it was none of his business. He returned to the car and drove slowly back through clean, respectable, somnolent Cap Ferrat until he reached the coast road that would take him into Nice.

Despite an initial mild and really quite unjustified feeling of anticlimax—Marie-Laure would probably never have remembered him anyway; or else closer acquaintance would have shown her to be a spoiled brat after all—Andre found himself enjoying his day off. Unlike Cannes, which slips into a kind of languid semihibernation once the festivals are over and the tourists have escaped, Nice remains awake all through the year. Restaurants stay open, markets continue, the streets are busy, the Promenade des Anglais is a-bob with joggers who like their exercise with a sea view, the traffic spits and snarls, the town breathes and sweats and lives.

Andre strolled through the lanes of Vieux Nice, with a stop at the Place Saint-François to admire some recently removed residents of the Mediterranean, now occupying slabs in the fish market. He sat outside and had a beer in the Cours Saleya, using his long lens again to take shots of the stallholders and their clients, the worthy housewives of the neighborhood, connoisseurs of the lettuce and the broad bean and the bargain. After a lunch of *moules* and salad and cheese, he shot three or four rolls of color in Auer and Alziari, bought some lavender essence for Noel, and—smiling at the thought of her wearing it—a genuine, made in the Pyrenees, guaranteed-*imperméable-à-l'eau* beret for Lucy.

It started to rain on his way back to Saint-Paul, a steady light drizzle that persisted through the night and into the morning, a change in the weather that

Andre welcomed. He always found it hard to leave the south of France; harder still if the sun was high and hot; less of a wrench under dripping gray skies.

The palm trees along the road to the airport, moist and morose, seeming to huddle under the rain, gave way to the glass and steel and concrete of the terminal. Andre returned his car to Avis and took his place in the check-in line among the businessmen (were they the same weary gypsies who had flown over with him from New York?) and a scattering of holidaymakers bearing sun-pink cheeks and noses.

"Hi! How you doing?"

Andre turned, to find his window-sensitive neighbor of the flight over beaming at him. He smiled back and nodded at her. It wasn't enough.

"So. How was your trip? I'll bet you had some great food. I went to this really neat place in Cannes, maybe you know it, Le something Rouge? Wait, I have the card somewhere." She produced from her bag a swollen Filofax. The line moved up one. Andre prayed for a full flight and a seat well away from his new friend.

4

LATE afternoon at JFK, a red sun dropping and the air like a knife, the banks of soiled snow a dismal contrast with the bright flower beds of Nice. Andre detached a hardened gobbet of lurid green chewing gum from the seat of the cab as he got in, and tried to make himself understood to the driver. It had been a smooth and mercifully crowded flight, the only distraction a movie in which one of Hollywood's steroid heroes had systematically wiped out the rest of the cast. There had been ample encouragement to close the eyes and think.

The scene at Denoyer's villa returned to nag at his thoughts, as it had several times during the flight. The incongruity of what he knew to be a very valuable painting being loaded, however carefully, into a local workman's van was impossible to forget. And there had been something else, which he had paid no great attention to at the time: The intercom set into the stone gatepost had been dead when he'd pressed the button. Normal enough, if the house had been closed up and there had been no one to answer. But

Claude had been there. It was as though the property had been deliberately disconnected from the outside world.

He felt a sudden impatience to see the photographs he had taken, a record more reliable than memory, and decided to go straight to the processing lab and get the film developed. Leaning forward to make himself heard over the swirls and torrents of sitar music, he gave the address to the back of the cabdriver's turbaned head.

It was almost seven by the time he pushed open the front door of his apartment. Dropping his bags, he went over and switched on the viewing box set into the top of his worktable. The glow flickered and spread into a sheet of pure white light as he laid the transparencies in vivid rows across the glass. The tiny images shone up at him—Claude, the Cézanne, the Zucarelli van and, presumably, Zucarelli himself. Andre rearranged the transparencies, putting them in chronological sequence, telling the story. The details were clear, the focus perfectly sharp even under the magnification of a loupe. As evidence it could hardly have been more conclusive.

But evidence of what? An innocent errand? Andre sat back on the stool, shaking his head. It wasn't right.

He stared at the bulletin board on the wall above his table, a jumble of Polaroids, bills, newspaper clippings, numbers and addresses on scraps of paper, a menu from L'Ami Louis, expense claim forms, unanswered invitations, unopened envelopes from the IRS, and, like a shaft of sunshine among the gloom of those loose ends, a photograph he'd taken of Lucy in the office. He had caught her during a call to Camilla, and she was holding the phone away from her ear as she looked into the camera, a wide, triumphant grin lighting up her face. It had been the day she'd negotiated his last fee increase with *DQ,* an increase that Camilla had finally accepted with very poor grace and a great deal of bluster.

Lulu. He'd show her the photographs, see what she thought, get a second opinion. He picked up the phone.

"Lulu? Andre. I just got back. There's something I want to show you."

"Is there a problem? Are you OK?"

"I'm fine. How about dinner?"

"It's Saturday night, Andre. You know? When working girls have dates and go out."

"A drink? A quick drink? It might be important."

A short silence. "Can you meet me where I'm having dinner?"

Andre was there in twenty minutes. He settled himself at the half-empty bar and looked around. The last time he had walked past, a few months before, the place had been a run-down hardware store, specializing in window displays of dusty small appliances and dead flies. Now it had been transformed into another SoHo restaurant hoping to be hip—stripped-down decor, hard surfaces, and a lighting level sufficiently high for anyone remotely celebrated to be easily recognized from across the room. The hostess—an aspiring actress, judging by the grease-paint—had the offhand manner and ceremonial swaying walk common to her breed, the menu sprouted with fashionable vegetables, and the wine list was heavily diluted with a dozen brands of mineral water. The owners seemed to have thought of everything; there was no reason why the restaurant shouldn't be a great success for at least three months.

It was still a little too early in the evening for the hoped-for invasion by models and their escorts, and the diners now reaching the end of their meals had the subdued look of customers who had been thoroughly intimidated by both the prices and the restaurant staff. Tunnel people, Camilla would have called them, who had come into the city from New Jersey and the suburbs for a glamorous evening. They were known to drink little and to tip sparingly, and so were treated with a coolness just this side of obvious disdain by the waiters. On the way home, they would tell each other, with a kind of perverse satisfaction, what a tough town New York was.

Andre could see the entrance to the restaurant reflected in the mirror behind the bar, and each time the door opened he glanced up, looking for Lucy's headful of black curls. When she finally did arrive he was caught by surprise and had to look twice, so little did she resemble the familiar office Lucy he'd been expecting. Her hair was pulled back, severe and shining, showing off the smooth long rise of her neck; her eyes and cheekbones were subtly accentuated by makeup; she was wearing earrings, two tiny gold studs in each lobe, and a short dress of dark silk, cut in the skimpy fashion of the day to look as much as possible like an item of expensive underwear.

Andre stood up and kissed her on both cheeks, breathing in her scent, conscious of the bare skin of her shoulders under his hands, his pleasure at seeing her tinged with jealousy.

"I'd have worn a tie if I'd known you were going to dress up." He let his hands fall to his sides. "What are you going to have?"

Lucy raised the barman's eyebrows by ordering a rum and water, no ice, sipping it slowly as Andre described what he'd seen on Cap Ferrat. He showed her the transparencies, watching the play of light on the angles of her face as she held them up and wondering whom she was having dinner with. The restaurant was becoming busy, and the bar was now under attack from modish young men, their sidelong glances surreptitiously comparing each other's stubble and haircuts while they waited for their drinks. Andre felt underdressed and overshaved.

"Well?" he said. "What do you think? That painting must be worth a fortune."

Lucy stacked the transparencies in a small pile on the bar with long, scarlet-tipped fingers. It was the first time Andre had seen her wearing nail varnish. "I don't know," she said. "If they were stealing it, why wouldn't they do it at night? Why hang around on the doorstep with it?" She took another sip of rum and smiled at the frown on his face. "Listen, if it bothers you, call Denoyer. Do you know where he is?"

"I can find out. It's odd, though, isn't it? You're right—I'll call him." He slipped the transparencies into an envelope and gazed at Lucy with what he hoped was a soulful expression. "All alone on Saturday night," he said, "the girl of my dreams promised to another." He sighed, a heavy, long-drawn-out sigh. "Pizza and TV, dirty dishes. Maybe I'll go mad and wash my hair. Maybe I should get a cat."

Lucy grinned. "You're breaking my heart."

"Who's the lucky man?"

She looked into her drink. "Just a guy."

"Meet him at the gym? That's what it was, love among the Nautilus machines. Your eyes met over the bench press. One look at his pectorals and you were lost." He sighed again. "Why don't these things ever happen to me?"

"You're never here." She looked at him in silence for a moment. "Right?"

Andre nodded. "Right. Anyway, he's late. He's

blown it. Why don't we go around the corner and get some real food, some . . ." A gust of aftershave made him look up, and the space between them was suddenly filled by a young man in a dark suit and an aggressively loud striped shirt. Andre was sure that red felt suspenders lurked under his jacket. What a ponce.

Lucy made the introductions; the two men shook hands with a marked lack of enthusiasm, and Andre surrendered his barstool. "Lulu, I'll call you tomorrow, after I've talked to Denoyer." He did his best with a smile. "Enjoy your dinner."

Walking home, the sidewalk treacherous with a skim of ice, Andre reflected on the often-quoted statistic that there were three unattached females in Manhattan for every one unattached male. It wasn't doing him much good at the moment; nor would it, he had to admit, as long as he spent most of his life somewhere else. Lucy was right. He stopped off at a deli for a sandwich, trying to avoid mental images of her and the striped shirt having dinner.

Later, to the celestial sound of Isaac Stern swooping through Mendelssohn, he searched the drawer where he tossed all the business cards given to him. Denoyer's, in the large and opulent French style, would be bigger than the rest. There. He picked it out and studied the classical black copperplate.

Two addresses, identified by seasons: *Eté,* Villa La Pinède, 06230 Saint-Jean-Cap-Ferrat. *Hiver,*

Cooper Cay, New Providence, Bahamas. No mention of Paris or Courcheval, so unless he was skiing, Denoyer should still be in the Bahamas.

Andre yawned, still on French time, four in the morning. He would call tomorrow.

———

Denoyer's voice, on a fuzzy line from Cooper Cay, was relaxed and amiable. Of course he remembered Andre, and those magnificent photographs. Many of his friends had complimented him on the article. He hoped that Andre was thinking of taking some pictures in the Bahamas. The islands were delightful at this time of year, particularly when the weather in Manhattan was so disagreeable. Denoyer paused, leaving direct questions unasked, and waited.

"In fact," said Andre, "I'm calling about France. I was on Cap Ferrat last week and passed by your house."

"What a pity we weren't there," Denoyer said. "It's closed up for the winter—but of course, you saw that. We don't go back until April."

"Well, the odd thing was, I did see your caretaker."

"Claude? I should hope so." Denoyer laughed. "I wouldn't want him anywhere else while we're away."

"Perhaps I should say that what he was doing was odd."

"Oh?"

"And I thought you should know. He and another man were loading one of your paintings—the Cézanne—into a van. A plumber's van. I watched them from the gate."

There was nothing but static on the line for a few moments, and then Denoyer's voice, sounding more amused than surprised. "Come, now, my friend. A plumber's van? You were at the gate, no? That's quite a distance from the house. Your eyes were playing tricks." He chuckled. "It wasn't after a good lunch, was it?"

"It was in the morning." Andre took a deep breath. "And I took photographs. Everything's very clear. Everything."

Another pause. "*Ah bon?* Well, I expect Claude was doing a little spring cleaning. I'll call him." And then, in a light, casual tone of voice, a mere afterthought, he added: "But it would be amusing to see the photographs. Would you mind sending them down?"

Light and casual it may have been, but not altogether convincing. There had been a suspicion of interest, something more than passing curiosity, and Andre found himself wanting to see Denoyer's face when he looked at the photographs. "That won't be necessary," he said. "I'll bring them." He found the lie came easily. "I've got to look at a house in Miami next week. It's only a hop over from there to Nassau."

After a few token protestations from Denoyer, it was agreed. Andre spent the rest of the morning arranging flights and trying to reach Lucy. She was out. Maybe the striped shirt had persuaded her to spend a rustic Sunday in the arctic wastes of Central Park. Maybe she had never come home after dinner. What a hideous thought, and what a waste. He had to stop traveling so much. He tipped the wrinkled contents of his bag into the laundry basket and played some Wagner very loud as he started packing for the Bahamas.

5

MANHATTAN was melting. Overnight, a warm front had crept into the city, turning the piled snow into gray ooze, exposing the heaps of uncollected garbage sacks to the pale sun, bringing joy to the hearts of those responsible for the strike. Soon the garbage would begin to announce its presence to the noses of several million passersby, and with the powerful endorsement of the stench, the union men could resume negotiations.

Andre waded through the streams and tributaries of West Broadway, stamping the worst of the slush from his feet before going up to the office. He found Lucy on the phone, a frown on her face, her voice terse. She looked up at Andre and rolled her eyes. He dug in his bag for the folder containing the shots he had taken of the icons and took a seat on the company couch.

"No." Lucy's frown deepened. "No, I can't. I'm tied up this week. I don't know when. Listen, I've got to go. Someone's waiting. Yes, I have your number. Right. And you." She put down the phone and blew out a long breath, shaking her head as she stood up.

Andre grinned. "I hope I didn't interrupt anything," he said, feeling sure that he had. "Not our friend in the striped shirt, was it?"

Lucy tried to scowl at him, then relented. "I should have gone around the corner with you while I had the chance. What an evening. And I thought he was a possible." She pushed her hands through her hair. "Have you ever been to a cigar bar?"

Andre shook his head.

"Don't."

"Too much smoke?"

"Too many striped shirts."

"And red suspenders?"

Lucy nodded. "Red, striped, floral, monogrammed, bulls and bears, cocktail recipes. One guy even had the Dow-Jones index printed on his. They take off their jackets when they get drunk." She shook her head again, and her shoulders twitched at the memory. "How did you know about the suspenders?"

"There'd be a slump on Wall Street without them. Most of the trousers would fall down. He was from Wall Street, wasn't he?"

"Let's just say he wasn't a smartass photographer." She came across and picked up the folder lying on the table. "Are these the shots from France?"

"I was going to ask if you could get them up to Camilla. I've got a plane to catch."

"There's a surprise." As Lucy looked through the transparencies, Andre saw her face soften. "These are nice. What a lovely old lady. She looks like Grandma Walcott without the tan. Is this her house?"

"It's an old mill. You'd like France, Lulu."

"It's beautiful." Lucy put the transparencies back in the folder and resumed her office manner, brisk and businesslike. "Well, where are we off to today?"

Andre started to describe his phone call to the Bahamas. As he spoke, he was aware that he might be reading a great deal into Denoyer's replies, his pauses and hesitations, his tone of voice. On the face of it, the man had said nothing suspicious; hadn't seemed astonished or even surprised by what Andre had told him; hadn't, in fact, seemed to show any more than polite interest until the photographs were mentioned. And yet, despite these reservations, Andre was positive that something was not quite right. Almost positive. Perhaps trying to convince himself as much as Lucy, he slipped unconsciously into a conspiratorial crouch, his head thrust forward, his expression grave.

Lucy was leaning back against the arm of the couch, her chin on one hand, smiling occasionally at his more animated gestures. As he became more intense, so he became more French, using his hands as visual punctuation marks, stabbing the air or kneading it with his fingers to underscore each phrase, each significant nuance. When he finished, it was with the full Gallic display—shoulders and eyebrows rising in unison, elbows tucked in to his sides, palms spread out, lower lip jutting—everything but the feet used to emphasize the undeniable logic of his conclusions. His old professor at the Sorbonne would have been proud of him.

"I only asked where you were going," Lucy said.

———

Those who travel to the Bahamas in winter tend to anticipate the weather, and many of the passengers at the gate were already in their tropical plumage—straw hats and sunglasses, beach-bright clothes, even one or two pairs of bold and premature shorts—and tropical mood too, with comments flying back and forth about skin diving, hot nightclubs in Nassau, and the delights of beach-bar cocktails with suggestive names. It was a festive crowd, ripe for self-indulgence and excess. Within twenty-four hours, Andre thought, most of them would be suffering from the island malady of Bacardi and sunburn.

His own relationship with the Caribbean was not a happy one. Some years earlier, during his first winter in New York, the idea of being only a short flight away from a white sand beach had been a constant temptation. Giving in, he had borrowed the money for what was touted as a bargain week on one of the lesser Virgins and was ready to come back after four days. He found the prices exorbitant, the food over-fried, heavy, and dull, and the few local residents he met addicted to gin and gossip. Subsequent working visits to other jewels of the Caribbean hadn't changed his opinion: He and small islands were not suited to each other. They gave him claustrophobia and indigestion.

And so it was with a sense of mission rather than pleasurable expectation that he strapped himself into his seat to the tinny strains of an airline calypso, followed by the pilot's welcoming address. How was it that all pilots seemed to have such rich, confident, infinitely reassuring voices? Was it an occupational requirement, along with navigational skills and perfect blood pressure? Did their refresher courses include tips on phrasing and elocution? The plane reached the limitless blue sky of its cruising altitude; Andre unbuckled his seat belt and tried to stretch his legs, conscious of rising damp from paddling through New York puddles. That, at least, would be a pleasure to leave behind for a day or two.

———

The light at Nassau airport made his eyes ache; the afternoon heat, like a moist towel wrapped around him, made his winter clothes cling to his chest and back, clammy and thick. He looked among the aging Chevrolets without success for a cab with air-conditioning, and spent the drive to Cooper Cay like a dog, his face hanging from the open window to catch the breeze.

Denoyer had arranged for him to have a room at the clubhouse, but before any visitor was permitted to penetrate that lush and heavily defended ghetto, there were some minor formalities to be completed. Forced to stop by a green and white striped barrier that blocked the entrance, the cabdriver sounded his horn. A burly, languid man in peaked hat, military uniform, and mirror-finish boots emerged from the gatehouse and sauntered over to the cab. He and the driver chatted like old friends—old friends with plenty of time on their hands and nowhere particular to go on such a pleasant day. Eventually, the two of them having brought their personal histories up to date, the uniformed man noticed Andre wilting in the back and asked whom he was coming to see. Returning at a slow march to the gatehouse, he picked up the phone to check with headquarters. It appeared that all was well. He nodded to the driver. The barrier was raised. The cab, with another blip on the horn, drove through, and Andre entered a Shangri-la reserved for those with a net worth in excess of ten million dollars and a good Bay Street lawyer.

The road began as a broad, straight avenue bordered by fifty-foot coconut palms before curving past a number of driveways that led to enormous white or pink houses. Discreet, crisply painted signs nestling among the bougainvillea identified each vast edifice, with equally vast false modesty, as a cottage: Rose, Coral, Seagrape, Palm (of course), Casuarina—their gardens trimmed to a whisker, their shutters closed against the sun. Andre found himself comparing the surroundings to Denoyer's other hideout, on Cap Ferrat. Despite the differences in the vegetation, in the quality of the heat and air, in the architecture, there was one striking similarity: the atmosphere of tranquil, somnolent wealth, the feeling that the rest of the world was a very long way away. Normal mortals, keep out.

The road curved again to skirt the emerald greens of the inevitable golf course, on which nobody walked. Progress from hole to hole, from shot to shot, was made by means of electric carts painted in the green and white livery of Cooper Cay. Passengers dismounted, hacked away, and remounted. Physical exertion was kept to a minimum.

Pulling up to the wide sweep of stone steps in front of the clubhouse entrance, the cabdriver showed a sudden burst of alacrity prompted by thoughts of a tip. He jumped out and wrestled Andre's bag from his hands, only to have it wrestled from him in turn by one of the club's bellboys, a giant with gleaming teeth and a green and white striped waistcoat. Andre distributed cash to waiting hands, the bills damp with perspiration, and made his way into the cool, high-ceilinged lobby.

He was shown to his room, overlooking the pool, and relieved of some more damp money. Without stopping to unpack, he stripped off his clothes and stood under a cold shower for five minutes before walking across the stone floor, dripping and naked, to look at his view. The long turquoise rectangle of the pool was empty, but along one side, positioned to catch the late afternoon sun, he could see a row of his fellow guests, oiled and motionless on their *chaises longues*. Middle-aged, leathery men, plump with good living; younger, leaner women, wearing pool jewelry and very little else; no children, no noise, no signs of life. He turned away from the window.

A cream-colored envelope was propped against a bowl of hibiscus on the table next to his bed. He dried his hands and opened it: an invitation to dinner with the Denoyers, complete with directions and a small map to facilitate the journey from the club-house to their cottage, through four hundred exquisitely clipped yards of jungle. He toweled himself off and emptied the contents of his bag onto the bed. Was Denoyer the kind of man who wore a white tuxedo when dining in the tropics? Did he expect his guests to do the same? Andre picked a white linen shirt and a pair of khakis from the tangle of clothes, hung them up in the bathroom, and turned on the shower to steam away the ravages that travel had wrought.

The front boy at the clubhouse entrance who tried to persuade Andre into a golf cart so that he could be driven to the Denoyers' cottage blinked in surprise when his offer was declined. Nobody *walked.* Not at Cooper Cay; not at night. And what a night it was: warm black velvet, a sickle of moon, the wink and glitter of stars, a faint, salty breeze coming off the sea, the coarse tropical grass dense and springy underfoot, an invisible orchestra of insects whirring and chirping away in the shrubbery—Andre felt a moment of particular well-being and had to admit that perhaps, after all, there was something to be said for the Caribbean in winter.

The house—which Denoyer had promoted from a common cottage by naming it *La Maison Blanche*—was, like its neighbors, imposing and immaculate, as was the dignified butler who opened the front door. Andre was escorted down a wide central hallway and out onto a terrace that ran the length of the house. From the terrace, a lighted pathway led past a swimming pool and through a grove of palms to a dock. Beyond that, darkness, and the lap and whisper of water.

"Monsieur Kelly! *Bonsoir, bonsoir.* Welcome to Cooper Cay." Denoyer's feet made no sound as he came across the coral flagstones of the terrace. He was dressed informally, Andre was pleased to see, in slacks, short-sleeved shirt, and espadrilles, the only sign of affluence a bulky gold watch—of the useful kind that is waterproof to a depth of five hundred feet—on one tanned wrist. His skin shone with health and sun, a warm smile softening his lined but still good-looking face.

He led Andre over to a group of rattan chairs arranged around a low glass table. "You remember my wife, Catherine?"

"Of course." Andre shook a slender, jeweled hand. Madame Denoyer was an older version of her daughter, elegant in a simple shift of pale-blue silk, blonde hair pulled back in a chignon, several generations of good breeding evident in her fine-boned, slightly haughty face. A graceful inclination of her head. "Do sit down, Monsieur Kelly. What will you drink?"

The butler brought wine. "Pernand-Vergelesses," said Denoyer. "I hope you like it." He gave an apologetic shrug. "We've never been able to get on with the Californian whites. Too old to change our tastes, I'm afraid." He raised his glass. "It's very good of you to come." As he sipped his wine, his eyes went to the envelope that Andre had put on the table, then they flicked away, as if it held no more interest for him than a package of cigarettes.

Andre smiled. "I was in the neighborhood anyway." He turned to Madame Denoyer. "I hope your daughter's well?"

"Marie-Laure?" There was a brief pout, a kind of facial shrug. "When she's here, she wants to be skiing; when she's skiing, she wants to be on the beach. We spoil her. *Non*"—she shook her finger at her husband—"Bernard spoils her." She looked at him, an equal measure of affection and mild reproach in her expression.

"Why not? It pleases me." Denoyer turned to Andre. "In fact, you just missed her. She went back yesterday to Paris, and then I expect she'll spend the weekend at Cap Ferrat." He smiled at his wife. "And Claude spoils her much more than I do." The mention of Claude seemed to remind Denoyer of the reason for Andre's visit, and he leaned forward, his eyebrows raised, a casual nod of his head in the direction of the envelope on the table. "Are these the photographs you took?" The nod was a fraction too casual, the tone of voice too offhand. Neither was convincing, or so it seemed to Andre.

"Oh, those. Yes. They're probably not worth looking at." Andre smiled.

Denoyer held up both hands, the picture of polite disagreement. "But you took all this trouble, came all this way." He reached over and picked up the envelope. "May I?"

The butler padded out from the house and murmured into Madame Denoyer's ear. She nodded. "Can they wait, *chéri*? Because I'm afraid the soufflé can't."

Despite its geographical location, it was a French household, with French priorities. The hideous thought of a soufflé collapsing into no more than a desolate withered pancake took precedence over everything else, and Madame Denoyer lost no time in leading them through to the dining room. As they sat down, Andre saw that Denoyer had brought the envelope with him.

The room was far too big and grand for the three of them, and they were seated around one end of an enormous mahogany table that could comfortably have accommodated a dozen. Andre had a mental picture of the Denoyers dining alone, one at each end of the table, with salt, pepper, and conversation being ferried up and down by the butler. "I expect you entertain a great deal down here, don't you?" he asked Madame Denoyer.

Again the fleeting facial shrug. "We try not to. All people here can talk about is golf, adultery, or income tax. We prefer to have our friends from France stay with us." She looked at the golden dome of the soufflé held out by the butler for her approval and nodded. "Are you a golfer, Monsieur Kelly? I'm told the course here is excellent."

"No, I've never played. I'm afraid I'd be a social disaster if I lived here." He broke through the top of his soufflé, inhaled a whiff of herbs, and spooned black *tapenade* into the fluffy cavity. "I'm not even very good at adultery."

Madame Denoyer smiled. The young man had a sense of humor, and such unusual eyes. What a pity Marie-Laure had left. *"Bon appétit."*

As a mark of due respect to the savory but fleeting lightness of the soufflé, there was no conversation while it was being eaten. Then came more wine, and with it Denoyer's views on the French economy, mostly gloomy, and some polite questions about Andre's work, life in New York versus life in Paris, favorite restaurants—pleasant, banal stuff, the social glue that holds strangers together during dinner parties, nothing probing or too personal. And nothing about the photographs, although Denoyer's eyes kept returning to the envelope beside his plate.

The main course was fish, but fish that had escaped the usual Caribbean death of suffocation by batter. It had been fried—lightly fried, in a coating of pumpernickel bread crumbs, garnished with slivers of fresh lime and served with *pommes allumettes* that snapped in the mouth in the most delicious and satisfying way. It was, Andre thought, fish and chips that deserved four stars and a mention in dispatches, and he complimented Madame Denoyer on her cook. "There's hope for Bahamian cuisine after all," he said.

Madame Denoyer picked up the small crystal bell beside her wineglass and rang for the butler. "That's kind of you." She grinned at him, mischief taking years off her face—suddenly she looked exactly like her daughter—and tapped the side of her nose. "But the cook's from Martinique."

Andre never ate dessert, preferring a last glass of wine, and Denoyer was quick to suggest they take coffee in the living room. This, too, was designed to hold a crowd, and they sat in a central island of armchairs under a slowly turning ceiling fan, surrounded on all sides by a sea of marble floor.

"Now," said Denoyer, "let's see what that old rascal Claude has been up to."

6

THE Monday night ritual of Rudolph Holtz had been strictly observed for several years. Business appointments ended at six p.m. sharp; social invitations were neither issued nor accepted. Monday evening belonged to him, and it followed precisely the same course each week. After an early light supper—the menu never varied—of smoked salmon from Murray's and a half-bottle of Montrachet, Holtz gathered together the latest sale catalogues and gallery announcements, together with his list of existing and potential clients, and climbed the steps to his four-poster bed. There, among the pillows, he plotted. It had become an invaluable part of his working week, an undisturbed period during which he had devised many profitable coups, some of them quite legitimate.

Beside him, Camilla was already asleep, her eyes shielded from the light by a mask of black satin. She was exhausted—quite drained, in fact—having spent the weekend with some madly social friends in Bucks County. She was snoring, a gentle, regular whiffle that reminded Holtz of a pug he had once been fond of, and he patted her absentmindedly from time to time as he sifted through the catalogues, occasionally jotting down a name next to a particular painting. This part of his work, which he thought of as a benevolent service—finding a loving home for art—he enjoyed a great deal; although, of course, it couldn't compare with the deeper satisfaction of depositing a seven-figure check when the sale went through.

He was considering a small but charming Corot, which he thought might fill a gap in Onozuka's Tokyo collection, when the phone rang. Camilla whimpered softly and pulled the sheet over her head. Holtz glanced at his bedside clock. Nearly eleven.

"Holtz? It's Bernard Denoyer."

Holtz looked at the clock again and frowned. "You're up early, my friend. What time is it over there? Five?"

"No, I'm in the Bahamas. Holtz, I've just seen something that I don't like at all. Photographs taken last week outside my house on Cap Ferrat. The Cézanne, Holtz, the Cézanne. Being loaded into a plumber's van."

Holtz was suddenly bolt upright, his voice louder. "Where are they, these photographs?" Camilla moaned and covered her head with a pillow. "Who took them? Not those bastards at *Paris Match*?"

"No, I have them here. The photographer left

them with me—a man called Kelly. He works for a magazine, the one that did the big article on the house last year. *DQ?* Something like that."

"Never heard of it." Camilla's moans continued. Holtz put a second pillow over her head. "Kelly— does he want money?"

Denoyer hesitated before replying. "I don't think so. He said he's going back to New York tomorrow, so I won't be seeing him again. But what's going on? I thought you were moving the painting to Zurich. That's what we agreed. To Zurich, and then to Hong Kong, and not a soul will know—that's what you said."

Holtz had dealt with many uneasy clients in the past. In most irregular transactions such as this one, there was a period of limbo—sometimes hours, sometimes days or weeks—when one side had to rely totally on the other to fulfill an agreement. Holtz made sure that the burden of trusting others never actually fell upon himself, but he could understand the insecurity that must accompany a decision to place your fate or your money in another man's hands. He settled himself back among the pillows and assumed his best bedside manner.

There was absolutely nothing to be concerned about, he told Denoyer, providing there were no more photographs in circulation. And that, he said, glancing at the sleeping body next to him, he was in a position to verify. Cutting Denoyer's questions short, he went on: Claude was not a problem. He would do what he was told. Loyalty would ensure his silence. As for the van, it was a simple disguise. The driver was not a plumber but a Holtz employee, a courier experienced in transporting various precious items without drawing attention to himself. Would anyone suspect an artisan's grubby old Renault of containing a valuable painting? Of course not. Denoyer could be assured that the Cézanne was now making its discreet way safely across Europe. Holtz omitted to mention that it would be stopping in Paris en route, but that was none of Denoyer's business.

"So you see, my friend," said Holtz, "you can relax. This is a minor inconvenience, nothing more. An accident. Enjoy the sunshine, and leave the rest to me."

Denoyer put down the phone and stared out at the soft Bahamian night. This was the first time in an honest and well-ordered life that he had worked with anyone like Holtz, and he was not enjoying the experience: the feelings of vulnerability, risk, lack of control, nervousness, even guilt. But it was too late now. He was too deeply involved. There was nothing to be done. He got up and poured himself a cognac. Holtz had sounded confident about tracking down the negatives and copies of the photographs, if indeed there were any. The young man seemed to be genuine. Perhaps he was making too much of a perfectly innocent coincidence. Even so, Denoyer would be relieved when it was all over.

As it happened, Holtz was far from being as confident as he had sounded. If what Denoyer said was true, he had only until tomorrow. Leaning over, he removed the pillows from Camilla's head and shook her awake. She pushed up her sleeping mask. One bleary eye opened, a narrow slit, looking curiously naked without its customary makeup.

"Not now, sweetie. I'm exhausted. Maybe in the morning, before the gym." Like many short men, Holtz made up for his lack of stature with a voracious libido, which Camilla often found rather tiresome. She patted his hand. "A girl needs a night off now and then, sweetie. Really."

It was as if Holtz had not heard her. "I've got to have the address of that photographer you use. Kelly."

Camilla struggled into a sitting position, the sheet clutched protectively to her bosom. "What? Can't it wait? Rudi, you know what a complete disaster I am without my sleep, and tomorrow's—"

"It's important. Something's gone wrong."

Camilla saw from the set of his mouth that further argument was useless—he could, as she knew, be quite a savage little brute sometimes—and got up to fetch her handbag, stubbing her toe on a Louis XV commode and hopping back to the bed on one leg in a decidedly unglamorous fashion. She took out her address book and turned to the Ks. "My toe's just going to balloon, I know it will. That bloody commode." She passed the book over to Holtz. "Am I allowed to know what this is all about?"

"I dare say you'll live, my dear. Let me make this call."

By now fully awake and highly curious, Camilla took a mirror from her handbag and adjusted her hair while she started to listen to Holtz's end of the conversation with someone called Benny. Then she rather wished she hadn't. She certainly didn't want to hear all the messy details. Not tonight anyway. Resuming her mask, she dived back into her burrow of pillows and feigned sleep.

But sleep for Camilla was some way off. She was drowsily aware of the conversation coming to an end, and then felt the soft, insistent touch of Holtz's hands on her body, turning her toward him. She looked down at the top of his head; somehow he was still short, even when horizontal. The hands persisted. Camilla gave in to the inevitable and sighed, moving her injured toe as far as possible from the risk of collision with Holtz's scrabbling feet.

———

Andre looked back through the rear window of the cab as the striped barrier swung down to guard Cooper Cay against invasion by the common herd. It was a perfect, shining morning, the flowers vivid against tropical green, the groundskeepers sweeping and clipping so that residents might be spared the horrors of seeing a fallen leaf or a dead bloom. He slumped down in the seat, nursing his disappointment, feeling as though he had spent the last twenty-four hours wasting his time.

Denoyer could hardly have been more charming or, for most of the evening, more relaxed. Far from reacting to the photographs with the astonished concern that Andre had expected, he appeared to have been more interested in the state of his garden than in the Cézanne. There had been only one revealing moment, and that only a sudden, puzzled frown when he'd seen the van, but recovery had been almost instantaneous. The plumber was an old *copain* of Claude's, he said, who often ran errands. The Cézanne was occasionally lent to a friend's gallery in Cannes. That must explain it, Denoyer had said, although he would certainly have a word with Claude about the casual method of transportation. And that had been that. Denoyer had been effusive in his gratitude for Andre's concern and had insisted on paying for his stay at the clubhouse. But the evening—indeed, the whole trip—had been an anticlimax.

There was some small consolation that afternoon when he reached New York to find that the thaw had continued and the sidewalk outside his building was no longer an ice rink. As he climbed the stairs to his apartment, he decided that he needed cheering up and, with thoughts of Lucy and dinner in mind, unlocked his door and made for the phone. He was halfway across the room before he stopped short and took in the chaos spread around him.

Every one of the cartons had been opened and upended. Books, pictures, clothes, souvenirs from trips, were strewn in muddled heaps across the floor and against the wall, as though flung by violent, angry hands. Andre walked over to his worktable, the harsh crackle of broken glass under his feet. The filing cabinets where he kept all his transparencies, organized by year and country, were open and empty. Next to them, the equipment storage closet had been stripped of everything except a collapsible tripod and an old plate camera he had been meaning to have restored. His other cameras, his lenses, his filters, his lighting gear, and the custom-made bags to carry them in were all gone. He went through to the galley kitchen, opened the fridge, and saw, without great surprise, that they had taken every roll of film. Welcome back to New York, home of the thorough thief.

In his bedroom, he found drawers sagging open, closets bare, clothes tossed everywhere, the mattress pulled from the bed. He felt stunned, numb. The outrage, the sense of being violated, would come later. Picking his way through the debris of his possessions, he perched on the stool at his worktable and began to make the calls that had to be made.

The police: polite, but weary. This was one of several hundred criminal incidents that had taken place in the city since the weekend, and on a list headed by homicides, rapes, overdoses, and the start of the hunting season in the subway, petty larceny ranked low. If Andre would like to bring the details into the precinct house, the burglary would be officially recorded. And there, barring an extraordinarily lucky break, the file would gather dust. Andre was advised to change his locks.

The insurance company: instantly defensive, with the professional skepticism and the barrage of fine-print questions that provide such comfort in times of crisis and misfortune. Were all doors and windows locked? Was the alarm system set? Did Andre possess all the required paperwork—receipts, dates of purchase, serial numbers, estimated replacement costs? No action could be taken without this crucial information. Meanwhile, he was advised to change his locks. As Andre hung up, he remembered the company's advertising slogan, delivered at the end of every commercial by a voice dripping with saccharine sincerity: something about a friend in need.

Lucy: and finally some sympathy. She told him she would be there as soon as she had closed up the office.

She stood in the living room surveying the wreckage, her face tight with dismay and anger. She was wearing the beret he had bought her in Nice. It was the best thing he had seen all day, and it made him smile.

"It suits you, Lulu. I think I'll get you a bike and a string of onions to go with it."

She took it off and shook her hair. "If you're going to be all manly and brave, I'm not going to take you out to dinner. Lord God, what a mess."

They started in the bedroom, Lucy quick and deft as she folded clothes, hung them up, or consigned them to the laundry basket. After seeing Andre's labored efforts with a sweater, she sent him off to the living room, hoping his domestic education had at least included lessons on how to operate a broom. Without thinking, he picked out a Marley CD and put it on, and it wasn't until he turned away from the stereo that something struck him as very odd: There shouldn't have been a stereo. Why hadn't it gone with everything else? And then, as he started to sweep up the shards of broken glass, he went over what had been taken; or, rather, what hadn't: not the stereo, not the TV, not the shortwave bedside radio, not the mobile phone, not even the half-dozen silver Art Nouveau photograph frames that were now lying on the floor beneath the shelf where they normally stood. It didn't make sense, unless the burglars were planning to set up as professional photographers. But if all they wanted was equipment, why take his transparencies? Why take his stock of film from the fridge? Why tear the place apart? What were they looking for?

Two hours later, although a semblance of order had returned to the apartment, Lucy showed no signs of slowing down; nor of hunger or thirst, both of which were starting to distract Andre from his household duties. He stopped her as she came across the room balancing a stack of books that reached up to her chin.

"Enough, Lulu, enough." He took the books from her and put them down. "You said something about dinner, or are you having too much fun to stop?"

Lucy put her hands on her hips and eased her back. "Well, it'll do for tonight. Do you have a maid service?"

"What?"

"No, I thought not. I'll get someone over tomorrow. The place could do with a good scrub. So could the windows. Have those windows ever been cleaned? And Andre? Yogurt doesn't last forever, even in a fridge. When it starts to glow in the dark, you get rid of it, OK?"

Andre suddenly had the feeling—a strange but pleasant feeling—that part of his personal life was coming under new management. He helped Lucy on with her coat. She picked up her beret and looked around the room. "You don't have any mirrors here, do you?" She tucked her hair in the beret, tilting it steeply over one eye, and caught him smiling at her. "This isn't how they wear them in France?"

"No. But they should."

Lucy took him to what she called her local, a small, warm, noisy restaurant on Duane Street. Mount Gay rum, Red Stripe beer, a Jamaican chef with an Italian wife. Both sides of the marriage were represented on the short menu.

Lucy sipped her rum. "I'm sorry about what happened."

"There's something about it I don't understand." Andre leaned forward, looking into his glass while he spoke. "They weren't interested in stuff they could sell on the street in five minutes. Just cameras—cameras and my shot files. My work. That's all they wanted. And they were pros. Didn't have to break the door down, knew how to cut off the alarm." He looked up. "Pros, Lulu. But why me? I mean, photographs of houses, furniture, pictures—it's not as if there's anything they could sell to the *Enquirer*. The only nudes are in the paintings."

The chef's wife squeezed her ample body through the tables to take their orders, kissing the tips of her fingers when Lucy ordered the jerk chicken and nodding with approval at Andre's choice of seafood risotto. "I choose the wine for you, eh? A nice Jamaican Orvieto." She cackled, and waddled off to the kitchen.

Lucy grinned. "Don't look so disapproving and

French. Angelica knows best. Now go back a bit, tell me about your trip."

Andre went through it, trying his best to keep the account factual, watching Lucy's face for reactions. She had that most attractive quality in a listener, complete and serious attention, and he barely noticed the arrival of Angelica with the food and wine. They sat back to give her space to put down the plates.

"*Basta,*" said Angelica. "Enough romance. Eat."

For the first few minutes they ate in silence. Lucy paused to take some wine. "You're right," she said. "It doesn't make sense, unless someone just wanted to make a mess of your work." She shook her head. "Do you know anyone who has a grudge against you? You know, in business?"

"Not that I can think of. But why would they want my old transparencies? There's nothing they could sell. And why would they take the whole place apart?"

"Looking for something, maybe. I don't know . . . something you'd hidden."

Angelica loomed over them. "How is everything?" She picked up the wine bottle and filled their glasses. "Your first time here?" she said to Andre.

He smiled at her and nodded. "Very good."

"*Bene.* Make sure she eats. She's too thin." Angelica moved away from the table, massaging her stomach with a chubby hand.

They ate and talked, avoiding any more theories about the burglary, slipping gradually from business gossip into an exchange of likes and dislikes, hopes and ambitions, the small revelations of two people feeling their way toward knowing each other. The restaurant was almost empty by the time they finished coffee, and when they went out on the street there was a damp chill in the air. Lucy shivered, tucking a hand under Andre's arm as they walked to the corner of Duane and West Broadway. He waved down a cab, and for the first time that evening there was a tentative, slightly awkward moment.

Lucy opened the cab door. "Promise me you won't do any housework when you get home."

"Thanks for everything, Lulu. Dinner was lovely. Almost worth getting robbed."

She stood on tiptoe and kissed the end of his nose. "Change your locks, OK?" And then she was gone.

He stood watching the cab's back lights blend into a hundred others, feeling surprisingly happy for a newly burgled man.

7

FLURRY reigned at the Madison Avenue offices of *DQ,* which were even more overwrought than usual as the latest issue was being put to bed. Camilla's plans had been turned upside down—completely *bouleversés,* as she said—by the unsolicited submission of an article on decorative bidets of the famous, accompanied by some simply ravishing pictures taken by a promising young Parisian photographer. Rarely had hygienic porcelain looked so rich, so sculptural, so much a part of today's well-dressed bathroom—and the end of winter was such a perfect time for readers to be reviewing their sanitary requirements. At the editorial conference, it was generally agreed that this was groundbreaking material, possibly even a first in magazine history. Also, as Camilla was quick to point out, there was the added cachet provided by the celebrated owners of the bidets. They were nowhere to be seen in the photographs, for obvious reasons. Nevertheless, they had granted permission for their names to be used. It was too good to pass up.

But the issue was already full, and one of the scheduled features would have to be dropped. Camilla stalked back and forth in the conference room beside the long table on which the dummy page spreads were laid out. She was shadowed, as always, by her junior secretary, notepad poised, and watched by the art director, the fabrics editor, the furniture editor, the accessories editor, and a flock of young assistant editors, looking like a row of solemn black-clad pixies.

Camilla came to a stop, nibbling her lower lip. She couldn't bring herself to defer the piece on the Duchess of Pignolata-Strufoli's medieval folly in Umbria, or the other major feature, which was the elaborate conversion by a dear little Swiss billionaire of a nunnery in the Dordogne. The social repercussions of a postponement might be awkward and could easily jeopardize the summer invitations that had been extended to her. Finally, she came to a decision. In the manner of a fairy exercising the vanishing powers of her wand, she tapped three of the dummy spreads with her Montblanc pen. "I hate to see these go," she said, "but icons are *completely* timeless, and bidets are somehow such a spring thing. We'll have the icons in the summer."

Amid much nodding and note taking—but not without some ritual sulking and tossing of curls from the art director, who would have to reassemble all his layouts—the meeting broke up. Camilla returned to her office, to find Noel on the phone in considerable distress.

"You poor, poor boy," he was saying. "One's treasures picked over by those horrible people. I'd be in tears. It's just too bad. Oh, here she is now. I'll put you through." He looked up at Camilla. "The most dreadful thing—Andre's been robbed. I think he needs a shoulder to cry on."

Camilla went to her desk and sat down. Andre—the very mention of his name provoked a vague and most unusual emotion. Could it be guilt? Anyway, he was the last person she wanted to speak to, and she tried to think of some plausible crisis that might have occurred between Noel's desk and her office that would allow her to avoid taking the call. The phone glared at her with a blinking red eye. She picked up, preparing herself to be shocked and sympathetic.

"Sweetie! What*ever* happened?"

As Andre began to tell her, Camilla slipped off her shoe to ease the throbbing ache of her toe. The relief was instant and made her think that instead of trying to squeeze her foot bravely into Chanel's best, she might consider dressing the part of the injured editor—trousers, of course, and a pair of those cozy monogrammed velvet slippers. Perhaps an ivory-topped walking cane. Didn't Coco herself use a cane in later years? Yes, definitely a cane. She started to make notes.

"Camilla? Are you there?"

"Of course, sweetie. Just stunned by the news. Absolutely distraught."

"I'll survive. At least they didn't get the icon shots. What do you think of them?"

"Sublime, sweetie. Perfect." Camilla took a deep breath. He was going to find out sooner or later. "But as a matter of fact, there's been a tiny change in plan because of last-minute advertisers, and I've lost some pages. Too dreary for words. It means we've had to reschedule, and the icons won't be in the next issue. I can't tell you how desolated I am."

Camilla broke the disappointed silence by calling to an imaginary lackey. "Do stop *hovering* out there. I'm coming." And then, to Andre: "Must fly, sweetie. I'll talk to you soon. *Ciao* for now." She put down the phone before he had time to answer and buzzed for the junior secretary, all traces of guilt forgotten, her thoughts already occupied with the details of her walking-wounded wardrobe.

———

Andre's week had started badly and became worse. His friends in need, in the time-honored way of insurance companies, were treating him like a mendacious crook, finding fresh obstacles to payment each time he called. The cost of replacing the equipment he was ordering had run into thousands of dollars. Camilla hadn't mentioned any new assignments. And although Lucy was beating the bushes for new business, nothing had come up so far.

Between calls, he spent his time picking up after the burglars. In a pile of old magazines, he came across the issue of *DQ* that had featured Denoyer's house, and paused to flick through the pages. He felt a prickle of curiosity return as he came to a shot of the main salon. There was the Cézanne above the fireplace, luminous with the colors of Provence, the focal point of the room. Where was it now? According to Denoyer, hanging in a gallery in Cannes. He stared at the painting, trying to remember if he had ever seen an art gallery in Cannes. There couldn't be many of them. It would be easy to check, and there would at least be some satisfaction in finding out. If the painting was where Denoyer said it was, the whole incident made some kind of sense, and he could forget about it.

Early the following morning, he was on the phone to a friend in Paris. After a two-minute search on the Minitel, France's electronic phone directory, the friend was able to give Andre the names and numbers of the handful of galleries in Cannes. One after the other, Andre called them; one after the other, with varying degrees of regret, they informed him that they had no Cézanne on the premises, nor did they know of any Monsieur Denoyer.

So he had lied.

———

"He lied, Lulu. Why would he do that if he wasn't up to something?" Andre perched on the edge of her desk, watching Lucy eat an apple. Eyes wide, she shook her head as she finished chewing.

"Andre, it's his painting. He can do what he wants with it."

"But why would he lie? Actually, I'm glad he did. I don't feel like quite such an idiot. There *is* something fishy going on."

Lucy held up both hands in surrender. "OK. Maybe you're right. But that's his problem. We've got our own." She picked up a sheet of paper from her desk and passed it over to him. "These are the magazines I've called to see if they have something for us. None of them has called back. By the way, did you talk to Camilla? Has she got anything?"

Andre shook his head. "You know what she's like when she's getting an issue ready: She can hardly think past lunchtime." He glanced at Lucy's list without great interest. "But she did tell me she'd dumped the icon feature. Too much advertising. So one way and another it's been a pretty good week." He looked as mournful as a caged hound.

"Andre, we all have lousy weeks. Listen, why don't you go and pick up your new equipment? You're going to need it by the time I've finished." She tilted her head and looked up at him. "And could we have a little less gloom? Please?"

He left the office and was walking down West Broadway, when his eye was caught by a display in Rizzoli's side window. A new Gauguin biography had come out, thick and bulging with scholarship, and behind the neat stacks of books was a poster showing the artist's *Woman with a Flower.* Something about the posture of the woman and the angle at which she had been painted was familiar. Despite the differences in color and technique, there was an echo of the older, stouter woman in Denoyer's Cézanne.

Andre went into the store and browsed through every book he could find on the Impressionists until he came to what he was looking for. It had been given a full page and a brief caption: "*Woman with Melons.* Paul Cézanne, circa 1873. Once the property of Pierre-Auguste Renoir, now in a private collection." Well, maybe it still was, thought Andre. Or maybe it was in the back of a plumber's van. But certainly not in a gallery in Cannes. He paid for the book and walked back to his apartment, readying himself for another skirmish with Doubting Thomas, the man with a hundred excuses, his nemesis at the insurance company.

The last pale wash of light from a dying sun left the tops of the buildings, and downtown Manhattan took on its evening glow. Andre consigned a final bundle of odds and ends to the trash and poured himself a glass of red wine. He looked around the apartment, now cleaner and more orderly than it had been since he moved in. The thought was crossing his mind that there is nothing quite like a good burglary to simplify one's life, when the phone rang.

"That's a relief. You haven't committed suicide yet." Lucy laughed, and Andre found himself smiling. "I've been thinking about your mystery painting. Is it still bugging you?"

"Well—yes, I suppose it is. Why?"

"I have a friend who runs a gallery around the corner. You know, if you wanted to talk to someone in the business." She hesitated. "We could drop by this evening and see him."

"Lulu, that's sweet of you, but you've heard it all before. Wouldn't you be bored?"

"Boring comes later. My cousin and his wife are in town from Barbados, and they've landed me with their friend on a blind date. A computer purchasing agent for the Bajan government, first time in New York, and he's very, very shy. Does that sound like a good time?"

"You never know, Lulu. Us shy people have hidden depths. I'll pick you up in ten minutes." Andre had a racing shower, put on a fresh shirt and too much aftershave, and left the apartment whistling.

The gallery was one flight up, in a fine old building on Broome Street; blond wood floors, tinplate ceiling, subdued lighting, and a surprisingly young proprietor. "Daddy's rich," Lucy had said as they were going up the stairs, "but don't let that put you off. David's a nice guy, and he knows what he's doing."

David waved at them from the end of the gallery, a slight, pale-faced figure in a dark suit and white T-shirt, standing behind a minimalist desk, with a phone tucked between an ear and his shoulder. Two other young men were propping canvases against the bare walls. The sound of Keith Jarrett's concert in Cologne rippled from hidden speakers.

David finished his call and came over to greet Lucy with a peck on the cheek, a soft handshake for Andre. "I'm sorry about the mess." He gestured at the large, spotless space. "We're getting ready for a new exhibition." He led them through a door at the back, into a more human, untidy room, sparsely furnished with two office chairs and a scuffed leather couch, a computer and a fax squeezed in between piles of artbooks.

"Lucy told me you're looking for a Cézanne." David grinned. "Me, too."

Andre went through his story, the young art dealer quiet and attentive, lifting one hand from time to time to finger a silver earring, his eyebrows going up as Andre described his series of phone calls to Cannes.

"You're taking it pretty seriously, aren't you?"

"I know." Andre shook his head. "And I know it's none of my business, but I can't seem to leave it alone."

David sucked in air against his teeth. "I wish I could help, but that kind of thing is out of my league. I'm just a kid dealer." He scratched his head and frowned; his fingers paid another thoughtful visit to the earring. "Let's see. You want somebody— ah, wait a minute." He swiveled his chair around to face the computer. "I know who you want." He carried on talking as he tapped the keys to open a file. "He's one of the uptown dealers, a friend of my dad's. He has one of those Fort Knox brownstones in the East Sixties." He scrolled through a list of addresses on the screen. "There you go—Pine Art, his little joke. His name is Pine, Cyrus Pine." David scribbled the address and number on a pad. "I've met him a couple of times. He's a character, deals in Impressionists, plugged in to all the big collectors." David stood up, passed the slip of paper to Andre, and looked at his watch. "Listen, I've got to go. The new show opens tomorrow. Say hello to Cyrus."

Back on the street, Andre took Lucy's arm

and steered her at a brisk pace toward West Broadway. "Lulu, you're a jewel, and you deserve the best that life can offer. Do you have time for a glass of champagne?"

Lucy smiled. It was good to see him cheerful again. "Not really."

"Great. We'll go to Felix. I'd like them to see your beret."

They sat at one end of the small bar, surrounded by a hubbub of French voices. A patient, world-weary dog was tethered to a chair outside the men's room in the corner, nose twitching at the smells coming from the kitchen. Overt smoking was taking place. On a night like this, you could almost believe you were in Paris. It was one of the reasons Andre liked to go there.

Lucy was looking puzzled as she tried to pick out a familiar sound from the torrent of noise. "Do they always talk so fast?"

"Always. There's a wonderful line in one of Chekhov's letters: 'The Frenchman, until advanced senility sets in, is normally excited.'"

"What happens when advanced senility sets in?"

"Oh, they go on chasing girls. But slowly, so they don't spill their drinks."

The champagne arrived, and Andre raised his glass. "Thanks again, Lulu. It's probably a waste of time, but I'd really love to know what happened to that painting."

A hundred blocks to the north, Rudolph Holtz and Camilla were also drinking champagne. It had been a satisfactory few days. There had been no further panic calls from Denoyer, and the Cézanne had arrived safely in Paris. A thorough check on the proceeds from the burglary had revealed no unpleasant surprises. The transparencies had been burned, the equipment disposed of through the slippery but capable hands of Benny's uncle in Queens.

"So we have nothing to worry about," said Holtz. "If Kelly were in a position to do anything, we'd know by now. He'd have been in touch with Denoyer."

Camilla wriggled her toe in its velvet cocoon. The pain had gone, but she was enjoying the attention caused by her cane and had developed what she thought was a rather fetching limp. "I don't know about that, but he's been calling the office every day."

"Of course he's been calling the office. He wants work." Holtz brushed a scrap of lint from the sleeve of his tuxedo. "But I think it would be wise not to have anything to do with him for a while. You can find another photographer, I'm sure." He put down his glass. "We should be going."

The limousine was waiting outside the entrance of

the building, ready to take them the four blocks to a private fund-raising dinner. Holtz was not looking forward to it; these charity evenings could bankrupt a man if he wasn't careful. He patted his pockets to make sure he'd forgotten his checkbook.

8

THE streets of Manhattan's Upper East Side tend to confirm the view of those who see the city as a frontier outpost on the brink of war. Apartment buildings are garrisons, patrolled around the clock by uniformed men called Jerry or Pat or Juan. Private houses are fortified against invasion: Triple-locked doors, thickets of steel bars, alarm systems, drapes so heavy they could be bullet-proof—every security device short of the domestic rocket launcher and the antipersonnel mine is prominently displayed or signaled. And this is the safe part of town. These urban bunkers are the seats of wealth and privilege, situated in highly desirable locations, properties that change hands for seven figures.

As Andre turned off Park Avenue to go down Sixty-third Street, he wondered what it would be like to exist in a permanent state of siege. Did it ever become something you took for granted and eventually didn't even notice? The idea of the prison home appalled him, and yet for some people it was normality. Denoyer, for instance, whether he was in

France or the Bahamas, spent his life behind barricades. And so, from the look of his house, did Cyrus Pine.

It was a fairly typical four-floor brownstone, perhaps a little wider than most, and noticeably well kept. The short flight of steps was scoured and spotless, the front door and the ironwork protecting the lower windows were sleek with fresh black paint, the brass bell push was dazzling in the noon sunshine. There was no sign to indicate that this was a commercial enterprise, but then it was hardly the kind of business that depended on passing trade or impulse purchases.

Andre pressed the bell and identified himself to the intercom. Sixty seconds later, the door was opened by a stray from Fifth Avenue—a willowy young woman who looked as though she had spent most of the morning and a good deal of her father's money shopping for her outfit for the day. A cashmere sweater, a silk scarf, a skimpy but luxurious flannel skirt, and the kind of shoes—high heeled and with paper-thin soles—that are priced by the ounce. The way she smiled at Andre, she might have been waiting for him all her life. "Follow me," she said. Which he did with pleasure as she led him across the black and white tiled hallway and into a small study.

"Mr. Pine will be right down. Can I get you an espresso? Some tea? A glass of wine?"

Andre asked for white wine, feeling a little

uneasy at being treated with such consideration. His call to Pine had been brief; while he had mentioned the young art dealer's name and the magic word Cézanne, he hadn't gone into any detail about the purpose of his visit. Pine must have assumed that he was a potential customer. He smoothed his jacket and looked down at his shoes, dull against the chestnut sheen of the study's parquet floor, and was standing on one leg, polishing a dusty toecap against the back of his trousers, when the girl returned.

"There." She gave him another smile and a crystal glass, misty with condensation. "He's just finishing a call. Please sit down and make yourself comfortable." She closed the door behind her, leaving a trace of scent in the air.

Andre gave up on his shoes and inspected the room. It had the feeling of a quiet corner in a comfortable, long-established gentlemen's club—paneled walls, armchairs of veined and cracked leather, a fine but faded Oriental rug, two good eighteenth-century occasional tables, the faint aroma of beeswax. Andre was surprised by the absence of paintings; or indeed of anything that suggested Pine's occupation. The only pictures in the room were two large black-and-white photographs hanging side by side over the small fireplace. He went to take a closer look.

The photographs showed the yellowing tinge of age, in contrast to the obvious youth of their subjects. On the left, a group of boys turning into men, formal in black coats and high starched collars, hands in pockets, displayed a variety of decorative waistcoats to the camera. The faces, under slicked-back hair, were round and serious, almost haughty, gazing into the distance as though the photographer weren't there. A caption beneath the figures read: *Eton 1954.*

The second photograph showed another, less formal group. More young men, this time dressed for tennis, with sweaters slung over their shoulders and rackets that looked decidedly old-fashioned held casually in front of them. They were tanned and cheerful, smiling into the sun. *Harvard 1958.* Andre was looking from one photograph to the other to see if he could find a face that appeared in both, when the door opened.

"I'm the pompous one on the far left who looks like he has a smell under his nose. How are you, Mr. Kelly? I'm so sorry to keep you waiting." Andre turned to see the beaming face and outstretched hand of Cyrus Pine.

He was tall and slightly stooped, with a full head of silver hair brushed straight back above a wide forehead, sharp brown eyes, and an impressive set of eyebrows, worn long. He was dressed in a gray tweed suit of European cut, a pale-blue shirt, and a butter-colored silk bow tie. Like his house, he appeared to be immaculately maintained. Andre put his age at around sixty. His handshake was firm and dry.

"Thanks for seeing me," said Andre. "I hope I'm not wasting your time."

"Not at all. It's always a pleasure to meet a friend of David's. Very bright young man, David. His father's a great friend. We were at college together."

Andre nodded at the photographs. "You had an interesting education."

Pine laughed. "I had wandering parents—never knew on which side of the Atlantic they wanted to be." He moved over to the photographs and pointed to one of the tennis players. "That's me at Harvard. You can see I no longer had a smell under my nose. Must have left it behind at Eton."

Andre was trying to place his accent, a charming and cultivated hybrid of an accent that seemed to fall somewhere between Boston and Saint James's. "You are English, though, aren't you?"

"Well, I still have the passport. But I haven't lived there for forty years." He glanced at his watch. "Now then. I hate to rush you, but a lot of my business is done with a knife and fork, and I'm afraid I have an early lunch date in half an hour. Let's sit down."

Andre leaned forward in his chair. "I'm sure you're familiar with Cézanne's *Woman with Melons.*"

Pine nodded. "I don't know the lady intimately, much as I'd like to. That painting hasn't been on the market for at least seventy years." He grinned, and Andre could suddenly see the young man in the photographs. "Are you buying or selling?"

Andre grinned back, already liking him. "Neither," he said. "Much as I'd like to. Let me tell you what happened."

Pine sat motionless, his chin resting on clasped hands, letting Andre speak without interruption. He had heard similar stories before—paintings that had slipped out of circulation, followed by unconfirmed rumors of their reappearance in Switzerland, in Saudi Arabia, in California, in Japan. He himself had assisted once or twice in discreet maneuvers designed to minimize inheritance taxes. Paintings valued in the millions were often too expensive to keep. These days, you had to be very careful when and where and how you died. As Andre talked on, Pine began to feel stirrings of interest. Odd little incidents like this deserved to be taken seriously in a business that had once been described as shady people peddling bright colors.

Andre finished talking and picked up his glass. "Mr. Pine, let me ask you something. What do you think that painting's worth? Just a guess."

"Ah. The same question occurred to me while you were talking. Let's start with what we know." Pine rubbed the side of his jaw reflectively. "A year or so ago, the Getty Museum bought a nice Cézanne—*Still Life with Apples*—for more than thirty million dollars. That was the reported price. Now, given certain obvious requirements, like proof of authenticity and the good condition of the painting, I'd have to say that *Woman with Melons* could fetch as much or more. The fact that it once belonged to Renoir doesn't hurt, of course; nor does its long absence from the market. Collectors sometimes find those things extremely attractive. It's difficult to put a price on them." He gave a mischievous smile, his eyebrows twitching upward. "Although I'd love to try. But let's be conservative and stick to thirty million."

"*Merde,*" said Andre.

"Indeed." Pine stood up. "Let me have your number. I'll ask around. The art business is an international village inhabited by gossips. I've no doubt someone will know something." Another twitch from the eyebrows. "If there's anything to know."

There was a gentle tap on the door, and Miss Fifth Avenue appeared. "Mr. Pine, you should be going."

"Thank you, Courtney. I'll be back by two-thirty. Make sure all your admirers have left by then, would you?" Courtney giggled as she opened the front door, her cheeks rosy with the faint traces of a blush.

The two men left the house together, with Andre murmuring something complimentary about the girl as they went down the front steps. Pine buttoned his jacket and shot his cuffs. "One of the advantages of being in a business where appearances are important is that you can hire pretty girls with a completely clear conscience. And they're deductible. I do love pretty girls, don't you?"

"Whenever I get the chance," said Andre.

They parted company on the corner of Sixty-third and Madison. As he was uptown, Andre decided to walk to *DQ*'s offices and see if he could catch Camilla. The last time they had spoken, she had brushed him off, and none of his subsequent calls had been returned. Her continued silence was beginning to puzzle him. It was unlike her; she wasn't pleased when he worked for someone else, and normally she called often, even when she had no job to discuss. Just keeping you warm, sweetie, she had once admitted to him.

The milder weather had brought out the usual rich variety of Madison Avenue street life: tourists wearing jeans and running shoes and apprehensive, about-to-be-mugged expressions; businessmen bellowing into cellular phones to make themselves heard above the din; boutique vultures, hair frosted, faces lifted, shopping bags bulging; beggars, Rollerbladers, massage parlor touts, vendors selling everything from pretzels to fifty-dollar Rolex ripoffs—and, drowning out conversation or even lucid thought, the unremitting cacophony of hoots and squawks, horns and sirens, the pneumatic grunting of buses, the squeal of tires and gunning of engines, the mechanical bedlam of a city in a perpetual hurry.

The midday exodus was at its height by the time Andre reached the *DQ* building, with a stream of humanity flooding across the lobby and out to lunch. He decided against taking one of the elevators up to the office, not wanting to miss Camilla coming down; and so he waited, facing the hundreds of figures pushing past him in their race to get through the doors. Why didn't anyone stroll in New York? They couldn't all be late.

Another elevator door slid open. Andre saw Camilla's oversized dark glasses and the shining bounce of her hair as she stepped out, surrounded by a flying wedge of editorial staff, the junior secretary in her official position at Camilla's shoulder. Andre moved toward the group, recognizing this as being one of Camilla's mobile meetings. They were frequent occurrences at the magazine, due partly to the sense of urgency and excitement that Camilla insisted came from thinking on one's feet, but mainly to her congenital unpunctuality. The meetings had been known to continue in the car taking Camilla to lunch or to Bergdorf's. They were part of the show: the successful, overworked editor not letting a second go to waste in the service of the magazine.

They were also most effective when used as a shield against the unwelcome approach of anyone Camilla didn't wish to speak to, and this was such an occasion. She saw Andre—she must have seen him; they were only five feet apart when he called out to her—and she looked straight at him for a moment before her head jerked away. And then, safely behind a wall of bodies, she was past him. By the time he had turned to follow her, she was through the door and into the back of a waiting car.

Caught between disbelief and mounting irritation, he stood watching the car cut uptown through the traffic on Madison Avenue. He and Camilla had worked together for more than two years. They weren't close friends, nor would they ever be, but he had developed a liking for her and had always thought that it was reciprocated. Apparently not. His calls were no longer returned, and now this deliberate and obvious snub. But why? What had he done wrong?

He hesitated outside the entrance to the building, wondering whether to go up and see Noel, who was usually able to make some kind of sense out of Camilla's signals. But then a mixture of pride and anger took over: If she was going to avoid him, he was damned if he would chase after her. To hell with her, and to hell with *DQ*. There were plenty of other magazines. On his way toward Park Avenue, he ducked into the bar of the Drake to celebrate a minor victory of independence over immediate need. And immediate need there was, as he had to admit when he looked at the cocktail napkin on which he'd added up the cost of his new equipment. If the insurance people didn't come through—and they were showing every sign of trying to delay settlement until well into the twenty-first century—he would start to feel the pinch very shortly. Work, that was the answer. He raised his glass in a silent toast to the next job. Lucy was bound to come up with something soon.

———

"OK, so it's not enough to retire on, but it's better than anything else in town." Lucy's face wore a puzzled, slightly defensive expression. "It's dead out there." She glanced down at her notepad. "I've tried just about everything except the *Plumbers' Gazette,* and the only other job anyone could come up with was a catalogue." She wrinkled her nose. She didn't like her photographers doing catalogues unless the alimony payments really had got them by the throat and they were desperate. She shrugged. "You never know. It might be fun."

The assignment was for an English magazine at an English fee, significantly lower than Andre's American rate. But Lucy was right. Shooting tapestries in a stately home was certainly better than the grind of working on dozens of room settings under the eye of an art director who wanted everything lit by searchlight. Andre had been through that when he was starting out, and he didn't feel like going back to it.

"Lulu, it's fine. Honestly. I don't have much choice at the moment. When do they want it done?"

Lucy consulted her notes. "Yesterday? It's a crisis. They had it all set up. Their regular photographer was down there, and then he fell off a horse and broke his arm."

Andre winced. "They don't expect me to get on a horse, do they? What was he doing on a horse, for God's sake?"

"How do I know? Grip with your knees, you'll be fine."

"You're a hard woman, Lulu. I wish I'd had you with me this morning." Andre described his unsuccessful brush with Camilla and saw a frown settling on Lucy's face. "So there I was," he said, "standing in the lobby like a *connard*—"

"A what?"

"A jerk—and she looked straight through me. And she saw me, I know she did."

Lucy got up from her desk. "Andre, she's a flake. You're always saying she's not so bad, she has her funny little ways but she knows her job, she puts out a good magazine. That may be true"—Lucy wagged a cautionary finger—"but it doesn't alter the fact that she's a flake. When she likes you she's all over you like a rash; when she doesn't, you don't exist. And for some reason, now she doesn't like you." Lucy folded her arms and cocked her head to one side.

"Are you sure nothing happened when you were in France together?"

Andre thought back to the evening in the Colombe d'Or and shook his head. "No. Nothing."

The frown on Lucy's face was replaced by the hint of a smile, a rather knowing smile. "Maybe that's the problem."

———

Cyrus Pine, beneath the carefully maintained veneer of affable, casual charm that he displayed to his clients, was highly competitive. It had been in his nature to want to win ever since Eton, when he had discovered that "coming top"—either in sports or in the classroom—afforded him a certain cushion against the minor brutalities of public school existence. And it was at Eton that he had learned to disguise his gifts, since it was very poor form to be seen to try too hard. Success that seemed to come as a result of accident or luck was acceptable; success as a result of obvious determination and hard work was not. By the time he finished at Harvard, the pattern was established: He appeared to be one of life's fortunate amateurs. This camouflage also worked well for him in business, but the reality was that he worked as hard and liked a deal as much as the next man.

Deals in the art world—or in Pine's rarefied part

of the art world—frequently depend on information acquired before anyone else. Occasionally, this will fall into your lap, the long-service award presented by an old contact after years of patient cultivation. More often, it comes from following up and sifting through the whispers and rumors that inevitably swirl around a business in which many millions of dollars are chasing a few hundred paintings. And for Cyrus Pine, who liked to joke that the ideal art dealer was an acrobat who kept his nose to the grindstone, his ear to the ground, and his eye on the main chance, no whisper was too faint to pursue.

When he returned to his office after a decorous and wine-free lunch with an elderly client who regularly pronounced herself bored with her collection of Pissarros and Sisleys (and just as regularly changed her mind), Cyrus settled himself by the phone. The young man's story might be nothing more than a curious, unimportant incident, but one never knew. With a glass of cognac to take away the taste of mineral water, he began to work his way through the Rolodex.

9

THE apartment had reverted to chaos, as though the burglars had come back for more. Outer cartons, inner cartons, skeins of torn plastic skin with cellulite puckers, Styrofoam in all its rich diversity—molds, blocks, wedges, countless drifting shards taking flight with every passing breath of air: the floor was a testament to America's passion for over-packaging.

In contrast, the long worktable at the end of the room was a picture of order. Camera bodies, lenses, Polaroid backs, film, and filters were laid out in line, waiting their turn to be stowed in the padded compartments of dark-blue nylon bags. It was a comforting sight. Andre had felt vulnerable without the tools of his trade, as if his eye and his professional skills had been stolen along with his equipment. But now, as he ran his fingers over the buttons and knurls and listened to the snick of a lens fitting into its housing, he felt his mood lift and his confidence return. Maybe after England he'd slip over to Paris for a couple of days, to see if he could get an assignment from one of the French magazines. A week or so in the south, shooting for *Côte Sud,* would be the perfect antidote to the frustrations of the past few days. He picked up the Nikon. It wasn't his old, battered familiar friend, but he enjoyed its heft and the way the shape of the camera body fitted into his hand. Taking it to the window, he squinted through the viewfinder at the early evening mosaic of shade and deep shadow, lights beginning to blink on. Screw *DQ,* and screw Camilla. He would manage without them.

He answered the phone on the second ring, expecting to hear Lucy and her usual pretrip nanny routine, making sure he had his tickets and his passport and plenty of clean socks, so he was taken aback for a moment when he heard the distinctive clipped drawl.

"Dear boy, it's Cyrus. I hope I'm not disturbing you. I expect you're tied up, but I'm calling on the off chance that you might be free to join me for a drink. I've been doing a little research. Thought you might be interested."

"That's very kind, Cyrus." Andre glanced at the littered floor. "As a matter of fact, I had a date with a roomful of garbage, but I've just canceled it. Where do you want to meet?"

"Do you know the Harvard Club? Forty-fourth, between Fifth and Sixth, number 27. It's quiet there, and you can actually see who you're talking to. I'm getting too old for dim bars. Shall we say six-thirty? Oh, I'm afraid you'll need a tie. They like ties."

"I'll be there."

It took Andre some time to find his token tie, rolled up in the side pocket of one of his jackets. The tyranny of the tie had often inconvenienced and irritated him, never more than when he had stayed at an outrageously expensive, outrageously pretentious hotel in Dallas. After a day of shooting in a Texan palazzo, he had wandered into the hotel bar, sober and respectable in his Sunday-best blazer, and had been refused admission because the snowy bosom of his freshly laundered white shirt was tieless. The authorities had lent him a whisky-stained length of violently patterned silk—the bar tie—and he was then permitted a drink, as though he was a pariah suddenly become socially acceptable. He had shared the bar with two boisterous men wearing bootlaces around their necks, and a woman who, apart from a cascade of jewelry, was practically naked from the waist up. One of the men had been wearing a large hat too, he remembered, a sartorial touch that would have been frowned upon in many parts of the civilized world. Ever since that experience, he had traveled with an all-purpose, black knitted silk tie in his pocket—crease-resistant, stain-friendly, and suitable for funerals. He adjusted the knot and set out, with a sense of expectation, for the haven where the great and the good of Harvard go to refresh themselves after a bruising day among the bulls and bears and lawsuits of corporate America.

Checking his coat, he found Cyrus Pine in a corridor off the lobby, studying the announcements pinned to the notice board, his smoothly tailored back to the cloakroom. Andre went over and stood beside him. "I hope they haven't issued a ban on photographers."

Pine turned and smiled. "I was looking to see if any of the members had been caught trying to entice young women into the steam baths. Those were the days." He nodded at a flyer pinned to the red felt. "Times have changed. Now I see we're having Japanese-speaking lunches. How are you, dear boy?" He took Andre by the elbow. "The bar's through here."

It is a bar without frills at the Harvard Club, the way bars used to be before hanging ferns replaced tobacco smoke and the jabber of jukeboxes and sports commentaries destroyed quiet conversation. There are, it's true, two television sets—recently installed, to Pine's considerable annoyance—but on this particular evening they were blank and mute. It was a slow night; of the four small tables, only one was occupied, by a single figure bent over his newspaper. Another member sat at the bar, lost in thought. There were no frivolous distractions from the peaceful enjoyment of alcohol.

The two men settled at one end of the bar, far

from the uproar made by the reading member turning the pages of his *Wall Street Journal*. Pine deliberated over his Scotch for a first long swallow, indicated his appreciation with a sigh, and settled himself on a barstool. Andre listened to the room. The loudest sound was the clink of bourbon against vodka as the bartender rearranged his bottles. "I get the feeling," he said, his voice low, "that we should be passing notes to each other, or whispering."

"Good Lord, no," said Pine. "This is lively compared with a place I sometimes use in London. You know? One of those really ancient clubs. Disraeli was a member—I dare say he still is. Let me tell you a quick story, supposed to be true." He leaned forward, his eyes bright with amusement. "The reading room there has a *very* strict rule of silence, and the armchairs on either side of the fireplace are traditionally taken by two of the oldest members for their afternoon meditations. Well, one day old Carruthers totters in, to find the equally old Smythe already in his chair, fast asleep, a copy of the *Financial Times* over his face as usual. Carruthers reads his paper, has his nap, leaves the reading room at gin time. Smythe still there, hasn't moved a muscle. A couple of hours later, Carruthers comes back. History doesn't relate why—probably left his false teeth under one of the cushions. Anyway, he finds Smythe in exactly the same position. Hasn't budged. Odd, thinks Carruthers, so he taps Smythe on the shoulder.

Nothing. He shakes him. Nothing. He lifts up the newspaper, sees staring eyes, wide-open mouth, and puts two and two together. 'My God!' says he. 'One of the members has died! Fetch a doctor!' Comes a stern voice from another member, snoozing in the shadows at the far end of the room: *'Silence, chatterbox!'"*

Pine's shoulders shook with mirth, his head nodding as he watched Andre laugh. "You see? Compared with that, what we have here is Rowdy Hall." He took another sip and dabbed his lips. "Now then, to business. Tell me something," he said. "Last time you saw this Denoyer fellow, did you get the impression that he was thinking of selling the Cézanne? A tear in the eye when he looked at the photographs? An unguarded remark? A quick call to Christie's? Anything like that?"

Andre thought back to the evening of anticlimax at Cooper Cay. "No. As I told you, the only thing that seemed not quite right was the fact that he wasn't surprised. Or if he was, he did a good job of hiding it."

"Does he strike you as an undemonstrative man?" The bushy eyebrows jigged up and down. "No disrespect to the French, but they aren't exactly famous for hiding their feelings. Impulsive, yes. Dramatic, often. Inscrutable, hardly ever. It's part of their charm."

"Controlled," said Andre. "I think that might be a better way of putting it. Perhaps it was just that I was a stranger, but I felt he always took an extra moment—just a second or two—before he answered a question or reacted to anything. He thought before he spoke."

"Good God," said Pine, "that *is* unusual. Where would the world be if everyone was like that? Luckily, it's not a habit shared by many people in the art business." He glanced up at the bartender, using a circling finger to semaphore his need for another Scotch. "I made a few calls this afternoon, not entirely truthful calls, I have to admit. Said I was acting on behalf of a serious collector—name withheld to protect my commission, naturally—who was in the market for a Cézanne. Client of outstanding probity, significant funds available, payment anywhere in the world, all the usual guff. Ah, thank you, Tom." Pine paused and sipped. "Now, here's the interesting part. Normally, when you dangle a worm in the water like this, it takes quite a while before there's a bite. But not this time."

Pine paused, cocked his head, and looked at Andre's attentive face for a few seconds in silence. The inspection seemed to satisfy him. "I'm going to be quite candid with you. If there is a deal to be done here, I'd like to be in on it. I'm not getting any younger, and these things don't come along every day of the week. And as you brought it to me, it's only right and proper that you take a share." Another pause, while the two men looked at each other.

Andre wasn't sure what to say and took refuge in his wine as he tried to gather his thoughts. Money had never crossed his mind; all he wanted to do was to satisfy his curiosity. "Do you really think that's likely? A deal?"

"Who knows? I could find three buyers tomorrow for that painting, if it was available—and if Denoyer would let me handle it."

"And you think it is available?"

Pine laughed, causing the member opposite to frown and look up from paying homage to his martini. "You're dodging the issue, dear boy. We won't know that for sure until we do some homework."

"We?"

"Why not? I know the art business, you know Denoyer. I have the impression that you're an honorable young man, and I am an absolute pillar of rectitude, although I say it myself. Two minds on the problem are better than one. All in all, it seems like a reasonable basis for collaboration. Let me get you some more wine." Pine kept his eyes on Andre's face while the finger circled once more at the bartender. "Well? Are you in? It might be fun."

Andre found Pine a difficult man to resist and couldn't immediately think of any reason why he should try. "I wouldn't be doing it for the money," he said. "The money's not important."

Pine's reaction was a clench of the face—so severe that his eyebrows almost collided. "Don't be ridiculous. Money's always important. Money is freedom." The eyebrows resumed their normal position, and Pine's face relaxed into a smile. "But if it makes you feel any better, you can do it for a good cause."

"What's that?"

"My old age."

Andre looked at the silver hair, the twinkling eyes, the jaunty, slightly lopsided bow tie. It might be fun, Pine had said, and Andre had a feeling that it probably would. "All right," he said. "I'll do what I can. But I have to work as well, you realize that."

"Good man. I couldn't be more pleased. We'll fit the work in, don't you worry. Now let me tell you what I heard this afternoon." Pine waited for the bartender to replace Andre's glass and glide back to his bottles.

"We mustn't get too excited," Pine said, "because this isn't even a grown-up rumor; more of a gleam in the eye than anything else. But as I said, the reaction was very fast, within a couple of hours of my dropping the word. There's a dear old soul who works at the Met—I give her lunch two or three times a year—and she has the longest ears in town. According to her, I imagine after listening to some conversation she wasn't supposed to hear or reading a memo upside down on somebody's desk, there is the merest breath of a hint that an important Cézanne will be coming onto the market within the next two or three months. Nothing firm, of course, and no details." Pine leaned forward for emphasis. "Except this: The painting is privately owned, no museums involved, and it hasn't made the rounds for a long time. Which fits our bill, doesn't it?"

Andre had instinctively leaned forward as well and caught himself looking over his shoulder. "There might be others, mightn't there? I mean, he was quite prolific."

"He certainly was. Must have done sixty paintings of Mont Sainte-Victoire, for a start, and practically died with a brush in his hand. But this is too much of a coincidence." Pine looked at their empty glasses and then at his watch. "Can you stay for dinner? Drinkable wine, good nursery food. Unless you're out on the town tonight?"

"Cyrus, if I told you about my social life at the moment it would put you to sleep. The only girls I spend any time with these days are the ones who tell me to fasten my seat belt."

"Really? You should give Courtney a whirl. Tasty little thing, but she doesn't have much luck with young men. I've met one or two of them—middle-aged at twenty-five, and thrilled with themselves. Dull beyond belief." Pine signed the bar chit and stood up.

"Suspenders and striped shirts?"

"Matching underwear, too, I'm sure. Let's go in, shall we?"

They left the bar and entered a double-level room that could easily have accommodated three hundred of Harvard's finest, with parking space to spare for a small army of flunkies. The decorative style fell somewhere between a baronial hall and a hunting lodge, with a profusion of stuffed and mounted trophies, many of them, so Pine explained, the victims of Teddy Roosevelt's hunting expeditions—heads of elephant and bison, horns and tusks, a gigantic rack of elk antlers. Human trophies took the form of portraits, men of substance with dignified expressions: "Either presidents of the club or presidents of the U.S.," said Pine, as they made their way through the main room. Above them, a wide balcony accommodated more tables, and Andre noticed several women among the diners, somehow surprising in such masculine surroundings. "We were the last of the university clubs to admit them, I think it was back in '73. Good thing, too. Makes a pleasant change from looking at all the wildlife on the walls."

Pine saluted an acquaintance at a nearby table—a tall, dapper man wearing an emphatic mustache with a fine Ruritanian twirl at each end. "That's Chapman, brilliant legal mind, plays the clarinet. The bushy-haired fellow with him runs one of the Hollywood studios. Hardly recognized him without his sunglasses. I expect they're up to no good. Now, what are you going to have?"

Andre chose clams and salmon hash from a list of

simple, unfussy dishes and watched as Pine wrote his selection down on an order form. It was Andre's first experience of dining in an American university club, and he found it old-fashioned and immensely soothing. There was none of the hovering and the breathless recitation of the specials of the day from an out-of-work actor that seems to be obligatory in many New York restaurants. The red-jacketed waiters murmured, if they spoke at all. They were deft and unobtrusive. They knew their business. Andre rather wished he had gone to Harvard, so that he could escape here whenever the racket of Manhattan became unendurable.

With the edge taken off their appetites by the first course, Pine resumed the conversation where he had left it in the bar. "Step one," he said, "or so it seems to me, is to find out where the painting is. What's your guess?"

"Well, we know it's not where Denoyer said it was, in a gallery in Cannes. I suppose it might have been sent somewhere for cleaning."

"Most unlikely," said Pine. "It's not that old, and the lady and her melons looked very healthy in the photograph you took for *DQ*. Next guess?"

"Reframing? It wasn't framed when they put it in the van. Sent up to his house in Paris? Stuck in a bank vault? God knows. It might easily be back in Cap Ferrat by now."

"Indeed." Pine nodded. "It might be. Or it might

not. That's all we have to go on at the moment, and I think that's where we have to go. Very agreeable at this time of year, as I remember."

"Cap Ferrat? Are you serious?"

"Where else, dear boy? If the painting's not where it should be, we might be onto something. If it is where it should be, we go down the road to Beaulieu and drown our sorrows at La Réserve. Haven't been there for twenty years." Pine looked like a schoolboy at the end of term. "I told you it would be fun."

Andre couldn't argue with the logic and didn't want to. It would be fun to take off with this amiable old rascal; in any case, he was leaving for Europe tomorrow. And so it was decided that they would meet in Nice, after Andre had finished his stately home assignment. The rest of the evening, which included some memorable cognac of great antiquity, was spent working out how they might get into the house on Cap Ferrat without encouraging the French police to join them.

10

HEATHROW on an early-spring morning. Fine, persistent drizzle leaking from a low gray sky; a frieze of sleep-deprived faces lining the carousel to watch the crawl of other people's luggage; announcements turned into gibberish by the scrambling devices that airports build into their loudspeaker systems; late arrivals; missed connections; anxiety attacks—the start of yet another day dedicated to the joys of travel.

Andre felt surprisingly fresh, having avoided alcohol and slept for six hours. If the traffic wasn't too bad, he could be down in Wiltshire before lunch, spend the afternoon and the following morning shooting, and be back at Heathrow in time for an evening flight to Nice. Encouraged by this cheerful thought, he made the mistake of smiling at the customs officer as he was going through the green channel. And was, of course, stopped.

"Open that one, sir, if you don't mind."

The customs officer looked at the array of equipment in the bag and lifted an eyebrow. "Amateur photographer, are we, sir?"

"Professional. I take pictures for magazines."

"I see." The voice flat and unconvinced. "Been at it long?"

"A few years, yes."

"But not with this equipment."

"No." Why did he feel guilty? "My stuff was stolen. I bought all this last week in New York."

A chilly smile, and permission to proceed.

Swearing never again to make eye contact with customs officials, he headed west in his rented Ford, among cars that looked like toys after the road monsters of America. He wondered how many smugglers were caught and what they were caught with. Care packages of China White? Items prejudicial to public safety? Or was it more likely to be a wicked extra bottle of duty-free brandy and a bootleg laptop? How would one smuggle something bigger, something like a painting? He pushed the car up to eighty, anxious to be done with the job and off to meet Cyrus Pine.

The drizzle gave way to heavy, windblown rain as he left the suburbs behind and reached the plump green hills and neat small fields of Wiltshire. What a beautiful country England would be if someone turned off the water. Andre peered through the metronome sweep of the windshield wipers, looking for the side road that led to the village where he was to ask for directions to his final destination.

He very nearly drove through it, Nether Trollope being not much more than a single-street hamlet. A straggle of beamed cottages, dour and dripping under the rain, a tiny post office and general store, and a pub.

The Lamprey Arms announced itself to passersby with a weather-beaten painted sign that showed a creature resembling a worm—rampant and with a prominent set of teeth—writhing above a peeling and indecipherable Latin motto. A supplementary inducement hanging from the bottom of the sign offered Pub Grub. Andre pulled into the car park and walked across waterlogged gravel, his footprints turning instantly to puddles.

Whatever conversation had been going on ceased as he pushed open the door and the half-dozen customers turned to stare at him. The other silent greeting was a strong whiff of beer and stale smoke, mingling with overtones of damp clothes. A hissing coal fire struggled for life in the grate, any warmth from it absorbed by the sleeping bulk of a venerable black Labrador, its gray muzzle twitching in dreams. Behind the bar, a stout, dark-haired woman glowed with the implausible radiance achieved by an over-generous hand with makeup.

"Morning, dear," she said. "Nice day for it. What's it going to be?"

Andre ordered a beer. The mutter of voices resumed, low and secretive, as though gardening and football were forbidden subjects.

"There you are, dear." The barmaid put Andre's beer in front of him. "Just passing through, are you?" She looked at him, her inquisitive eyes bright against the pools of midnight-blue eye shadow.

"I wonder if you can help me," said Andre. "I'm looking for Throttle Hall."

"Off to see his lordship, are you?" She puffed on a cigarette. That, too, had been cosmetically enhanced, by a smear of lipstick on the filter. "It's only five minutes up the road. Big iron gates, with one of them nasty things on the top. You can't miss it."

"Nasty things?"

"It's your lamprey, isn't it? Like the one on the sign. Sort of an eel with teeth, gives me the shudders, but there you are. I'd much rather have a nice dog and duck or a royal oak, but seeing as it's Lord Lamprey's pub, we have to grin and bear it."

"That's a historical creature, Rita." One of the customers joined in. "Dates back. Traditional."

"I don't care." Rita lit a fresh cigarette from the stub of her old one. "Gives me the shudders," she said again. "It's the teeth."

Andre removed his elbow from a beer slick on the bar. "Does Lord Lamprey come in often?"

Rita sniffed. "Not so's you'd notice. Daphne does, though. His daughter." She nodded two or three times and winked. "Saturday nights." She gave Andre a significant glance under lowered eyelids. "Likes her little bit of fun, does Daphne. Oh, yes."

Andre ignored the unspoken invitation to ask exactly what Daphne did on Saturday nights. "And Lady Lamprey? Do you see much of her?"

Rita abandoned her post behind the beer pumps to edge closer. "Lady L.," she said, her voice hardly above a whisper, "did a runner, didn't she? Went off with a solicitor from Salisbury." She applied more lipstick to her cigarette. "*Years* younger than her, he was. But you know what they say."

Andre didn't, and he didn't think he wanted to. He distracted Rita from making further revelations by ordering what was advertised on the blackboard as a Ploughman's Lunch. This turned out to be a small log of bread, a foil-wrapped pat of Dairy Fresh butter, a slab of cheese, and two large and viciously overpickled onions. The paper napkin showed a fat man in a chef's hat waving a banner that said *Hearty Fayre*. Andre used it to muffle the acrid smell of the onions. He felt sorry for ploughmen.

Half an hour later, with lunch a solid, unforgiving memory in his stomach, Andre got out of the car and pushed open the gates to a wide gravel drive that curved away through parkland dotted with stands of magnificent old chestnuts and oaks. He drove through, then walked back to close the gates. A group of sodden sheep turned to examine him. One of them bleated, a thin, plaintive sound that barely carried above the drumming of rain on the gravel. Andre shivered and headed up the drive.

Pringle's *Guide to the Stately Homes of England* lists Throttle Hall as "an imposing manor house of sixteenth-century origins and subsequent additions," a benevolent description that glosses over four hundred years of architectural mayhem. Previous Lord Lampreys, when in funds, had indulged themselves with extensions, annexes, follies, buttresses—some of them flying—crenellations, pediments, and Gothic flourishes, until the Elizabethan symmetry of the original building was completely hidden. Now, approaching the twenty-first century, Throttle Hall was a rambling barracks of spectacular ugliness. As Andre parked the car and got out, he was grateful that exteriors weren't part of the assignment.

His first tug of the bell pull hanging by the studded double doors produced nothing except the rasp of iron against stone. He pulled harder and was rewarded by the sound of distant barking, which quickly became closer and more agitated. He heard paws scrabbling against the other side of the door, then a curse, and finally the screech of an unoiled lock. He stepped to one side as the door opened and a group of lanky, rust-colored dogs tumbled out, whining and wriggling with excitement, leaping up to pin him against the wall.

"You'll be the photographer, I suppose."

Andre pushed one of the dogs away from his groin and looked up to see an elderly figure in a long apron over black trousers and waistcoat, shirtsleeves rolled above scrawny mottled forearms, hands in grimy white cotton gloves. The face, beneath strands of hair plastered across his skull, was narrow and pale, the only touches of color provided by a tracery of broken veins on his cheeks.

Andre nodded. "That's right. Lord Lamprey?"

"Watching the racing." The custodian sniffed and jerked his head. "Follow me." With an escort of scampering dogs, he led Andre into the gloom of the interior, walking with short, careful steps, his body tilted forward, as if the floor were covered in ice. They passed through a somber flagstone hall, beneath the gaze of past Lampreys in their cracked gilt frames, and down a paneled corridor. It was cold, colder than outside, the particular damp English cold that works its way up from the ground and creeps through the body, leaving chilblains and rheumatism and bronchitis in its wake. Andre looked in vain for radiators.

As they approached an open door at the end of the corridor, Andre could hear the high-speed babble of a television commentator, interrupted by a deeper, more patrician bellow: "Give him the whip, you bloody fool. Give him the whip!" And then a groan of disappointment.

They stopped in the doorway. The old man coughed loudly. "The photographer, my lord."

"What? Ah, the photographer." Lord Lamprey continued to stare at the television as the horses cantered back to the enclosure. "Well, go and fetch him, Spink. Bring him in."

Spink raised his eyes to the ceiling. "He's here, my lord."

Lord Lamprey looked around. "Good God, so he is." He put his glass on a side table and pushed himself up from his armchair, a tall, burly man with a ravaged, once-handsome face and a florid outdoor complexion. Andre could see scuffed suede shoes and brown corduroy trousers below the hem of a long tweed overcoat, its collar turned up against the brisk nip in the air.

"Lamprey. How d'you do." The hand he extended to Andre felt like chilled leather.

"Kelly." Andre nodded toward the television. "Don't let me take you away from the . . ."

"There's half an hour before the next race—plenty of time for a dish of tea. Spink, what about a dish of tea?"

Spink muttered to Andre out of the side of his mouth. "First he tells me to clean the silver. Now he wants tea. I've only got one pair of effing hands, haven't I?" And then: "Darjeeling or China, my lord?"

"I think Darjeeling. We'll take it in the long

gallery, so that Mr. Kelly can have a squint at the tapestries."

Lamprey led the way down the corridor past a succession of large rooms, their furniture covered with dust sheets, before stopping at the foot of a wide oak staircase. He stopped on the first step and patted the carved banister. "Elizabethan," he said. "The place is a bit of a warehouse, as you may have noticed. My ancestors were magpies, always coming home with something or other—statues, paintings, unsuitable wives." They had reached the top of the stairs, and Lamprey threw out a hand toward the tapestries. "And these, of course."

The gallery extended on either side of the staircase, a run of perhaps sixty feet, with tapestries stretching the entire length, some hanging on rods, others framed as panels. "Gobelins, most of them," said Lamprey. "Rather splendid, don't you think?"

Andre murmured in agreement as he walked slowly past the beautiful muted colors, his mind taken up with the technical difficulties of shooting in the narrow, badly lit gallery. Whatever else had been changed at Throttle Hall over the centuries, the original electrical fixtures remained—early twentieth century, with plug sockets rationed to one per wall. Lighting would be a problem.

Tea arrived, dark brown and thoroughly stewed. Spink showed no sign of wanting to return to his silver cleaning but stood with his arms folded, sucking his teeth. Andre warmed his hands on his teacup and caught Lord Lamprey looking at his watch as he turned away from the tapestries. "They're magnificent," said Andre. "How long have they been in the family?"

"Brought back from France in the eighteenth century." Lamprey walked across and ran his fingers over one of them. "Priceless now, of course."

Spink edged sideways until Andre was in range of a whisper tinged with gin. "Nicked, they were. All nicked, every last one. Never paid a penny for them." With the back of his hand, he wiped a dewdrop from the end of his nose and sniffed. "Talk about daylight robbery."

"Well," said Lamprey, "mustn't hang around here getting in your way."

"Mustn't miss the start of the two-thirty," muttered Spink.

———

After a frustrating hour spent rigging the lighting, replacing blown fuses, and overcoming the eccentricities of wiring that was well past retirement age, Andre was able to start shooting. From time to time, Spink would appear at the foot of the staircase and look upward, with pursed lips, before returning to the servants' quarters and the comforts of his gin. Of Lord Lamprey there was no sign. By seven o'clock, when he was bidden by Spink to change for dinner, Andre felt satisfied that he was more than halfway there; if the electricity held out, another three hours in the morning should see the job done.

He was spending the night in what Spink referred to as the Blue Room, an appropriate name that matched not only the curtains but the effect the temperature had on the skin color of guests. While waiting for a reluctant trickle of hot water to cover the bottom of the bath, Andre made a tour of his bedroom. Despite the good, if shabby, antique furniture, the room held the promise of an acutely uncomfortable night. The springs of the large bed had given up, creating a sagging trough in the middle. A small lamp cast a vestigial glow over one bedside table. On the other table, a tooth glass and a half-empty decanter of whisky had been provided, doubtless to provide numbness that would compensate for the lack of warmth. There was a gas heater, but investigation showed that there was no gas. Andre bathed by sections in three inches of tepid water, dressed as warmly as he could, and made his way downstairs.

The cocktail hour at Throttle Hall was celebrated in one of the smaller sitting rooms, a dim cavern decorated, after the fashion of the Harvard Club, by an enthusiastic taxidermist. At the far end of the room, Lord Lamprey stood with his back to the log fire, his jacket hoisted up to permit the unimpeded passage of warm air to the noble rump. In a corner, Spink pretended to busy himself over the drinks table, holding glasses up to the light and buffing them with his sleeve. As Andre walked across the room, dogs converged on him in a paroxysm of welcome.

"Kick 'em if they bother you," said Lord Lamprey. "Splendid people, Irish setters, but no sense of decorum. Fitz! Fitz! Get down!"

The dogs took no notice. "Which one's Fitz?" Andre asked.

"They all are. *Down,* damn you! Never could tell them apart, so it was easier to give them the same name. What are you drinking?"

Spink, it appeared, had already decided. He thrust a tumbler on a silver tray under Andre's nose. "Whisky." The word came from the side of his mouth, in his confidential mutter. "Wouldn't trust the sherry, and we've run out of gin."

Andre was glad to see there was no ice. He pushed his way through the dogs to join his host by the fire. "Snaps going well, I hope," Lamprey said. "I expect you heard about the last chap, did you? Led into bad ways by my daughter, I'm afraid, and fell off a horse."

"So I heard."

"Trouble is, Daphne thinks everyone can ride like her, but she's been on horses since she was three. Rides like a man. Wonderful seat."

The two of them shared the fire in silence, and for the first time since his arrival, Andre began to feel warm. It was not to last. With the look of someone weighed down by the burden of grave organizational problems, Spink approached them, tapping his watch as he came. "Cook said seven-thirty, or it'll spoil."

Lamprey sighed. "Where's Daphne? Damned women. Why are they always late? Eh, Spink?"

Spink leered. "Titivating, my lord, I dare say."

"We'll have to go in without her. Wouldn't do to upset cook." Lamprey drained his glass, handed it to Spink, and dislodged a dog that had been lying across his feet. He led Andre through the door and across a hallway, grumbling as he went about his daughter's cavalier sense of time—wouldn't keep her bloody horses waiting, treats the house like a hotel, young people nowadays all the same, punctuality a thing of the past. He was still developing what was obviously a favorite theme as they entered the dining room.

Here were more portraits, this time of the Lamprey women. Some of them, with their sharp faces and glassy eyes, bore a strong family resemblance to the giant badger whose mounted head snarled above the fireplace. The long oak table was set for three beneath a heavy chandelier, and Andre half expected to see the tiny candle-shaped bulbs start to gutter in the stiff breeze coming through chinks in the leaded windows.

Lord Lamprey settled himself at the head of the

table, ringing a small silver bell vigorously before reaching for the wine bottle. He peered at the label and grunted. "We're in luck. It's the '69 Latour. I thought Spink had drunk it all." He poured a little into his glass and sniffed it. "Splendid. Are you a wine man, Kelly?"

"I certainly am."

"Pity." He reached over and half filled Andre's glass.

"Has Spink been with you long?"

"Thirty years, maybe longer. Started helping out belowdecks, in the scullery. Stayed on." Lamprey chewed on his wine. "Funny old cove, but we're used to each other now, and he pretty well runs the house. I'm quite fond of him, really. You know how it is with servants."

Andre was spared the need to reply by the simultaneous arrival, through different doors, of Spink shuffling in with a soup tureen and, with military, booted step, the daughter of the house, a strapping young woman dressed in riding breeches, roll-neck sweater, and one of the bulky down vests so beloved by rural Englishwomen. "Sorry I'm late, Daddy. Percy's got colic." Her voice, resonant and slightly strangulated, echoed through the room; in the orchestra of human voices, hers was a trumpet.

She turned to look at Andre as he stood up.

Lord Lamprey drew back from an examination of his soup. "Mr. Kelly, this is my daughter, Daphne."

Spink, standing by Andre's side with tureen poised, whispered, "The *Honorable* Daphne," his emphasis making Andre wonder if he was supposed to curtsy or drop to one knee. She was staring at him with an intensity that he found disconcerting, her eyes very wide and very blue against the ruddiness of her complexion. Her brown hair was pulled back and tied with a black ribbon, and her forehead showed the faint line left by a recently discarded riding cap. In fifteen years' time, she would probably have thickened, with her skin coarsened by too much wind and weather. But now, in her early twenties, she had the healthy glow of a well-exercised animal in prime condition.

Lord Lamprey waved his spoon at a small rubber thimble that was bobbing on the surface of his soup. "Spink, what the devil's this?"

Spink hurried over and rescued the thimble with his ladle. "Ah. Cook's been looking for that. It must have slipped off the finger she burned." He transferred it smoothly to his handkerchief. "She *will* be pleased. It was her last one."

Andre bent his head over his soup, on the lookout for any other lost objects hidden in the depths of the thick Brown Windsor. Somewhat to his surprise, he found it to be good—heavily laced with sherry, warm and comforting. He felt he was being watched, and looked up to see Daphne staring at him.

"D'you ride?" she asked.

"Afraid not. Well, I did once," he said. "A long time ago, my parents took me to the seaside at Arcachon, not far from Bordeaux. They had donkeys on the beach. I think I managed about ten minutes without falling off." He smiled at her. "But it was a very quiet old donkey."

The mention of France roused Lord Lamprey from his soup to deliver a lecture on the pernicious nature of the French—their dedicated self-interest, their arrogance and complacency, their snobbery, their preoccupation with food. Frogs, for God's sake, and snails. And now the bloody franc was so overvalued you couldn't afford to go there. It was a well-worn point of view that Andre had heard expressed many times before by English acquaintances. They seemed to harbor some deep resentment toward their neighbors, as though fate had given the French preferential treatment. And yet still they went, the English, across the Channel in their millions every year, to return with horror stories about a cup of coffee costing five pounds and the legendary rudeness of Parisian waiters.

Andre waited for Lord Lamprey to run out of bile. "The funny thing is," he said, "the French say much the same about the English—apart from the food, of course. I wouldn't want to repeat their comments about the food. But arrogance, snobbery—particularly snobbery—you'll hear all the same things on the other side of the Channel. I think we enjoy being irritated by each other." He smiled at Daphne. "I'm actually half French myself," he said, "and I have to say that we're not all bad."

Daphne snorted. "Very sound on horses, the French," she said. "You mustn't take Daddy too seriously. He loathes everybody. You should hear him about the Germans. Or the English, for that matter. Get him going on politicians—all you have to say is Blair—and we'd be here all night."

"Say one thing for the French." Lamprey filled his glass and, with obvious reluctance, passed the bottle grudgingly over the other two glasses. "They make a very decent wine." He grinned at Andre and proposed a toast: "To your glorious country." An added undertone: "Wish it were ours."

Spink had cleared away during the exchange and now reappeared with the main course, a charred carcass in a sea of roast potatoes and brussels sprouts. After testing the blade on his thumb, he handed Lamprey a bone-handled carving knife and fork.

"Nothing like a free-range fowl," said Lamprey as he stood up to make the first incision. He attacked with a violent lunge of his carving fork, but the armor of blackened skin resisted the prongs, and the chicken skidded off the plate and halfway down the table, scattering sprouts and potatoes as it went. Lamprey followed its progress with alarm. "Good God, the damn thing's not dead. Spink!"

"Maybe we were a little hasty with the first pass,

my lord." Spink used a napkin to retrieve the bird, and put it back on the plate. "Might I suggest a less sudden hand with the fork? And then in over the horns with the knife." He started to gather up the escaped vegetables, watching Lamprey out of the corner of his eye.

"Horns? What horns? It's a bloody chicken."

"Old bullfighting term, my lord."

Lamprey grunted, successfully impaled the chicken, and began sawing away with the knife.

Spink smirked. *"Olé,* my lord."

Andre found it difficult to decide which was the tougher, the sprouts or the bird, but the others ate with uncritical country appetites and evident enjoyment, coming back for second helpings. When all that remained on the plate was a stripped rib cage, Lamprey declared a truce. The skeleton was removed, to be replaced by a decanter of port and the remains of a large Stilton.

The conversation drifted on, with Daphne and her father discussing horses, a recent point-to-point meeting, and the prospects for next year's pheasant shooting. They were entirely taken up with their own world, showing no curiosity about Andre or his work, which suited him very well at the end of a long day. After a cup of tepid coffee in the sitting room, Lord Lamprey announced his intention to watch the latest disasters, as he called the ten o'clock news, and Andre took the opportunity to make his excuses and go upstairs.

He sat on the edge on the bed, a tot of whisky in his hand, delaying the moment of getting out of his clothes to slip between sheets that felt more like frozen glass than cotton. The alcohol was fighting a losing battle with the temperature, and undressing assumed the significance of a health hazard. He was trying to decide whether to be a man about it or get undressed in bed, when there was a sharp rap at the door. Hoping to see Spink with a heated brick or a hot-water bottle, he went to open it.

And there was the Honorable Daphne.

"Fancy a gallop?"

"What?" said Andre. "In the dark?"

"We can keep the light on if you like." And with that, she applied a firm hand to his chest, pushed him backward, and closed the door behind her with a kick from her booted foot.

11

YESTERDAY'S rain had gone, spring's warm breath was on the breeze, and even the hideous facade of Throttle Hall looked a little less offensive in the glow of the afternoon sun. Andre, mission accomplished and farewells made, stowed the last of his bags and closed the trunk of the car. Spink lurked on the front steps, keeping out of work's way until the moment came to swoop in and claim his tip. Andre walked to the front of the car, but Spink, showing a surprising turn of speed, beat him by a head and opened the driver's door with a deferential leer. He palmed the twenty-pound note Andre gave him, after a downward glance to verify the denomination and assess the degree of gratitude.

"Very kind, sir, very kind." With the money safely in his pocket, he felt he could afford to satisfy his curiosity. "Comfortable night, sir? Warm enough? Took advantage of the amenities, I trust?" His face contorted into what he thought was a subtle wink.

Andre couldn't help smiling at the old gargoyle.

He fastened his seat belt and started the engine. "Never slept better, Spink, thank you."

I knew it, Spink seemed to be saying to himself. I could tell by the way she was looking at him over dinner, measuring him up. Saucy little piece. Takes after her mother. He glanced at his watch, apparently wondering if he had time to go into the village and get a bottle of gin from Rita before Lord Lamprey surfaced from the afternoon siesta that was his habit on days when there was no racing on television.

Driving back to Heathrow, Andre shook his head at the memory of his night of high-impact aerobics with the Honorable Daphne. After her initial greeting, she had confined her remarks to instructions of a technical nature and demands for greater effort over the jumps. While recuperating between bouts, she had worked her way through the whisky on the bedside table and dozed, virtually ignoring his attempts at conversation. It was clear that he was there to provide a service rather than small talk, and service he gave, to the best of his ability. At dawn she had left him, facedown and exhausted, with a parting swipe across the buttocks and the comment that she'd had worse.

Met at Heathrow by a messenger from the English magazine, Andre handed over the rolls he had shot of the tapestries, then collapsed in the departure lounge. Muscles he'd forgotten he had were aching; another night like that and he would need crutches and a physiotherapist. He noticed tremors in his hands as he reached for the phone to call Lucy.

"Andre! Where are you?"

"Heathrow. I'm waiting for the flight to Nice. The magazine sent someone to pick up the film, so you can invoice them whenever you like." He yawned. "Sorry. The last couple of days have been a bit of a rush."

"How was it?"

"Cold. Wet. Weird. Cook, butler, ancestral portraits, wall-to-wall dogs, hundreds of rolling acres, and no heat. Lord Lamprey complaining that you can't get boys to go up and sweep the chimneys anymore. I didn't know people still lived like that."

Lucy's giggle came across three thousand miles. "Sounds like your kind of place. Did you have time to do any riding?"

"Lulu, I didn't have a minute to myself. Promise." Which was perfectly true, Andre thought. "How's everything over there?"

"It's OK. Things are still slow, but Stephen's back from Florida, so now I get to leave the office and go out to lunch."

"Save one for me, will you? I'm meeting Cyrus Pine tonight, but we should be back in a couple of days. I'll take you to the Royalton and we can wave at Camilla."

"Fine," said Lucy. "I'll bring a gun."

Andre heard the garbled squawk announcing that his flight was boarding. "Lulu, I'll call you from Nice."

"Now, that sounds like a place to have lunch. Have a good trip."

Andre took his seat in the back of the plane. He was asleep before takeoff, his last conscious thought being of Lucy sitting opposite him in an open-air restaurant overlooking the Mediterranean. When the flight attendant came to wake him just before landing, she saw he had a smile on his face.

————

At Cyrus Pine's suggestion, they had booked into the Beau Rivage, a small, pleasant hotel behind the Promenade des Anglais, not far from the opera. Visiting divas stayed there, Cyrus had told Andre, and he had a soft spot for divas, being very partial, as he'd said, to a statuesque bosom. He had flown overnight to Paris before coming down to Nice, checking in a few hours ahead of Andre and leaving a note at the front desk: *Gone out for fish and chips. See you in the bar at ten.*

Andre put his watch forward to French time and saw that he had half an hour. He unpacked and showered, inspecting his body for scars and contusions, feeling the abundant hot water ease away the aches. He swore to himself that he would never be unkind about French plumbing again, and went down to the bar feeling human for the first time that day.

Pine arrived shortly after ten, looking dapper and faintly theatrical in a houndstooth check suit and plum-colored bow tie; he was full, in every sense of the word, of the meal he had just eaten. "I'd forgotten how marvelously they do things in France," he said. "I'm sure I reek of garlic. Have you ever had lobster ravioli?"

Andre was reminded of his most recent meal, a pick-up lunch in the kitchen at Throttle Hall. "I thought you were having fish and chips."

"I was full of good intentions, but that pretty girl at the desk recommended a place called l'Esquinade, down by the port, and I gave in to temptation. An old habit of mine, I'm afraid." Pine paused to order a cognac from the bartender. "Anyway, you'll be pleased to know that the coast is clear. I made the call, as we agreed, and Denoyer's still in the Bahamas. I spoke to him. Seemed rather nice."

"What did you say?"

"I told him I was vice-president of international customer services at AT&T and that I wanted to send him a platinum card entitling him to seventy-five percent off all long-distance calls." Pine smiled into his cognac. "He was delighted. Nothing the rich like more than saving money. He told me to send the card to Cap Ferrat—he's arriving there next week. So tomorrow it's just us and the caretaker."

Andre grinned and raised an imaginary hat. "Did you bring the swatches?"

"Dozens, dear boy. We're all set."

———

By nine the following morning they were in the car, driving into the sun on the coast road to Cap Ferrat. Pine had modified his wardrobe for the occasion, and instead of a suit he was wearing a blazer and salmon-colored slacks, forsaking his customary bow tie for a silk paisley cravat.

"What do you think?" he asked Andre. "Could I pass as a decorator? I might have overdone it with the trousers. They're a relic from a weekend on Fire Island."

"To tell you the truth, Cyrus, the only decorator I've ever met was a woman—great beefy creature, very pleased with herself. She did cushions, I remember. In fact, I think she was wearing some of them when I met her." Andre turned off the N98 and took the small road to the Cap. "Don't worry. Your outfit's fine. The big mistake down here is to wear an Armani suit. If you do, everyone thinks you're a chauffeur."

"I did a bit of homework on the plane," said

Cyrus. "A book about the Riviera. King Leopold of Belgium had a place on Cap Ferrat, and he used to go swimming with his beard stuffed inside a rubber envelope. Fascinating. Are we nearly there?"

"Two minutes," said Andre. He had thought he would be feeling nervous; he was, after all, about to talk his way into someone's home under false pretenses. But his cheerful companion seemed to be having such a good time—his confidence so contagious—that Andre's feelings were more of anticipation and optimism. He was sure they could get into the house. And then the worst that could happen would be to find the Cézanne there after all, hanging in its rightful place. Anticlimax, followed by a good lunch. He shrugged and turned to Cyrus as he slowed down.

"It's just past this bend. Do we need to stop and do any more rehearsing?"

"Never," said Pine. "I think we know the basic plot. Spontaneity is the breath of life, dear boy. Just get us in, and leave the rest to me."

"Remember that Claude probably knows some English."

"I shall be the soul of discretion."

Andre grinned. "Not in those trousers." He stopped the car in front of the iron gates and pressed the buzzer.

The voice came over the intercom, tinny and abrupt. "*Oui?*"

"*Bonjour,* Claude. It's Andre Kelly—you remember? The photographer. Monsieur Denoyer asked me to bring a friend of his to the house. He's going to do some work in the salon."

"*Attends.*" There was a click, and the gates slowly swung open. Andre turned to Cyrus with a sudden thought. "We'd better not use your real name."

"You're quite right, dear boy." He adjusted his cravat. "How about Paisley? Frederick Paisley," he added, "the third. Old Palm Beach family. Scottish ancestors."

"Don't get carried away." Andre took his foot off the brake and let the car roll slowly down the drive. The gardeners had obviously been busy preparing for Denoyer's return. Lawns had been razor-cut, cypresses and palm trees shaped and trimmed, flower beds freshly planted. The spray from an invisible sprinkler system turned to rainbows in the sun, with the distant shimmer of the Mediterranean visible beyond the house.

"Denoyer does himself rather well," said Cyrus. "I wouldn't mind a summer here myself. Is that the faithful retainer I see on the doorstep?"

"That's him." Andre pulled up, and they got out of the car as Claude came forward to meet them, a stocky figure in cotton trousers and an old polo shirt, his face already tanned, a glint of gold in his smile. He shook Andre's outstretched hand and nodded.

"You're well, Monsieur Kelly?"

"Too busy, Claude. Too much traveling. I wish I could spend more time here. And you?"

"*Ouf.* Older." Claude's eyes went to Cyrus, who was standing to one side, his arms filled with books of fabric swatches, a sheaf of paint color samples, and a clipboard.

"Claude, this is Monsieur Paisley from New York." The two men exchanged inclinations of the head. "He'll be doing the redecoration of the salon, and he needs to choose colors and take measurements before he can make his proposal to the Denoyers."

"*Ah bon?*" Claude's amiable face became puzzled. "They said nothing of this to me."

"No? How bizarre." Andre pretended to think for a moment, then shrugged. "Well, that's easy. Why don't we call them?" He turned to Cyrus and repeated what he'd said, this time in English.

Cyrus took his cue. "Do you think we should?" He juggled what he was carrying so he could look at his watch. "It's three in the morning over there, and you know how Bernard likes his sleep."

Andre explained the problem to Claude. "And unfortunately," he added, "Monsieur Paisley has a rendezvous this afternoon in Paris. This is the only time he has."

There was a silence. Andre tried not to hold his breath. Claude pondered, looked at his own watch for inspiration, then finally shrugged. "*C'est pas grave,*" he said. He picked up an invisible telephone and held it to his ear. "I will speak to Monsieur Denoyer later." He nodded. They were in.

Claude took them across the tiled entrance hall and opened the double doors to the salon. The long, high-ceilinged room was dark, and they had to wait while Claude opened the heavy curtains and, with a slow deliberation that Andre found excruciating, the shutters. As the sunlight flooded through the windows, he saw the ornate sconces, the faded peach-colored walls, the fussy, precisely arranged furniture, the Aubusson carpet, the books and bibelots on the low tables. It was exactly as he had photographed it. Exactly.

"But this is *fabulous.*" Cyrus walked into the room, laying his swatches and color sheets on a couch before throwing his arms wide. "The proportions are heavenly, the light's exquisite, and *some* of the furniture is really quite exceptional." He put his hands on his hips and stood tapping one foot on the marble floor. "Mind you, I'm not mad about the sconces, and the less said about those curtains the better. But I see possibilities. I see great possibilities."

Andre barely heard him. He felt flat, all optimism gone. He stared at the painting above the fireplace, and Cézanne's *Woman with Melons* stared back, precisely where she was supposed to be. Even the frame, he noticed gloomily, was the same. It had all been a waste of time.

Claude took up a position by the door, his arms folded. It was obvious that he had decided to stay with them. Andre tried not to sound disappointed. "Is there anything I can do to help?"

Cyrus passed him the clipboard and a pen. "Would you mind taking notes as I dash around? Thanks so much." His voice gave nothing away. If he was feeling let down, he was concealing it very convincingly. "Now, it seems to me," he said, "that the focus of the room is the Cézanne, which is quite superb. So we mustn't have anything fighting with that, must we? Colors, finishes, fabrics—they must all work with the painting. Cézanne knows best. So that's where we start. Come along."

He took a bundle of swatches over to the fireplace and stared intently at the painting, occasionally holding up a scrap of fabric next to it before calling out a reference number, which Andre dutifully recorded on the clipboard. The process was repeated with the paint colors, and repeated again and again as second and third thoughts occurred to Cyrus, who seemed mesmerized by the painting. For two hours this continued, with Claude a silent, bored presence in the background and Andre's spirits lower with every pointless note he made on the clipboard.

It was close to noon before Cyrus had taken some measurements and one final, long look at the painting. "I think I've seen enough," he said. "Are you sure you've got it all down?" Without waiting for

Andre to answer, he went across to Claude and pumped his hand vigorously. *"Désolé* to make you wait like this, my dear fellow. You've been most kind. Many thanks. *Merci, merci. Vive la France."*

Claude turned a bemused eye to Andre, who added his thanks as they went out to the car. They drove through the gates without speaking. Once out of sight of the house, Andre pulled onto the side of the road. "Cyrus, I don't know what to say. I don't know how you managed to go through all that nonsense." He shook his head, staring through the windscreen. "I'm sorry. You were terrific, and that makes it worse."

"You weren't to know, dear boy. But the painting's a fake."

"What?"

"A wonderful, wonderful fake. I'm sure of it." Cyrus watched with amusement as Andre's face was split by a smile that almost reached his ears. "Well, don't just sit there. Drive on."

"Where to?"

"Lunch, dear boy. Lunch."

———

There are few better settings for a sunny lunch than the terrace of the Voile d'Or, overflowing with geraniums, high above the port of Saint-Jean-Cap-Ferrat. Cyrus hummed with contentment as they were seated at a table beneath the shade of an old olive tree. Andre left him in peace as they studied the menu after ordering a bottle of rosé. Finally, curiosity overcame him.

"How do you know it's a fake?"

"Mmm? The roast *crevettes* sound rather good, don't you think?"

"Come on, Cyrus. How do you know?"

"Well," said the older man, "I think it's mainly the result of years and years of looking very closely at the real thing, and I've handled quite a few Cézannes since I started. In time, your eye learns. Did you go to the Cézanne exhibition in Philadelphia last year? I spent two days there, looking and looking. Quite wonderful. Ah, good man."

The waiter uncorked the bottle, murmuring something about the complexion of a young girl as he poured the delicate, smoky-pink wine into their glasses. He took their order, nodded with approval, and padded back to the kitchen.

Cyrus held up his glass to the sun before tasting his wine. "There's nowhere quite like France, is there? Now, where was I?"

"Philadelphia."

"Indeed. The point I was making is that it's a matter of getting your eye accustomed to the way an artist paints, his use of color and light and perspective, his tricks of composition, his brushwork, which can be fast or slow—it's sometimes as distinctive as a signature. It must be the same with you photographers, surely. I mean, you could tell the difference between a genuine Avedon and an imitation." He smiled. "Or a genuine Kelly, for that matter."

"Not quite the same league, Cyrus."

"But you understand what I'm saying. There isn't a formula for spotting fakes. It's your eye, your experience, and your instinct—or your gut reaction, as it's sometimes rather indelicately called. There are tests you can do to establish the age of the canvas and the paint, the stretchers and the nails, but even tests are far from foolproof. Take canvas, for instance, or wood. There are thousands of old, undistinguished paintings floating around. A competent forger will pick one up for a few dollars—of the appropriate period, obviously—and use it for his fake. The more recent the painting, the easier it is to find materials of the same age, and Cézanne only died ninety years ago." Cyrus drank some wine. "To think that the forger undoubtedly got paid a great deal more than Cézanne ever received for the original! It's a wicked old world."

The waiter came, murmur at the ready. "*Les crevettes pour monsieur, et le Saint-Pierre avec la sauce gaspacho. Voilà. Bon appétit, messieurs.*"

Further questions from Andre had to wait while they paid due attention to their food. They were sharing the terrace with a few other couples, who revealed their origins by their choice of tables: the locals in the shade, the northerners sitting in full sun, making up for a long gray winter. Beneath them, the port was quiet, the rows of yachts and dinghies empty, their owners hard at work in their faraway offices to pay for the mooring fees. In July and August they would come down, the two-week sailors, to spend their vacations squeezed hull-to-hull among thousands like themselves. But today the seagulls owned the boats.

Andre mopped up the last of his sauce and saw Cyrus casting an appraising eye over the cheese board. "I'm beginning to think I've lived in America too long," Cyrus said. "I've been conditioned by the propaganda: Cheese is bad for you, the sun is bad for you, and don't even think about alcohol or tobacco. Remarkable how the French manage to survive to a ripe old age, isn't it? They must be doing something right."

"Would you ever think of living out here?"

"Adore to, dear boy, but it's a question of pennies. The house in New York is mortgaged, and I'm still paying off the last wife. But you never know—one big deal could change everything."

"Do you think this could do it?"

"Maybe. But there's a long way to go. We've got to get hold of the painting first."

"You said that the one in the house isn't just a fake but a wonderful fake. Is that any kind of clue?"

"Oh, I know who must have done it. There's only

one man who's that good on Impressionists. If I hadn't spent so much time with my nose practically touching the canvas I'd never have spotted it. Fine, fine work. But while I know who did it, the problem is finding the rascal." Cyrus beckoned to the waiter with the cheese board. "He won't be in the yellow pages."

"What good would it do to find him? He's hardly likely to tell us anything, is he? He's a crook."

"Exactly," said Cyrus, "and crooks can always be bribed. A certain subtlety may be necessary, but I'm sure we can manage that between us. Think about it. The only other person who's involved as far as we know is Denoyer, and he's not going to come clean. He's already lied once. My word, look at those cheeses. Do you think I could risk the Camembert? It looks as if it's going to attack at any moment."

He pointed to the cheese, and the waiter cut him a slice, dripping ripe and unctuous. "*Avec ça, monsieur?*"

He took some Cantal and a baby *chèvre,* ordered a glass of red wine to see it down, watched with interest as Andre made his choice. "How about you?" Cyrus asked. "You seem to like it here, you speak the language. I can see you in a little studio in Paris. Or even Nice. It's not as if you have to turn up at an office every day."

Andre looked out over the port. "I've thought about it quite a lot recently," he said. "But New York is where the good jobs are." He shrugged. "Or were, until a couple of weeks ago." And he went on to tell Cyrus about the cold shoulder he was getting from Camilla and *DQ*. "It happened overnight," he said. "As soon as I got back from the Bahamas, she wouldn't even take my calls."

Cyrus frowned over his Camembert. "That's interesting. She doesn't know Denoyer, does she?"

"Well, yes. She came with me on the shoot last year and met him then. But she's never mentioned him since."

"Don't you think it's odd—the timing, I mean? You see something you weren't supposed to, and then . . ." Cyrus drew a finger across his throat.

"I don't know. Probably just a coincidence."

Cyrus grunted. "The older I get, the less I believe in coincidences."

————

Bernard Denoyer was a troubled man as he performed his dutiful fifty laps in the swimming pool at Cooper Cay. Claude's call from Cap Ferrat had woken him at six, and what Claude told him had made a disquieting start to the day. Initially, he had thought—he had hoped—that his wife, Catherine, might have been organizing some redecoration as a surprise. But when he had asked her, she knew nothing about it; nor did she know anyone called Paisley.

He reached the end and turned, lowering his head in the cool water as he pushed off, watching the slow progress of his shadow on the bottom of the pool. If this scheme of Holtz's didn't work out, he would be in trouble. It had sounded so foolproof, too. A simple substitution of the Cézanne by a wonderful forgery, the original discreetly sold, the proceeds hidden away in Switzerland. No death duties, and plenty of cash to cover those unfortunate losses incurred during the Crédit Lyonnais fiasco. And now this. Why was the young photographer so interested, and who the hell was this Paisley? He finished his laps, put on a toweling robe, and went to his study, shutting the door behind him before picking up the phone.

For once, Rudolph Holtz was unable to provide any reassurance. He, too, was a troubled man as he finished speaking to Denoyer and climbed down the steps from his bed. The photographer was becoming a pest; more than a pest. He was becoming dangerous. Holtz shaved and showered, and sat brooding over a cup of coffee in the kitchen. The scam he devised had seemed foolproof, and indeed had worked for two years without a hitch. Like all the best scams, it was relatively straightforward. Camilla, through *DQ,* could gain access to the homes of the rich. She could spend hours, even days, roaming through the art-encrusted rooms, ingratiating herself with the owners and their servants, taking

Polaroids, making notes. By the time she was finished, she would have the material for one of her predictably fawning articles. But that was merely the front.

The other purposes of her research—and these, naturally, never appeared in print—were to establish two things. First, the owners' pattern of absence, the dates on which they regularly left their principal residences for the delights of the Caribbean or the ski slopes. And second, the extent and sophistication of the security arrangements, which were often out-of-date or surprisingly inadequate.

Armed with this information, Holtz then briefed the specialists: his forger and his removal men. A chosen painting would be copied (and the Dutchman was a genius, no doubt about it), and when the owners were safely on some distant alp or beach, the removal men—artists, too, in their own stealthy way—would tiptoe in and substitute the fake for the original. To all but the most expert and suspicious eye, nothing would have changed. The original would find a new home in a gloater's vault or a Tokyo penthouse. The Swiss accounts of Holtz and Camilla would swell in comfortable secrecy. Nobody would be any the wiser. And in this particular case, with Denoyer as a willing accomplice, there should have been no risk at all, nothing to go wrong. In theory.

Holtz's reflections were brought to an end by the

return from the gym of Camilla, in sunglasses, leotard, and the calf-length chinchilla that had been her bonus from their last big score. She bent down to kiss him on the forehead.

"Why the furrowed brow, sweetie? You look as if the maid's run off with the Renoir." She took a bottle of Evian from the refrigerator and made her breakfast by adding a slice of lemon to the glass before taking off her coat and coming to sit down.

Normally, Holtz found Camilla in her leotard a stimulating sight that had frequently caused him to put her through a second workout, but today such things were far from his mind, and he found her bright mood intensely irritating. "That goddamned photographer of yours," he said. "He's poking his nose in again."

Camilla removed her sunglasses, always a sure sign of concern. "Nothing to do with me, sweetie. I haven't spoken to him for weeks, just as you told me. What's he done now?"

"He's been in Denoyer's house with someone called Paisley, who says he's a decorator. D'you know him?"

Camilla looked blank. "Doesn't ring a bell. He can't be one of the top forty. I know *all* of them."

Holtz dismissed the top forty with a flick of his hand. "Bunch of fabric salesmen."

Camilla bridled. "They're very useful to us, Rudi, and you know it. And some of them are my dearest friends. Gianni, for instance, and that lovely man with the difficult name I can never remember."

"Screw Gianni." Holtz leaned forward and tapped the table with a stubby finger. "You've got to do something about the photographer before he makes any more trouble."

Camilla, who actually had screwed Gianni (and it was very nice too, she remembered) after a particularly cozy lunch, realized that this was not a morning for levity. She glanced at her workout watch, the one that the salesman at Cartier had assured her was sweatproof. "Sweetie, I'm running late. What do you expect me to do about him?"

"Get the schmuck out of circulation. Think of something. If you can't, I will. I don't want any more surprises."

———

Camilla stared at the back of the chauffeur's head as he drove downtown to the *DQ* office. Thinking cap on, sweetie, she said to herself. Divine green eyes or not, Andre would have to be dealt with.

12

THERE was nothing more they could usefully do in France. Cyrus changed his reservation so that he and Andre could travel together on the direct flight from Nice to New York, both men reluctant to leave but impatient to get back.

Cyrus had suggested that they bypass the efforts of the gourmet in the sky, and before leaving for the airport they had spent an enjoyable half hour wandering through the market in Nice, collecting ingredients for a picnic. As soon as they were settled in the modest comforts of business class, Cyrus summoned a flight attendant and handed her a shopping bag containing smoked salmon, an assortment of cheeses, fresh baguettes, and a bottle of white Burgundy. "When the moment comes," he said to her, "perhaps you could do the honors with this. It's our lunch."

The flight attendant's smile faltered as she took the bag, but Cyrus gave her no chance to reply. "You're a dear girl," he said, with a beam. "We have rather sensitive stomachs. Oh—could you make sure the wine doesn't get too cold? It should be chilled but not startled."

"Not startled," she repeated gravely. "Right."

Andre watched her go to the galley with the bag and wondered why he'd never thought of doing this himself. The well-meaning gastronomic contortions that airline chefs put themselves through never worked, no matter how glowing the descriptions on the menu. Lamb, beef, seafood, veal, *meunières* of this, *fricassees* of that—airline food invariably looked and tasted like airline food: mysterious, congealed, and dull. And the wines, even if they had been "specially selected by our flying sommelier," seldom lived up to their labels.

"Do you often do this, Cyrus?"

"Always. I'm amazed more people don't. The only things I ever accept on a plane are brandy and champagne. They can't do much to that. I see the bottle is coming our way. Shall we?"

The 707 went through its preliminary flexing and rumbling as it pawed the ground before takeoff. The two men nursed their champagne and looked through the window at a knot of figures waving goodbye from the airport's terrace. It was a change—a very pleasant change —for Andre to have a traveling companion, and it was a reminder that much of his life recently had been spent alone. His own fault, he had to admit. There was Lucy, sweet unattached Lucy, and what had he done about her?

Called her from airports and left her to the mercies of men in red suspenders. He was resolving to try harder with Lucy—in fact, to start trying as soon as he got back—when Cyrus turned to him as if he had been reading his thoughts.

"Ever been married, Andre?"

"Nearly." He was surprised to find that her face was only a blur in his memory. "About five years ago. Then I started getting work that involved going away, and I guess she got bored waiting for me to come back. She married a dentist and moved to Scarsdale. I suppose it was inevitable. Too much traveling, the story of my life."

Cyrus sighed. "I didn't do enough. They say there's nothing like distance to make a marriage last. I've had two stabs at it; both of them ended in tears." With a philosophical twitch of his eyebrows, he took a mouthful of champagne.

"Still like women?"

"Absolutely. The trouble is, I've never been able to spot the fakes."

It was the first time Andre had seen Cyrus with anything less than a good-humored expression, and he decided to leave a discussion about the perils of matrimony for another time. "Tell me about this forger. You said you know who he is. Have you met him?"

"Good Lord, no. He keeps his head well down, which is quite understandable in his line of work. You're not likely to bump into him at gallery cocktail parties, handing out business cards. I don't even know which country he lives in." Cyrus frowned as the in-flight video came on at full blast, the cheerful voice suggesting useful tips in the event of a crash and imminent death. He leaned closer to Andre to make himself heard. "His name is Franzen, Nico Franzen, originally from Amsterdam. The Dutch are pretty good at this sort of thing. Have you ever heard of the Vermeer man?"

Andre shook his head.

"Another Dutchman. His name was van Meegeren, and he specialized in faking Vermeers—used ancient canvases, hand-ground paints, all the tricks—and made a bundle at it, so they say. Fooled them all, for a while. You have to take your hat off to top forgers, in a way. They may be rogues, but immensely talented. Anyway, our man Franzen sticks to Impressionists, and as we've seen, he does them brilliantly. In fact, I've heard rumors that some of his work is hanging in museums and private collections, assumed by one and all to be genuine. He must get quite a kick out of it."

"How can that happen? Aren't paintings examined by experts?"

"Of course they are. But famous paintings come with a pedigree, a history, a string of learned opinions and endorsements, rather like precedent in law. When a painting has been accepted as genuine for a number of years, that's a very powerful recommendation. Experts are only human; they believe experts. If they're not expecting to see a fake—and if the fake's good enough—there's a better than even chance they won't spot it. Under normal circumstances, I'd have said Denoyer's Cézanne was genuine, because it's so beautifully done. But thanks to you, dear boy, I had my eye skinned for a fake." Cyrus paused. "And a fake is what I saw."

Andre shook his head. "The whole thing sounds like the emperor's new clothes."

Cyrus smiled, and waved his empty glass at the flight attendant. "Something like that. People see what they're conditioned to expect. What makes our little investigation unusual is that the owner is in on the scam. Denoyer wants the original to disappear, for whatever reasons, but he can't do that by himself. Apart from our friend Franzen, and the old boy who looks after Cap Ferrat, there must be others involved. Not just family. Outside people."

Cyrus stopped to charm the flight attendant as she poured more champagne, and his earlier comments about coincidence came to Andre's mind. "I never thought to tell you," he said, "but when I got back from that trip to the Bahamas, my apartment had been ransacked, and all the photographic stuff was taken—cameras, film, files of my old transparencies. But nothing else."

The Pine eyebrows registered surprise. "Well, well. And then your editor stopped taking your calls."

"Camilla?" Andre laughed. "Somehow I can't see her sliding down the fire escape with a sack of cameras."

"I'm not suggesting she did." Cyrus stirred his champagne thoughtfully with a plastic swizzle stick. "It's just the timing."

———

They parted company after sharing a cab from JFK. Cyrus was to put feelers out among the inhabitants of the art world, to see if he could get some idea of the forger's whereabouts. Andre had agreed to make another attempt at getting back on speaking terms with Camilla, and as the cab took him into the city he considered the alternatives. It was pointless to go on calling her at work and impossible to call her at home, since she kept her home number a national secret. The ambush in the lobby of the building had been useless. It looked as though the only answer was to surprise her with an early morning frontal assault on her office, cap in hand and claiming to be desperate for work.

The trip with Cyrus had done him good; his hunch had been proved right, and despite the time change he felt alert, ready to move on and find out more. He let himself into his apartment, dropping his bags inside the door as he went over to check the messages on his machine.

"Sweetie, where *are* you? I've been frantic with worry." It was Camilla, using her best seduction voice, low, throaty, and dripping with insincerity, the voice she always used when she wanted something. "I've called that little girl at your office, who seems to know absolutely nothing. I'm desperate to see you. It's been far, far too long, and I've got some rather exciting news for you. Come out of your burrow and call me. *Ciao.*"

And then:

"Welcome home, traveling man. Guess what? The war's over. Camilla's called twice, and she was almost polite. It must have killed her. Anyway, she says she has a big project for you. Oh, by the way—I didn't tell her where you were. Give me a call, OK?"

Andre looked at his watch, knocked off six hours, and saw that it was just after five. He called the office.

With the first brief exchange out of the way, Andre took a deep breath. "Lulu, I've been thinking, and I've decided that I've been a distant admirer for too long and it's going to stop. No, wait, that's not exactly what I meant to say. What I mean is the distant part is going to stop. I hope. I'd like it to. Well, that is if you . . . oh, shit. Listen, I can't really explain over the phone. Can I pick you up at six, and we'll have dinner?"

He could hear Lucy's breath, and another phone ringing in the background. "Andre, I have a date."

"Cancel it."

"Just like that?"

"Yes." Andre nodded decisively to himself. "Just like that."

There was a pause that seemed endless.

"Andre?"

"Yes?"

"Don't be late, and don't tell me you're going to the airport."

Half an hour later, showered and shaved, Andre was walking up West Broadway, whistling and holding a single long-stemmed white rose. One of the regular West Broadway bums, his radar attuned to passersby in such obvious good humor, shuffled up to him and was startled to receive a broad smile and a ten-dollar bill.

It was a few minutes before six when Andre pressed the buzzer, put the stem of the rose between his teeth, and poked his head around the edge of the office door.

Lucy's partner, Stephen, looked up from his desk. "Why, Andre! This is so sudden. I never knew you cared."

Andre felt himself blushing as he removed the rose from his mouth before coming in. "Where's Lucy?"

Stephen grinned. "Putting on her false eyelashes. She won't be long. How are things?"

Andre heard the door open behind him and turned to see Lucy, in blue jeans and an oversized white turtleneck that set off the chocolate cream of her skin. She looked at the rose in Andre's hand.

"Here," he said, offering it to her. "Something to go with your sweater."

Stephen's head swiveled from one serious, intent face to the other. "Too bad, Lucy," he said. "You missed the entrance." He turned to Andre. "Is that what they do in France? Chew roses?"

Andre picked up Lucy's coat from the couch and helped her on with it. His fingers brushed the back of her neck as he freed the hair that had become caught under the collar. He swallowed hard. "Remind me to send your charming partner a large bouquet of poison ivy."

Stephen watched them leave with a smile on his face, pleased to see that what had been obvious to him months ago was finally getting somewhere. He picked up the phone to call his girlfriend. He decided to take her somewhere nice for dinner, maybe bring her some flowers. Romance was contagious.

———

Cyrus Pine had started working through his list of contacts within minutes of getting home. But although he had a more or less respectable story, the respectable art dealers of his acquaintance were all giving him the same line. We handle only genuine work, they told him, and he could almost see their noses in the air. He knew perfectly well that most of them had been fooled at least once, but reminding them of it would get him nowhere. He gave up on them and started looking through his Rolodex for someone who lived closer to reality. He had almost given up when he reached the letter V and saw the name Villiers. He remembered the rumors and the subsequent public disgrace. If anyone could help him, Villiers could.

Villiers had been the darling of the eighties, when money was sluicing through the New York art world in a seemingly endless torrent. Thin, pinstriped, English, and distantly related to the aristocracy (a connection that became miraculously closer with every year he spent in America), he had been blessed with an infallible eye. The auction houses consulted him. Museums deferred to him. Collectors invited him, somewhat apprehensively, to visit their homes. He was, so everyone told him, destined for eminence, for seats on the boards of foundations and museums, and, eventually, for the rewards that come to important cogs in the establishment wheel.

Eventually wasn't good enough. Eventually couldn't compete with immediate cash, and Villiers began to do favors for owners of paintings whose provenance was open to some doubt. His approval was like money in the bank to the owners, who showed their gratitude in a time-honored and practical way. Villiers prospered and then became greedy, certainly no sin in the art world. But worse, he became overconfident and careless. And, perhaps worse still, ostentatious. His duplex, his vintage Bentley, his place in the Hamptons, his stable of blondes, and his parties featured in the gossip columns. Art's golden boy, they called him, and he lapped it up.

His fall was swift and noisy, being reported in the media with the special relish that journalists display when they catch a man more fortunate than themselves with his pants down. It started when a seventeenth-century painting that Villiers had declared genuine was sold for several million dollars. The new owner, at the request of his insurance broker, had the painting tested. There were doubts, then more tests. These suggested that the nails securing the canvas to its stretcher were eighteenth century and that the canvas itself was even more recent. The painting was deemed to be a dud. Word got out, and other owners who had acquired Villiers-approved paintings joined the rush to the laboratories for scientific tests. More counterfeits came to light. In a matter of weeks, the golden boy turned into a suspected swindler.

Suits and countersuits forced Villiers to sell his

assets. The blondes disappeared, as blondes tend to do in these circumstances. The establishment turned its back on him, and he was reduced to eking out a living consulting for people who were more interested in his eye than in his tattered reputation. Cyrus Pine's call, coming as it did during a particularly barren period, was welcome. Less than thirty minutes after putting down the phone, Villiers was sitting in Pine's study, making short work of a large vodka.

"Good of you to come, Mr. Villiers. As I mentioned to you, it's a matter I'd like to get under way without wasting any time." Pine shrugged apologetically. "You know what clients are like, I'm sure—they want everything done yesterday."

Villiers was a slight, rather seedy figure, showing signs of neglect. His chalk-striped suit, although well cut, needed pressing. His shirt collar was starting to fray, and his hair, lank and curling over his collar, was overdue for a visit to the barber. He smiled at Cyrus, exposing dingy teeth. "I'm not too busy at the moment, actually," he said, swirling the ice around his glass. "I might be able to fit something in."

"Splendid, splendid." Cyrus put down his drink and leaned forward, his eyebrows cocked. "This is between us, of course." A nod from Villiers. "My client has a very decent collection—Impressionists, mostly, with one or two of the more modern fellows like Hockney. He keeps some of them at his apartment in Geneva and the rest in the family home in Tuscany. Very nice too, I might add. Anyway, he's getting a little nervous. There was a rash of burglaries down there not long ago, which you may not have heard about. It was hushed up by the powers that be—bad for tourism, bad for investment, all the usual excuses. In any event, my client is not too happy about leaving valuable paintings protected by an alarm system and a caretaker who's a bit of an antique. Are you with me?"

In fact, Villiers was well ahead of him. He'd heard it all before. The cover story came first, before they got to the point. And the point was invariably shady. He saw the prospect of money. "It must be a great worry," he said. "Do you think I could have another vodka?"

"My dear fellow." Cyrus continued talking as he made Villiers another drink. "There are two paintings in particular that he's concerned about, and so I've offered him a piece of advice." He handed Villiers the glass and sat down. "Tuck the originals in the bank," I told him, "and get copies made. What do you think?"

Here we go, Villiers said to himself. He wants a forger. "Very wise."

"He thought so too. But he insists on first-class copies."

"Of course. Can you tell me who your client is?"

"He'd prefer to remain anonymous. They all do, don't they? But I can tell you he has substantial resources." Cyrus looked at Villiers for a moment before adding, "And he's not an ungenerous man. I'm sure there won't be a problem over the fees."

This was going according to the script, Villiers thought. Money for old rope. "Who are the artists?"

"There's a Pissarro and a Cézanne."

"Hmm." Villiers multiplied by two the figure he had first thought of. Franzen was the man, the only man. But he would have to clear it first. "I may be able to help you, Mr. Pine. Can you give me twenty-four hours?"

In the cab taking him back to his apartment, Villiers wondered how much of the introduction fee he would have to share, or whether he should risk contacting Franzen directly and keep it all. Better not, he decided regretfully. It was bound to come out, and then there would be one more person who would never give him work again. Vindictive, greedy little swine. What difference would a few thousand dollars make to him? As the cab pulled up, Villiers looked with distaste at the drab building where he now lived. He undertipped the driver and scuttled across the sidewalk, his shoulders hunched against the stream of abuse that followed him.

With another vodka for luck, he placed the call.

"Holtz residence."

"Is he there, please? It's Mr. Villiers."

"Mr. Holtz is dining, sir."

"It's important." Jesus, what a pain butlers were when they weren't yours.

A minute passed. There was a faint click as the call was transferred. "Yes?"

Villiers forced himself to be genial. "Sorry to bother you, Rudi, but something's just come up that might interest you. A job for Franzen, and I know you like to deal with him yourself."

"Who is it for?"

"Cyrus Pine, fronting for some European. Wouldn't tell me the name. He needs a Pissarro and a Cézanne."

Holtz looked through the open door of his study. The sound of Camilla's laughter came from the dining room across the hall as he thought it over. He knew of Pine and had seen him often at gallery events. The man had a good reputation and might be useful in the future. As long as Holtz kept himself out of the way, Villiers would catch any possible unpleasantness. "Very well," said Holtz. "I'll call Franzen tomorrow. Wait until you hear from me before you give his number to Pine. Although"—Holtz made a sound that might have been mistaken for a laugh—"I don't know that 'give' is quite the right word."

Villiers winced. The little toad never missed a trick. "Well," he said, "I might charge him a small fee."

"Naturally. But I wouldn't expect to share in that. Let's just say a case of Krug for my services, shall we? I'll talk to you tomorrow." Walking back to the dining room, Holtz had every reason to feel generous. The fifty percent he would take of Franzen's fee would run into six figures. Every little bit helps, he said to himself. He smiled at his guests as he sat down. "Forgive me," he said. "My mother eats dinner early in Florida, and she thinks we all do the same up here." He took a mouthful of spring lamb and wondered if sixty percent might not be more appropriate, considering the ruinous price of international phone calls.

Meanwhile, Villiers surveyed the contents of his refrigerator—a half-empty bottle of vodka and an elderly, curling packet of liverwurst—and decided to go out and treat himself to dinner on the strength of his fee. There'd be plenty left over after he'd bought that cheap bastard his champagne. He would get the nonvintage.

13

THE ringing went off eighteen inches from Andre's ear, jerking him from sleep, the shrill, determined nag of the bell penetrating the pillow he pulled over his head. He felt movement next to him, and then the warmth of bare skin and the weight of a body on his chest as Lucy slid across him to pick up the phone.

He was dimly aware of her voice, a sleepy hello, before the pillow was lifted from his face. Lucy nibbled the lobe of his ear. "It's Camilla." She passed him the phone and rested her head on his shoulder. Andre tried to muffle a yawn.

"*There* you are. I'm so glad I caught you." Camilla's voice, bright and loud, made him flinch and hold the receiver away from his ear.

"How are you, Camilla?"

"Couldn't be better, sweetie, and simply longing to see you. Lots to talk about. Listen, I've just had a cancellation, and I thought I could take my favorite photographer to lunch. Just the two of us."

Andre heard Lucy's whisper against his neck. "My favorite photographer. Jesus."

"Andre?"

"Right. Sure. That would be fine."

"Wonderful. One o'clock at the Royalton?"

"The Royalton. One o'clock."

Camilla, unable to resist: "Andre, who answered the phone just now?"

"Oh, that was the cleaning lady." Lucy raised her head and grinned before biting Andre's neck, causing him to let out an involuntary grunt. "She comes in early on Thursdays."

"It's Wednesday, sweetie. See you at one."

Andre dropped the phone and spent half an hour saying good morning to Lucy before she pushed away his hands and jumped out of bed. "I'd better be going. Save the rest for later, OK?" She put the pillow back over his face. "And don't lose the place."

He heard the distant drumming of the shower as he drifted back toward sleep, lazy and filled with an unfamiliar contentment, smelling her scent on the sheets, wondering why it had taken them so long. Her touch on his shoulder and the smell of coffee brought him back to wakefulness.

"Andre, it's time you stopped living like a bum."

He sat up and held the mug in both hands, inhaling the steam. "Yes, Lulu."

"That fridge is like a science laboratory. There's life in there. Things are breeding."

"Yes, Lulu."

She bent down to kiss him. "Stay out of trouble, you hear?" He was starting to miss her before he heard the front door close.

Four hours later, still feeling pleasantly light-headed, Andre waited to be shown to Camilla's table at the Royalton. As he was led across the room, faces turned to focus on him like pale camera lenses—brief, searching glances to see if he was sufficiently well known to merit a prolonged stare. There was no attempt to disguise their interest; nor any attempt to disguise the lack of it as the faces turned away.

Andre recognized it as a screening process common to a number of restaurants dedicated to the high-voltage New York lunch. The success of these establishments is based not on the quality of the cooking, which can often be excellent, if largely unnoticed, but on the status rating of the clientele. And for these fabulous creatures—the models, actors, and writers of the moment, the cream of the media cream, players alert to every nuance of the game—it is crucial to be well placed. Exile to an obscure table can turn the carpaccio of tuna to ashes in the mouth, and it seems that the law laid down by Brillat-Savarin has been rendered obsolete. "Tell me what you eat," the great man used to say, "and I will tell you what you are." Those simple days are gone. "Tell me where you sit, and I will tell you what you are" is a more appropriate motto, and it can only be a matter of time before the special of the day is not a dish, but a celebrity—the *personnage du jour,* whose presence in the restaurant is announced discreetly as the menu is delivered.

With these thoughts running through his mind, Andre was seated at a prominent banquette and fussed over with the ceremony due the honored guest of one of the restaurant's most devoted fixtures. She was, of course, late. When she finally did arrive, finding her way through the tables mostly by memory (her vision being impaired by large dark glasses), her progress attracted a ripple of interest and a salvo of long-distance air kisses.

"Andre!" It was as though his presence at her table was a total surprise, bringing joy to an otherwise cheerless day. "How are you? Let me look at you." Which she did, tilting her head first to one side, then to the other, the dark glasses at half-mast on her nose. "I detect a definite twinkle in the eye, sweetie. And what's that on your neck?"

Andre ducked his head and grinned. "You're looking well, Camilla. I haven't seen you for ages. Been busy?"

"Frantic, sweetie. Night and day, working out my little surprise for you. But tell me all your news. Did I hear somewhere you've been to Europe?"

"A few days in England." Andre gave her an edited account of his trip, filling it out with descriptions of Lord Lamprey and the tapestries at Throttle Hall.

He was finishing the story of the runaway chicken when he was interrupted by the ringing of Camilla's handbag. He ordered while she was taking the call; the waiter hovered until the phone was back in the bag. Camilla specified her preferred combination of green leaves and turned to Andre with the rueful sigh of an overworked and indispensable executive. "Where were we, sweetie?"

"You were just going to tell me about this project that's kept you so busy."

Sitting back, not knowing what to expect, Andre was then exposed to half an hour of Camilla at her most persuasive. The dark glasses came off, her eyes fixed on his with unblinking intensity, her hand fluttered back and forth, squeezing his arm gently for emphasis. Her plateful of leaves remained undisturbed. An observer would have thought her completely oblivious to everything except the young man sitting next to her. It was an act that she had perfected over the years, and despite the fact that Andre had seen it before, aimed at others, he found himself drawn in by her performance. And, he had to admit, he found himself attracted to the idea she was trying so hard to sell him. She knew him well, and she had chosen the bait with great care.

It was a book; no, it was more than a book. It was a definitive record of the most extraordinary residences on earth, all photographed by him, all expenses paid by the magazine. One of Garabedian's associate companies would be responsible for publication and promotion. Great houses of the world, sweetie, Camilla said, her voice emphasizing the words with the vibrant sincerity of a politician making a campaign promise. And your name—here she paused to sketch it large in the air with her hands—your name *above the title.* There would be a promotional tour, there would be foreign editions—Germany, Italy, Japan, the universe—an exhibition of the pictures, a CD-ROM. It would establish him as the world's most important photographer in his field. And of course, there would be money in profusion—from the foreign rights, from serial rights, from royalties. It would just pour in. Camilla shook her hair at the excitement of it all and waited for Andre's response.

For a moment, he was genuinely at a loss for words. It was, as Camilla had said, the opportunity of a lifetime, the dream assignment that exactly matched his ambitions. Under normal circumstances he would have been calling for champagne and threatening to spoil Camilla's composure, and possibly her makeup, with an enthusiastic embrace. But even as he searched for a suitable reply, the worm of suspicion was at work in his mind. It was too pat, too perfect.

"Well," he said at last, "you'll have to forgive ⸲, but I'm stunned. It's going to take a while to sink in. Tell me how you see the timing. I mean, it's not exactly a ten-day shoot."

Camilla dismissed such trivial considerations with a wave of her hand that brought the waiter running. "Take all the time you need, sweetie." The waiter gave her a confused look, making a tentative lunge at her salad before a second wave sent him away. "This is going to be a *monument* of a book. I see St. Petersburg, Jaipur, Scottish castles, Marrakech, Bali, Venice—God, Venice." The hair shook again. "A year, eighteen months, whatever it takes." Her voice became lower and more confidential. "As a matter of fact, I've mapped out the first leg, and there is just the *tiniest* urgency at the very beginning. It's the most fantastic old taipan's house in Hong Kong, and one can't be sure about Hong Kong."

"Can't one?"

"The Chinese, sweetie. They've taken over, and who knows how long it will be before they turn all the grand houses into dormitories for the women's revolutionary land army? So it's important that you get out there before our little friend Mr. Choy gets cold feet and decides to scamper off to join his money in Beverly Hills." She pushed her plate away and leaned her elbows on the table. "As soon as possible, really."

The worm of suspicion was working overtime. "Have I got time for coffee?"

Camilla beamed and patted Andre's hand. "I'm *so* glad you like the idea, sweetie. It's absolutely you."

She left him at the entrance to the hotel with instructions to get inoculations and visas, and to call Noel about tickets and expenses. In the car going back to the office, she congratulated herself. He seemed to have swallowed it, and with any luck he would be on his way to Hong Kong within a week. Rudi would be delighted.

Andre went back to the lobby and called Cyrus Pine. The art dealer didn't give him time to speak.

"Good news, dear boy, good news—I've tracked Franzen down, and thank God he lives somewhere civilized. You're not averse to a trip to Paris, I hope?"

"Cyrus, I've just had lunch with Camilla, and the plot seems to be thickening. When are you free?"

"Let's see. I've left a dear old trout downstairs with a couple of rather nice watercolors. She seems to be itching to take out her checkbook. Wouldn't want to disappoint her. How about this evening?"

"Can you come downtown? There's someone I'd like you to meet."

Cyrus chuckled. "Is she pretty?"

"Stunning."

They arranged to meet at Felix. After calling Lucy, who was full of questions but too busy for long answers, Andre had the afternoon to kill. On an impulse, he decided to walk to SoHo.

A long, unhurried stroll down Fifth Avenue on a crisp spring afternoon is one of the treats of Manhattan. When New York skies are blue, they are piercingly blue, and when New Yorkers feel that winter is over, they loosen up their hunched shoulders, raise their faces to the sun, and occasionally even smile at strangers. The weather suited Andre's mood, and although he felt he should be trying to work out what was behind Camilla's offer, he found that his attempts to unravel the puzzle were pushed aside by mental pictures of Lucy, and Paris. It was a distracting combination.

He passed the seething racket of Forty-second Street and the New York Library lions, massive and benign in the sunshine, looking as dignified as lions can look with garlands of pigeons clustered on their heads. Then the shops and offices of lower Fifth Avenue, modest and workmanlike in contrast to their glamorous uptown neighbors. Every other block he checked his watch, counting the minutes. He dawdled through Washington Square and stopped for a cup of coffee, savoring the novelty of his impatience to be with somebody. It had been years since he had felt the tug of a human magnet.

His resolve—to arrive at the office as it closed—collapsed when he reached West Broadway shortly before five and almost ran the last hundred yards, hoping to find Lucy alone.

Stephen met him at the office door. "You're early, I'm leaving, Lucy's gone home to change, and if you make her late for work again tomorrow, I'll sue. Have a nice evening."

"Stephen, since you're here . . ." Andre pushed him gently back into the room. "I was wondering . . . well, the thing is, I was hoping you could do without Lucy for a day or two. You know, a long weekend. Maybe a week."

Stephen smiled and shrugged. "Do I have a choice?"

"I haven't asked her yet."

"Where are you going?"

"Paris."

Stephen put his hand on Andre's shoulder, his face serious. "Go ahead and ask her. But there's one condition."

Andre nodded.

"If she turns you down, I'm coming."

They left the office together. Andre waited outside the building, his head turning toward every cab that slowed down. Evenings were gradually becoming longer now, and softer. Dusk, mysterious and flattering, had covered the imperfections and sharp edges of West Broadway. The lights glittered a welcome to the evening, and Andre felt a quickening in his blood as a cab stopped, the door opened, and one slim brown leg emerged. Say what you like about New

York cabs, he thought, but whoever designed them must have been a leg man. He watched approvingly as a second leg appeared, then he walked across the sidewalk to help Lucy out.

She was wearing a dark-gray dress, short and simple, with a black coat slung around her shoulders, her hair pulled back, her eyes shining in the street light. She straightened the collar of his shirt. "You're early," she said.

"I was just passing by," he said, "hoping my luck would change."

Arm in arm, they walked slowly toward Grand Street. "Lulu, I've got a surprise for you."

She looked up at him, light catching the silver studs in her ear. "Let me guess. You cleaned out the fridge."

"Even better than that."

"You made Camilla eat french fries at lunch."

He shook his head. "Have you ever been to Paris? Would you like to go?"

"Paris!" It was almost a scream, loud enough to make two passing men stop; they waited to hear more. "Paris! Are you serious?"

"It's all set. I spoke to Stephen. You're getting a week off for good behavior. We're meeting Cyrus now to fix up the dates, and . . ."

She reached up to his face, and West Broadway was treated to the sight of a kiss that threatened to stop traffic. One of the passersby nudged the other. "They've got to come up for air soon." His friend sighed and shook his head. "Would you?"

———

By the time they reached the restaurant, Lucy had her excitement sufficiently under control to sit at the bar, order a rum and water, and start asking questions—Was this a job? What was the weather like in Paris? Where were they going to stay? Would she look dumb over there in her beret? Was Cyrus coming? Would he like her?—dozens of them, tumbling out in a stream that gave Andre no chance to reply. Eventually, he picked up her drink and put it in her hand.

"A toast," he said, "before you lose your voice. Your first time in France."

They touched glasses and watched each other drink. Andre was leaning forward—to kiss or to whisper, he hadn't decided which—when there was a diplomatic cough behind them. Andre turned, to catch Cyrus studying Lucy with evident enjoyment, his eyebrows going up as he took in the curve of her body and the brevity of her dress, which was accentuated by her perch on the barstool.

Andre put down his glass. "Lulu, this is Cyrus."

She held out her hand, which Cyrus cradled in both of his. "Delighted to meet you, my dear. I haven't been to SoHo for years, but if the girls are all as pretty as you, I shall be down more often."

"If you'd like to give her back her hand, Cyrus, you'll find it easier to deal with this." Andre passed him a Scotch, complimented him on his red and white spotted bow tie, and steered them away from the bar to a nearby table.

They sat down, Lucy between the two men. "Where shall we start?" said Andre. "Cyrus, you want to go first? Lulu knows everything that's happened so far."

Cyrus was a man who liked a story properly told. He began with an account of the rise and fall of the unfortunate Villiers, before going on to describe their first meeting, the brief negotiations that followed, and a second meeting, which took place in the lobby of a bank on Park Avenue, where Franzen's phone number was to be exchanged for five thousand dollars.

Lucy whistled softly. "Isn't that a lot for a phone number?"

"Everyone takes a cut in situations like this," Cyrus said, "and the cut gets bigger as you get closer to the painting. I shudder to think what Franzen's prices are like. Anyway, there I was, lurking by the door with an envelope full of cash. Villiers arrives, looks around as if he's being followed by half the CIA, and comes sidling up to me. It was the most suspicious thing you've ever seen in your life. I kept expecting someone to jump out of the woodwork and wave a gun at me. So we exchanged envelopes, and then the cheeky little bugger made me wait while he counted the money. And off he went." Cyrus looked at his empty glass with a faint air of surprise.

"Let me get you another one." Andre went over to the bar, and Cyrus turned to Lucy. "One of the privileges of reaching my age is that I feel I can ask impertinent questions." There was a quick twitch of the eyebrows. "Are you and Andre—how shall I put it?—close?"

Lucy grinned. "We're getting there. Maybe you should ask him."

"No need to, my dear. It's perfectly obvious to me. I don't think he's looked at me more than once since I got here. I couldn't be happier. I've become very fond of him; he's a good man."

Lucy pushed her glass around. "Yes," she said. "I think he is. Cyrus, before he gets back—would you mind if I came to Paris too? He asked me on the way here, but I don't want to—"

Cyrus cut her short with an upraised hand. "Not another word. If you don't come, I shall be extremely disappointed."

She leaned across to kiss him on the cheek, and Andre, arriving at the table with a Scotch in his hand, could have sworn that Cyrus was blushing. He looked from one to the other as he sat down. "Do you two want to be left alone?"

Lucy winked at Andre. Cyrus cleared his throat. "I was waiting for you to get back and hear the end of it," he said. "But I was attacked by our traveling companion. Now then." He took a swig of his drink. "I called the number that Villiers gave me, and spoke to Franzen, who seemed quite interested, although we obviously didn't go into details over the phone. We're meeting him next week, on what he calls neutral territory. I must say the man has an expensive sense of humor. He wants to meet at Lucas-Carton, for the artistic ambience. He said it was one of Toulouse-Lautrec's favorites."

Andre shook his fingers as though he'd burned them and saw the puzzled expression on Lucy's face. "It's one of the best restaurants in Paris," he explained, "on the Place de la Madeleine. I went there once, on my birthday."

"Not cheap," said Lucy.

"Not exactly."

Cyrus put aside financial concerns with a shake of his head. "My dears, you must consider this trip an investment. The possibilities here are enormous. Besides," he said, looking at Andre, "I had a very good afternoon—the old girl bought both watercolors for her grandson, and I'm feeling flush. We won't be short of funds."

Andre frowned. "I don't know, Cyrus. You've already laid out a lot."

Cyrus raised a finger at him. "You have to speculate to accumulate, Andre. What did I say that painting might be worth? Thirty million plus." The finger went down, and Cyrus leaned back as if he'd just won an argument. "Now, tell me about your editor."

Andre started to go through Camilla's proposal, with occasional muttered remarks from Lucy, while Cyrus listened without speaking. As Andre was describing the details of the book and its publication, he sensed growing skepticism coming from his companions, and when he finished, it was with a shrug and the comment that it seemed like a good idea at the time. Even to him, this sounded rather lame.

Lucy was the first to break the short silence. "She's a piece of work, Camilla. Does she really think you can take off for eighteen months just like that, with a few days' notice? The woman's crazy." She turned to Cyrus. "As you may have noticed, I'm not a fan."

"Lulu, it's all possible." Andre ticked off the points on his fingers. "She has the contacts, she has Garabedian's money behind her, the idea makes sense, and she knows I don't have much work coming in. Cyrus, what do you think?"

Cyrus was shaking his head. "Fishy, dear boy. Lulu's quite right—it's the timing. If I were a cynical man, I'd have to say that all the guff about exhibitions and foreign editions and God knows what else is a smoke screen. The whole pitch—and I admit it's ingenious—is designed to get you on a plane. She wants you a long way away, preferably by yesterday."

"OK. But why?"

"Ah," said Cyrus. "There you have me. But it's not for your health, and I don't think it should get in the way of our little expedition. Would you agree, my dear?"

Lucy's answer was a huge, infectious smile that spread around the table. "I think I'm going to like Paris."

"You've talked me into it," said Andre. He beckoned to a waiter and asked for menus. "Let's have some practice before we go."

14

THE squeak of wheels across the floor and the rasp of a heavy zipper being unfastened made Andre sit up, groggy and disoriented, conscious only that he was in a strange bed. A smaller, feminine bed, altogether more dainty than his own mattress on box springs, a bed half covered, as he now saw, with piles of clothes. At the end of the room, under the soft glow of a shaded lamp, he could see Lucy crouching over an open suitcase, a human island surrounded by more clothes. She was wearing a white T-shirt and a guilty expression as she heard him move and turned to look at him.

"Lulu? What are you doing?"

She put a hand to her mouth, her eyes wide as she stood up. The T-shirt was just long enough to keep her out of jail. "Andre, I'm sorry. I didn't mean to wake you. I couldn't get back to sleep, so I thought I'd just . . . you know." She flapped a hand vaguely at the suitcase and shrugged. ". . . start packing."

Andre fumbled with sleep-clumsy fingers on the bedside table for his watch. "What time is it?"

Lucy shrugged again. "Oh. Well, kind of early." A flash of white teeth. "Unless you're going to Paris."

He found his watch and squinted at it. "Lulu, it's four a.m. The flight doesn't leave until eight tonight. How long do you need to pack?"

Lucy came over to sit on the edge of the bed and pushed the hair back from his forehead. "You don't understand. I have things to put together here. I don't want to look like some little hick next to all those fancy Parisian babes." She smiled down at him; her hair, lit from the back, formed a tangled black cloud around the paler triangle of her face.

Andre let his hand slide along the top of her thigh, feeling the long muscle move under his touch, thoughts of sleep leaving him. "You're right," he said. "And those Parisian babes can cook, too."

She pushed him back, pinning his shoulders to the bed, and leaned over him. "Not with my ingredients, they can't."

———

They met Cyrus in the Air France departure lounge, after a day that had seemed to them curiously like Christmas Eve in early April: packing, repacking, farewell phone calls, last-minute errands, a sense of celebration. They had stopped for a late lunch of pasta and a bottle of champagne, and by the time they reached JFK they were both pleasantly giddy from a mixture of fatigue and excitement. Cyrus, peering at them over the top of a folded copy of the *New York Times,* looked as though he had done nothing more strenuous with his day than visit his tailor for a fitting.

"Good evening, my dears. How are you on cross-word puzzles? I need a five-letter word for 'City of Light.' Do you think that might be Paris?" Smiling as he put down the paper, he stood up and kissed Lucy on the cheek. "The beret looks very fetching," he said. "You'll be the talk of Saint-Germain. Andre, you're a fortunate young man."

The start of an adventure shared among friends is one of the better moments in life and one of the few remaining pleasures of modern travel. Agreeable company, with the added lift of anticipation, provides a certain immunity from the tedium of formalities. Delays, fractious ground staff, security checks, and the usual feeling of being an inconvenient and troublesome piece of human baggage fade into insignificance and become part of the background. With Cyrus and Andre taking turns to tell Lucy about their favorite corners of Paris—the Ritz bar, the flea market, the Musée d'Orsay, the Pont Neuf, the food and flowers in the Rue de Buci—they scarcely noticed the slow shuffle of the herding process that eventually deposited them in their seats.

Lucy studied the flight attendants, stylish in their dark-blue uniforms, the men physically smaller than their counterparts on American airlines, the women groomed to a hair and wearing the expression of polite hauteur that is such a distinctive part of the official French face. She nudged Andre. "I was right about the babes. They all look like they're taking the day off from Dior."

Andre winked at her. "That's just the part you can see. French women spend more money on underwear than anyone in Europe. I got that from the lingerie correspondent on the *Wall Street Journal.*"

Lucy leaned over to watch a pair of strictly-corseted hips swaying up the aisle and nodded thoughtfully. As the plane eased away from the gate, she reached for Andre's hand to give it a squeeze. "Don't get any ideas, buster. You're booked." Her head settled against his shoulder, and with the suddenness of an exhausted child, she was instantly asleep.

Cyrus was less fortunate with his immediate neighbor, a skittish middle-aged woman from Washington, D.C., who seemed eager for conversation and guidance, this being her first trip—solo, as she pointed out with an inviting smile—to France. Further personal details followed and even more were hinted at, but after half an hour Cyrus decided to have a headache. He pushed back his seat, closed his eyes, and reviewed once again his chances of handling a thirty-million-dollar sale for a man he had never met.

They were as slim as they had been the last time

he had thought about them. A lot would depend on Franzen—his relationship with Denoyer, his discretion (or, with luck, his lack of it), his reaction to the three of them. Forgers were understandably nervous by nature, quick to suspect and slow to confide, their professional lives conducted with one eye looking permanently over their shoulder. What did a man like Franzen tell his friends he did for a living? Would he be inclined to trust anyone introduced by a little rogue like Villiers? On the other hand, who else was likely to bring business to a forger? Certainly not a curator at the Met.

As for selling the Cézanne, Cyrus could see no serious problems. The unofficial market for fine art was, as he knew, extensive. There were the gloaters, who would keep the painting insulated from public view in a vault, to be visited and enjoyed in secret; there were the Japanese, who could benefit from an obliging Japanese law that protects private property from discovery; there was Hong Kong, where treasures of all kinds could conveniently disappear. He was confident that a quiet, judicious sale could be arranged. There was never a shortage of rich and acquisitive people.

Cyrus glanced across the aisle at Lucy and Andre, their bodies slumped together in sleep. He weighed the prospect of dinner against more revelations by the enthusiastic lady from Washington, and decided to contain his appetite until he could do it justice in Paris.

But Paris was not to be reached without a struggle. The flight was delayed by congestion in the pale-blue morning skies above Roissy. More delays were provided by the immigration inspectors, who were on a go—slow, limbering up for the annual summer strikes. And traffic from the airport into the city was moving at the speed of congealed syrup. Plans for a café breakfast were discarded as the taxi made its way down the autoroute in a series of short lurches and sudden stops, and it was past eleven by the time the three travelers crossed the Seine to join the crawl of cars in the narrow streets of the Left Bank.

They were staying at the Montalembert, in a small side street off the Rue du Bac, *vieux Paris* on the outside, cool and contemporary within, a hotel much in favor among the black-uniformed ornaments of the fashion world. Andre had chosen it not simply for its looks and its location but because the staff were charming, young, and—flying in the face of Parisian convention—genuinely friendly. There was also the bar.

The bar at the Montalembert, just to the left of the lobby, is a place where one could easily spend an entire day. Breakfast, lunch, and dinner are served there. Drinks flow from late morning onward. The world comes and goes, deals are done, love affairs begun (seldom ended, for some reason; perhaps the lighting is too cheerful for tears and remorse). There are no TV sets. The entertainment is human.

As they were waiting to check in, Lucy cast an appraising eye over two wafer-thin, high-gloss women sitting with glasses of champagne, puffing cigarettes and recoiling after each puff, with a twist of long and elegant necks, from the smoke. "Babes," said Lucy. "Look at them. They're comparing cheekbones."

Cyrus patted her shoulder. "Two suburban house-wives, my dear. Probably discussing what to give their husbands for dinner."

Lucy pursed her lips, trying to imagine either of them anywhere near a kitchen. Andre turned away from the front desk, two keys in his hand. "Lulu, stop staring at those nice old ladies."

He gave one of the keys to Cyrus and shepherded them into an elevator of that particular Gallic size which encourages close personal relationships. If the occupants are strangers at the beginning of the ride, they certainly aren't by the end.

Lucy investigated their room with the thorough-ness of a Michelin inspector, running her fingers over the rosewood, testing the bed in its crisp navy and white striped cover, admiring the steel and slate of the bathroom, throwing open the tall casement windows that overlooked a tumble of Parisian rooftops, rooftops like no others in the world. Andre smiled as he watched her dart from one discovery to the next.

"Well?" he said. "Will it do?"

"I can't believe I'm here." She took his hand and pulled him over to the window. "Look," she said. "*Paris!*"

"So it is," he said. "What do you want to see first?"

"Everything."

———

There are several thousand starting points for such an ambitious enterprise in Paris, but few more pleasant or fascinating for the first-time visitor than Deux Magots, the quintessential café on the Boulevard Saint-Germain. Its critics may say that there are too many tourists; that the waiters, world-weary and flat of foot, have made an art form of curmudgeonly service; that the prices are inhospitably severe. Much of this may be true, but there is nowhere quite like a table on the terrace for watching Parisians do what Parisians do so well: strolling, posing, inspecting each other's spring outfits, exchanging multiple shrugs, pouts, and kisses, seeing and being seen.

As morning gave way to noon, it had become mild and sunny, with a light breeze off the Seine, the best kind of street weather. The leaves on the trees, not yet made dull by gasoline fumes, shone against their branches as though they had been freshly painted a clean, strong green. It was the kind of day that had turned April in Paris into a song.

Lucy sat between the two men, enthralled. She could have been watching tennis, her head swiveling from side to side, not wanting to miss anything. How unlike New York it all was. There were so many smokers, so many dogs, so many old and beautiful buildings, a feeling of spaciousness that was impossible in a skyscraper city. The coffee was stronger, the air tasted different, even Andre was different. She watched him with the waiter. When he spoke French, his body changed gear and became more fluid, his hands and shoulders constantly on the move, his jaw and bottom lip thrust forward as he pronounced those words that sounded so exotic to ears accustomed to the harsher cadences of Anglo-Saxon speech. So fast, too. Everybody spoke so fast.

Cyrus suggested they eat lightly, saving themselves for what was likely to be a long and elaborate dinner, and after coffee they ordered glasses of Beaujolais and ham sandwiches, substantial half-baguettes, Lucy's first taste of true French bread and Normandy butter. She took a first appreciative bite, then stopped eating to look at Andre.

"Why isn't everyone in Paris fat?" she said, waving a hand at the people around them. "Look at the stuff they're putting away, and the wine. And then they're going to do it all over again at dinner. How do they do it? Do they have some special diet?"

"Absolutely," said Andre. "No more than three courses at lunch, no more than five courses at dinner, and they never drink before breakfast. Isn't that right, Cyrus?"

"Something like that, dear boy. Don't forget the daily bottle of wine and a small cognac at bedtime— oh, and plenty of butter in the cooking. Very little exercise, too. That's important. And a pack of cigarettes a day."

Lucy shook her head. "OK, maybe it was a silly question. But so far, I haven't seen a single fat person. Not one."

"It's part of what they call the French Paradox," Andre said. "Do you remember? There was a big fuss about it a few years ago. I think it all started when they did a survey of twenty countries and their eating habits. They were looking at the relationship between national diets and the incidence of heart disease."

Cyrus looked thoughtfully at his wine. "I'm not sure I want to hear about this."

Andre grinned. "You'll be fine as long as you stay here. When the results came out, they showed that the country with the healthiest diet was Japan—not surprising, really, when you think that they mainly eat fish and rice. But the big surprise was the runner-up. Number two out of twenty countries was France;

despite the bread, the cheese, the foie gras, the sauces, the three-hour lunches, the alcohol. So of course, people wanted to know why. They thought there must be a secret, some kind of diet trick that allowed you to eat what you wanted and get away with it. And what they came up with as the explanation was red wine."

Cyrus nodded. "I remember now," he said. "It was on television, wasn't it? Most of the liquor stores in America sold out of Cabernet Sauvignon in forty-eight hours."

"That's right. Then someone started talking about the incidence of cirrhosis of the liver in France being higher than in the States, and everyone went back to hamburgers and Coke."

"Where did America come on the list?" Lucy asked.

"Oh, way down. Something like fourteen or fifteen, I think. Red wine isn't going to change that. Actually, my theory is that red wine has less to do with it than people think. Obviously, what you eat and drink is important, but so is *how* you eat and drink. And there's an enormous difference in national habits. Food for most Americans is fuel—eat in the car, eat on the street, finish dinner in fifteen minutes. Food for the French is treated as a pleasure. They take their time over it. They concentrate on it. They like being at the table, and they don't eat between meals. You'll never catch the President of

France sucking up potato chips at his desk. Cooking is respected here. It's accepted as an art. The top chefs are almost like movie stars." Andre paused and finished his wine. "Sorry. That sounded like a lecture. But it's true." He turned to Lucy. "Wait till you see the food tonight."

"I didn't tell you," said Cyrus. "I called Franzen from the hotel."

"Is everything OK?"

Cyrus rolled his eyes. "He's an enthusiast. Couldn't stop talking about the menu—apparently Senderens is one of the great chefs, and Franzen sounded as though he already had his knife and fork out. We're meeting him there at eight. He seemed very friendly, I must say, told me to call him Nico. I have a feeling we're going to get on."

Lucy was watching a tall blonde in black leather stride through the boulevard traffic with a borzoi, ignoring the cars, both girl and dog walking with haughty, head-high grace. The effect was marred by the dog's decision to cock his leg against the rear wheel of a parked motorcycle while the owner was attempting to get on. The owner expostulated, his leg also cocked across the saddle. The girl ignored him and strode on.

Lucy shook her head. "In New York, they'd be in a fight by now. Then the dog would be sued." She shook her head again and turned to Cyrus. "Can we talk business?"

"Of course."

"Do you think I should wear black tonight? No, I'm kidding. What do you hope to get out of Franzen?"

"Well, let's see." Cyrus straightened his bow tie, his eyes looking across the boulevard at the Brasserie Lipp. "I'd like him to feel comfortable with us, to feel that he can trust us. I'd like him to tell us how he came to work for Denoyer and to see what he knows about the original painting—where it is, where it's going." He looked at Lucy and smiled. "I'd like him to tell us all the things he shouldn't be telling us."

Lucy frowned. "Do you have a plan?"

"Certainly," said Cyrus. "Get him drunk and hope for the best."

————

Camilla was livid. She paced back and forth in front of Noel's desk with short, agitated steps, her elbow crooked, her cigarette held up at shoulder level. It really was too bad. She had offered Andre the chance of a lifetime, a chance any photographer would kill for, and now he'd disappeared. Disappeared. She must have called his apartment a dozen times over the past two days. His flight to Hong Kong was booked, arrangements had been made—complicated arrangements that had required the most servile pleadings on Camilla's part—and where was he? Vanished. The irresponsibility of creative people! The arrogance! The ingratitude! She felt like banishing him forever from her Filofax.

"Try his office again, Noel. Talk to that little Walcott girl. Maybe she knows where he is."

Camilla stopped pacing to stand over Noel as he made the call. He was shaking his head as he put the receiver down. "She's not there. On vacation until next week."

"On vacation." Camilla sniffed. "Package tour to Jones Beach, I suppose. Well, keep trying Andre's home number."

Noel watched her march back into her office, rigid with irritation, and sighed. It was going to be one of those difficult days.

15

THEY met in the lobby shortly before eight, Lucy in her best black, Andre with the sense of imminent strangulation that wearing his tie always gave him, Cyrus in a boulevardier's suit of Prince of Wales check. With a courtly swoop, he took Lucy's hand and bent over it. "You look ravishing, my dear. Quite the prettiest girl in Paris."

Lucy flushed and then became aware that one of the young bellboys was standing behind Cyrus, trying to catch her eye. She smiled at him and was assailed by a torrent of French: A taxi had just dropped off a guest at the hotel. It was empty and available. He would be delighted to hold it for mademoiselle if she wished. Judging by his moonstruck expression, he would have much preferred to hold mademoiselle. The puzzled Lucy turned to Andre, who was standing to one side, a half-smile on his face. "What did he say?"

"He says he has known many women, but none to compare with you. He wants to take you home to meet his mother."

The cab took them down the Boulevard Saint-Germain, and as they drove across the Pont de la Concorde, Lucy caught her breath at the sight of the Seine, a great dark ribbon beneath the glitter of the bridges. Andre was watching her face. "I had them turn the lights on for you, Lulu. Over on the right are the Tuileries gardens, and straight ahead is the Place de la Concorde. It beats West Broadway on a wet Monday morning, doesn't it?"

Lucy nodded slowly without taking her eyes off the extraordinary beauty of her surroundings: buildings painted by floodlight, the formal precision of the lines of trees, the sculptural fall of dense shadows on massive stone walls. She said nothing, stunned into silence by her first glimpse of Paris by night.

The driver was clearly in no mood for the leisurely delights of sightseeing. He accelerated hard out of the Rue Royale, hurtled into the Place de la Madeleine, cut sharply in front of a startled motorcyclist, ignored the vituperation that followed, and pulled up at the curb with a grunt of triumph. Another perilous voyage accomplished without loss of life. After inspecting his tip and finding it adequate, he muttered *"Bon appétit"* before thrusting his way back into the traffic, leaving the three of them on the sidewalk in front of the restaurant's entrance. This had a faintly theatrical quality, with the name of the star—chef Alain Senderens—given above-the-door billing just below the main title.

The origins of Lucas-Carton date back to the eighteenth century, when a bold Englishman, Robert Lucas, opened his Taverne Anglaise to provide gastronomically deprived Parisians with cold meat and steamed pudding. This unlikely combination found favor with the local gourmets, so much so that the name and reputation of Lucas endured long after his death. When the restaurant changed hands a hundred and thirty years later, the new owner renamed it Taverne Lucas. The good times continued, the premises were given an Art Nouveau face-lift at the start of the century, and in 1925, another owner took over, Francis Carton.

There is probably little difference today from the way the interior looked more than ninety years ago: maple, sycamore, and bronze in wonderfully flowing shapes, mirrors and decorative carved panels, bright splashes of fresh flowers, the murmur of voices coming from behind large, cream-colored menus, a general air of *luxe et volupté*.

Cyrus rubbed his hands and took a deep, pleasurable breath, as though he were inhaling a whiff of particularly potent oxygen. "I feel I should be wearing a frock coat and top hat," he said, looking around the room. "Do you see our man here?"

Most of the tables were occupied by neat, soberly dressed groups of businessmen, the unglamorous but essential mainstay of any expensive restaurant. A few women stood out among the clumps of dark suits; some wore conspicuous jewelry with makeup to match, others the tailored uniforms that identified them as conscripts in the international army of corporate management. And in a corner seat at the far end of the room was a solitary figure immersed in his menu, the back of his unkempt head reflected in the mirrored panel behind him.

The maître d'hôtel led them to the table, and Franzen looked up over the top of reading glasses, his round blue eyes taking in Andre and Cyrus, widening at the sight of Lucy. He got to his feet with some difficulty, crouching over the table as he extended a meaty paw to each of them in turn. He was big, a bear of a man, made even bulkier by a suit of brown corduroy that looked thick enough to withstand bullets. A checkered shirt, the top button open, was given a wrinkled semblance of formality by a tie of yellow wool.

His head was large, capped by a shaggy halo of salt-and-pepper hair that sprouted in all directions above a high forehead, a long, straight nose, and a carefully clipped mustache. When he spoke, it was in the almost too perfect English that Dutchmen seem to acquire at nursery school.

"Do I look surprised?" he said. "You must forgive me. I was expecting only Mr. Pine." He clasped his hands over his menu, nodding amiably at the others. "So tonight is social, no?"

"Maybe we can manage a little work as well,"

said Cyrus. "Miss Walcott and Mr. Kelly are my colleagues. I can promise you they're very discreet."

The waiter who had been adjusting the placement of an ice bucket by the side of the table pulled up a dripping bottle until the label was visible. Franzen turned his head to peer at it, nodded, and smiled at Cyrus. "The house champagne," he said. "I'm sure you'll approve. It's very good." In the pause that followed, the sound of the cork being drawn, no louder than a sudden exhalation of breath, was followed by the whisper of bubbles rising in the glasses.

Cyrus leaned across the table, his voice low. "I hope it's understood that I will take care of the bill tonight. I insist."

The Dutchman appeared to give this his consideration as he fingered the stem of his glass. This was a promising start, he thought; not at all like that stingy little bastard Holtz, who made every centime a subject for negotiation. With a slight inclination of his head, he said, "Most generous. I can see it will be a pleasure to collaborate with you, my friend."

Cyrus looked around the table and raised his glass. "To art," he said.

"To business," said Franzen. "But not on an empty stomach, eh?"

Lucy and Andre, their knees touching under the table, let the two older men continue to bat courtesies back and forth while they shared a menu, Andre murmuring translations of the dishes, Lucy the picture of rapt attention. An observer might have thought they were discussing marriage. In fact, Andre was doing his best to explain *bigorneaux.*

"They're winkles, Lulu. You know—winkles. From the sea."

"Like a fish? Like a crab?"

"Not exactly, no. More like a snail."

An involuntary shudder. "How about *ris de veau?*"

"Delicious, but I don't think you want to hear about it."

"That bad?"

"That bad."

"OK. I'm feeling lucky. Let's go for *cuisses de grenouille.*"

"Lovely. Like the most tender chicken."

"But not chicken?"

"No. Frogs' thighs."

"Oh."

Franzen lowered his menu to look at Lucy. "If I could make a suggestion," he said. "There is one dish here that you cannot find anywhere else in France, or perhaps the world: the *Canard Apicius.* The recipe dates back to the Romans, two thousand years ago." He paused to drink some champagne. "It is a duck, but a duck like no other, a duck roasted in honey and spices, a duck in ecstasy. You will remember this duck for the rest of your life." He raised a hand to his lips, made a bouquet of his fingertips, and kissed them loudly. "You will tell your grandchildren about this duck."

Lucy grinned at the three faces turned toward her. "You know what?" she said. "I think I'll have the duck."

By the time the waiter came to take their order, Franzen had assumed the responsibility of orchestrating everyone's meal, a task that he performed with huge enthusiasm and a great deal of knowledge. As he, the waiter, and the sommelier matched recipes with vintages, theirs became by far the liveliest table in the restaurant, a fact that Andre pointed out to Franzen when the ordering was finally done.

"It's very simple," the Dutchman said. "Most people come to restaurants like this for the wrong reason. They come to impress, to show that they can afford to spend a few thousand francs on dinner. And because money is holy to them, they behave as though they're in church." He joined his hands together and looked up to the ceiling, an ancient cherub. "No laughter, not too much wine, no *gusto*. Now, for the waiters, for the sommelier, this is not amusing. You know? Where is the satisfaction of serving food and wine to people who are more interested in price than taste? *Pah!*" He drained his glass and winked at the waiter for more.

"But us, we are different. We are here to eat, to drink, to enjoy. We are enthusiasts. We believe in *joie de manger,* we are an audience for the chef. This is appreciated by everyone who works here. Already, they find us sympathetic. By the end of dinner, they'll be buying us drinks."

Franzen's attitude was irresistibly contagious, and helped along by an uninterrupted flow of Burgundy and Bordeaux to accompany some of the most exquisite cooking in Paris, the four of them quickly fell into a comfortable camaraderie. Cyrus bided his time, watching the wine and the company doing their work on Franzen, waiting for an appropriate moment to get down to the purpose of their meeting.

It came as they were resting after the main course, and it was Franzen himself who brought it up.

"The duck has made me wish I could eat here every night," he said, dabbing his mustache carefully with his napkin. When he continued, it was as though he were talking to himself, musing out loud. "A standing reservation, the same table each night, the wine already in the bucket, my little preferences known, from time to time a visit from the chef. How agreeable that would be." He tucked his napkin carefully back into the collar of his shirt, patted it smooth, and, with the air of a man who had reached a decision, leaned toward Cyrus. "With an ambition like that, I shall need to work. What is it you want? Our mutual friend in New York didn't give me any details when I spoke to him. Tell me."

Cyrus, conditioned by many years' experience of the tender sensibilities and rampant egos of the art world, started to feel his way cautiously, anxious to reassure the Dutchman that his status as an artist was respected. Franzen shook his head, smiling, and held up one hand.

"My friend," he said. "You're not talking to Picasso. I'm a businessman with a brush."

"Delighted to hear it," said Cyrus. "In that case, I'll get right to it. I need a Cézanne."

Franzen's eyebrows shot up. "How extraordinary. I hadn't done him since '92. Now, this year, I've just finished my second, and here you are wanting another one. The old boy must be in vogue. It sometimes happens like that."

Before Cyrus had a chance to respond, the waiter arrived to attend to the matter of dessert, and Franzen was immediately distracted. "Go to the back of the menu," he said. "There's something you must try." As the others followed his instructions, Franzen went on: "Traditionally, you have cheese with red wine, but take a look at this—Camembert with Calvados, Epoisses with Marc de Bourgogne, Vieux Brebis with Manzanilla. The combinations are magnificent. Such imagination! Such research!" Shaking his head, Franzen continued to gaze at the list of nearly thirty different cheeses, each with a specially chosen liquid accompaniment. It was some time before he surrendered the menu and returned to the subject of Cézanne.

"I have a great admiration for him," he said, "and

not just for his work. Can I trouble you to pass the bottle, and I'll tell you my favorite Cézanne story." He poured out the last of the Bordeaux, held his glass to the light, sighed, and drank. "Like many artists, he was often unappreciated during his lifetime and frequently criticized by people who weren't fit to clean his brushes. This was down in Aix, as I'm sure you know, not exactly the capital of the world as far as painting was concerned. Anyway, there was an exhibition of his work—well attended, as usual, by the local critics—and Cézanne found himself standing behind one of them. The man was droning on about one of the paintings, getting more offensive by the minute, and then, after one particularly ignorant comment, Cézanne could restrain himself no longer. He tapped the critic on the shoulder. The man turned around. 'Monsieur,' said Cézanne, 'I shit on you.' No answer to that, is there? How I wish I'd seen the critic's face. Ah, here comes the cheese."

Once they had finished eating, Cyrus, exercising tact combined with a large cognac, managed to steer the increasingly convivial Dutchman back to business. It was agreed that they would all meet with clear heads in the morning at Franzen's studio to settle the details. After that, said Franzen, it was possible that they might wish to celebrate their new relationship with a little light lunch; he knew just the place. In the meantime, he scribbled down his address in the Rue des Saints-Pères, adding the entry code that would open the main door of the building. In return, Cyrus gave him the number at the Montalembert.

They were the last to leave the restaurant, with an honor guard of three waiters, the sommelier, and the maître d'hôtel to wish them good night. It had been a formidable dinner, and as they helped the Dutchman into a taxi, Cyrus felt that it had achieved as much as he'd hoped. Tonight had made them friends. Tomorrow, with any luck, would make them accomplices.

They drove back to the hotel, warm with wine and drowsy with jet lag. Lucy saw the lights of Saint-Germain as a blur through half-closed eyes and felt her head nodding forward. "Andre? You know that walk we were going to take tonight, over the bridge? Could we do that tomorrow?" There was no reply. "Andre?" Nothing. "Cyrus?"

She caught the cabdriver's eye in the rearview mirror. "*Dodo,*" he said. "All sleeping. Very nice."

———

Franzen let himself into his apartment, the familiar smell of oil paint and turpentine cutting through the fumes of alcohol in his head. He walked through the main room, which he used as a studio, to the little galley kitchen and started to brew coffee. A very charming man, Cyrus Pine, he thought, so unlike

Rudolph Holtz. He stared at the percolator, feeling all the old resentments return: Holtz was greedy; he was a bully; he was mean; he was untrustworthy; but, sadly, he was the source of most of Franzen's income, and they both knew it. How pleasant it would be if this new job, for a new and civilized client, led to others. Perhaps tomorrow he would show Pine the two canvases before they were packed up and sent off. Side by side, so the dealer could appreciate the workmanship.

With a cup of coffee and positively the last cognac of the day, Franzen settled into a battered leather armchair and was fishing in his pocket for a cigar, when the phone rang. And didn't stop ringing. Telling himself that one day, maybe even tomorrow, he would buy an answering machine, he lurched across the room and picked up.

"Franzen? This is Holtz. I trust you had an enjoyable dinner with Mr. Pine."

Franzen yawned. It was always like this with Holtz. He was on your back from the first contact until the time the paint dried—checking, nagging, making sure he was going to get his cut. "Yes, I did. He's a very sympathetic man."

"What does he want?"

"A Cézanne."

"I know he wants a Cézanne, for God's sake. Villiers told me that before I called you. Which one is it?"

"I don't know yet."

Holtz grunted. The painting dictated the price of the fake. How could they have spent the whole evening together without discussing the job? He tried to keep the irritation out of his voice. "When are you going to find out?"

"Tomorrow. They're coming to the studio at ten, and then we'll—"

"They? Who are they? I thought it was just Pine."

"Oh, no. He brought a couple of others—a young fellow and a girl."

Holtz felt a tremor of alarm, a goose walking over his grave. "Names—what were their names?"

"Kelly was the man. Andre Kelly. The girl was called Lucy. Don't remember her last name."

Holtz was silent, only his labored breathing audible.

"Holtz? Are you there?"

"You've got to get out, take the paintings and get out. Tonight. Now."

"Why? I don't understand."

Holtz took a breath. When he spoke, it was with the barely restrained impatience of someone trying to reason with a stubborn child. "Take the paintings. Go and check into a hotel. When you've checked in, call and tell me where you are. I'll stay by the phone. Is that clear?"

Franzen looked at his watch. "Do you know what time it is here?"

"For Christ's sake, this is serious. Just do as I say. Now."

Franzen looked at the dead phone in his hand and shrugged. He had half a mind to ignore the call and go to bed, but professional caution got the better of him. Whatever else Holtz might be, he wasn't a man who panicked. And he had said it was serious. Franzen put down the phone and went to fetch the two canvases from their hiding place.

———

Holtz sat in his study, his tiny feet in their black suede evening pumps tapping an agitated tattoo on the Aubusson. That goddamned photographer. What the hell was he doing in Paris? He should have been in Hong Kong.

"Sweetie?" Camilla stood in the doorway, dripping with silver bugle beads, dramatic in her most serious makeup *de soir,* ready to give her all in support of the charity of the evening. "Sweetie? We're going to be late."

"Come in and shut the door. We're not going anywhere."

16

AN exasperated and suddenly sober Franzen walked quickly down the quiet midnight street toward the alley where he rented a lock-up garage. He carried an overnight bag in one hand, a large aluminum art case in the other. Sharing the case, swaddled in layers of foam rubber and bubble wrap, were two canvases—*Woman with Melons,* by Paul Cézanne, and *Woman with Melons,* by Nico Franzen. Combined value: sixty million dollars and change.

Normally, the idea of wandering alone through the backstreets of Paris by night with such valuable baggage would have caused the Dutchman considerable apprehension. But as he turned into the gloom of the alley, any nervousness he might otherwise have felt was pushed aside by a growing irritation, some of it directed at himself. He had never liked Holtz, never trusted him. The saying in the business was that if you shook hands with Rudolph Holtz you should count your fingers afterward. And yet here he was doing exactly as Holtz told him—walking away from a warm bed and the prospect of a profitable job, a puppet being jerked around by a little man with galloping paranoia. What could be so serious? Pine had been checked out; he was a genuine dealer, well known in the art world. Suspected of being honest, too. Villiers had made a point of saying so. Would a man like that shop someone to the police? Of course not.

Franzen stopped in front of the garage door and fumbled with the padlock, watched by a cat with ragged ears and wide, inquisitive eyes. He hissed at it, remembering the time his neighbor's cat had got into his studio and sharpened its claws on a perfectly acceptable Seurat while the paint was still drying. He hated cats. No respect for art.

He pulled open the doors and switched on the light, aiming a kick at the cat as it crouched to jump on the dust-smeared hood of a Citroën DS. Stacked against the garage walls were dozens of old canvases and stretchers arranged more or less by age, the spoils of a hundred visits to flea markets and house clearance sales, the diligent forger's raw material. The big man squeezed his bulk along the side of the car, loaded the two cases into it, started up, and pulled out of the garage. The clatter of the idling diesel engine echoed against the wall of the alley as he went back to turn out the light and lock up. The cat gave him a reproachful look from a safe distance. Franzen set off in search of a bed.

It was past one in the morning, not a time anyone

would choose to be knocking on hotel doors. Franzen thought wistfully of a suite at the Crillon as he cruised the dingy streets behind the Gare de Lyon. Station hotels, he assumed, were accustomed to clients who kept curious hours. By the time he saw the flickering sign of the *Hôtel Léon Tout Confort,* with a vacant parking spot opposite, he was too weary to be anything but grateful.

The concierge, a sleepy Algerian with a transistor radio and a dog-eared copy of *Lui* magazine, took cash in advance before handing over a key and nodding toward a dimly lit flight of concrete stairs covered with balding orange carpet. Franzen made his way along a narrow, sour-smelling corridor and unlocked the door to his home for the night: an iron-framed bed, a liberally stained candlewick bedcover, two thin and defeated pillows. A barely successful attempt had been made to turn a closet into a bathroom. The surfaces of the chest of drawers and the bedside table were scarred with old cigarette burns, and above the bed hung a faded poster of the Eiffel Tower, across which a previous guest had written *MERDE* in emphatic, angry capital letters. It was a long way from the elegant comforts of dinner at Lucas-Carton.

Franzen slid the art case under the bed and searched through his overnight bag for the exercise book in which he kept addresses and numbers. His hand was automatically reaching toward the night table before he realized that the hotel facilities didn't extend to room phones.

Had the bed looked faintly inviting, or even sanitary, he might have postponed the call until the morning. Instead, clutching his exercise book, he trailed back down the stairs to confront the concierge, who barely raising his eyes from the centerfold, pushed the phone toward Franzen and clicked on a switch to activate the small machine on his desk that recorded time and cost.

Holtz picked up after the first ring.

"Where are you? Give me the number."

"Don't bother. I'm only in this fleabag for tonight. Now, what's the problem?"

"It's Kelly, the man you met with Pine. He saw the painting being taken from Denoyer's house."

"So?"

"He's suspicious. Why do you think he's with Pine? Why do you think he's in Paris? He could screw everything up."

The concierge turned his magazine sideways, to enjoy a different view of the pneumatic young lady smiling at him from the pages, and lit a cigarette. Franzen half closed his eyes against the smoke. "I don't understand. Pine isn't Interpol; he's a dealer, and if I do a job for him, he'll be involved. He's not going to—"

"You don't have to understand. You're paid to paint, not think. Now listen. I don't want you going anywhere near your studio. Just vanish, and let me know where you are. And forget about working for Pine."

Franzen chewed at his mustache, trying to hold down his anger. "You're asking me to forget a lot of money."

"I'm telling you: Work for Pine, and you're finished."

"I don't like threats, Holtz. Or is that a promise?"

Holtz listened to the static coming over the line and made an effort to soften his voice. "Nico, Nico, why are we arguing like this?" The sudden geniality, prompted by the fact that the paintings were currently in the Dutchman's possession, continued as Holtz attempted to mend his fences. "Think of all the jobs we've done together—all the jobs we're going to do together. Let's be reasonable, eh? I'm coming over to Paris tomorrow. We'll work everything out. Leave your number at the Ritz."

Franzen looked around the tiny, shabby reception area, the greasy plastic plant on the desk, the concierge licking a finger to turn the pages of his magazine. "The Ritz," he repeated.

"I'll see you tomorrow night, my friend. Don't forget to bring the paintings."

Franzen paid for the call and went back to his room. He emptied the contents of his pockets onto the night table, pausing to glance at Cyrus Pine's card, with his hotel number scrawled on the back, the souvenir of a job that would never happen. Franzen looked with distaste at the bed, which appeared to have been recently occupied by several people with dandruff. Unwilling to risk immersing himself in the sheets, he lay down fully clothed, staring at the ceiling, thinking of Holtz. What a little shit he was.

———

"That Dutch clod," said Holtz. He glared at Camilla, sitting with her legs tucked under her in an armchair. A chastened Camilla, who was still recovering from the tongue-lashing she had just received. She watched his manicured white fingers drumming on the top of the desk, his head sunk into his shoulders, his face pinched with anger, a furious gnome in a tuxedo.

Her voice, when she broke the silence, was tentative. "Anything I can do?"

Holtz stood up, his hands flat on the desk as though he were addressing a meeting. "Get us on the Concorde to Paris tomorrow. Call the Ritz and reserve a room."

"You want me to come?"

"You might be useful. That would make a change."

Camilla looked at his expression and decided that any comment from her would be ill advised. This is not the moment, she said to herself. And besides, look on the bright side, sweetie. April in Paris. She went off to make the calls and start packing. Spring was so difficult, she thought. One never knew what the weather might do.

Holtz sat down and went over his conversation with Franzen. The cretin didn't seem to take in the gravity of the situation. That was the trouble with workmen, however skilled they might be: they didn't think. Or, rather, they thought only of their own petty concerns, never of the big picture, never the future. No vision. If this mess was allowed to develop, if Denoyer ever found out that a second fake had been made, if Pine and that photographer talked, it could become disastrous.

Holtz reviewed the alternatives. On the one hand, a continuation of his luxurious, privileged existence, cushioned by the millions that came in each year. On the other, complications, God knew what unpleas-antness with Denoyer, publicity, the reputation of Rudolph Holtz destroyed, and years of work wiped out. One had only to look at Villiers to see how unforgiving the art world could be when one of its members slipped from his pedestal. Being guilty, of course, was not the sin; being found out, that was what could ruin a man.

In fact, ruin was still a long way from staring into Holtz's face, but he had no intention of letting it get any closer. Extreme problems called for extreme solutions. He looked at his watch and reached for the phone. What should he offer? Seventy-five? A hundred? As he waited for the call to go through, he shook his head at the punitive cost of doing business. Not even deductible, either.

Phone calls at irregular hours were an occupational hazard for Bruno Paradou. In his occupation—he was described on his business card as Security Executive—panic was normal. Clients were always impatient, sometimes desperate. Even so, he was hardly at his best at three a.m., and the growl with which he answered the phone would have discouraged any but the most determined caller.

"Paradou? This is Holtz. I have something for you."

"*Attends.*" Paradou left the bed and his gently snoring wife, and went to take the call in the living room. He looked at the time, collected cigarettes and a notepad, preparing himself—as he always had to whenever he dealt with Holtz—for a bargaining session. "*Je vous écoute.*"

Holtz described the job, emphasizing the urgency. Paradou mentally raised the price as he repeated the details and prepared himself for the inevitable haggle.

"It's worth thirty thousand," said Holtz.

"Each?"

"Are you mad? For all of them."

"Impossible. You're only giving me a few hours to

set everything up—I have to get in, I have to look, I have to arrange the material. Big hurry, big risk, big price. *C'est normal.*"

Holtz sighed. He had no options, and he knew it. "Your idea of a big price—what would that be?"

"A hundred thousand."

There was a whimper, a sound like an animal in pain, before Holtz recovered sufficiently to mutter: "Fifty."

"Seventy-five."

"You're a hard man. I'll be in Paris tomorrow night, at the Ritz. Call me there."

Paradou dressed and began to sort through the equipment he thought he would need. He was a compact, stocky man, his black hair still cut *en brosse,* the way it had always been during his time in the Legion. He had first come to Holtz's attention some years before, during his early civilian days, when he had worked as a bodyguard for celebrities. There had been a party following an art auction, and Paradou's client of the evening, a much-divorced film actress, had objected to the persistent attentions of a gossip journalist. Holtz had been greatly impressed by the discreet efficiency with which Paradou had broken the journalist's nose and arranged for his departure by ambulance. Since then, Holtz had employed him several times, on occasions when his business affairs had required Paradou's particular skills.

But tonight's job was in a different league, altogether more ambitious than routine intimidation or the breaking of a few bones, and Paradou found himself humming happily as he zipped his bag closed. Simple violence, as much as he enjoyed it, was no longer enough. He needed a challenge, something that would allow him to use everything the Legion had been kind enough to teach him. And this was his chance, a true test of planning and expertise, not to mention the fee. There was no doubt about it; he was about to move up a level in his chosen profession.

From his apartment in Montparnasse to the Rue des Saints-Pères, the streets deserted and still, took no more than ten minutes. Paradou drove carefully, respecting the traffic lights in case some officious little *flic* was lurking in a side street, and found a parking spot fifty meters from Franzen's building. He looked at his watch. Four a.m. He would have liked more time. Slipping on a pair of latex gloves, he checked through the contents of his bag, locked the car, and moved off on silent, rubber-soled feet.

The building was typical of many in the neighborhood, three sides arranged around a courtyard that was sealed off from the street by a high wall and massive double doors. An electronic key pad was set into the wall, its entry code changed each month for the guaranteed security of the residents. Paradou smiled in the darkness. If only they knew, the poor suckers. Landlords in Paris were all the same: too slow and too mean to keep up with modern technology. He took a slim box from his case, placed it over the key pad, switched it on, and read off the display of six digits that flashed up on the tiny screen. Removing the box, he tapped in the entry code, and the heavy door moved inward under his hand.

Standing for a moment in the shadow, feeling the pleasant buzz of adrenaline, Paradou looked around the courtyard. It was unlit except for a lamp above the front door, the squat shapes of flower tubs a deeper black against the cobblestones, the upstairs windows shuttered and dark. So far, so good.

It took him ten seconds to cross the courtyard to the front door, and an old-fashioned lock offered no resistance to the pick. By the light coming into the entrance hall through the glass transom, Paradou could make out a bicycle leaning against the far wall, and the graceful curve of a stone staircase. He went up two flights to the top floor, came to the door on the right of the landing, and found another rudimentary lock that an eight-year-old could have picked. Paradou shook his head. The trust that people put in these flimsy pieces of junk was extraordinary.

Closing the door behind him, he placed his bag carefully on the floor. Up until now, it had been a joyride. Now came the interesting part. Paradou switched on his flashlight.

The beam of light revealed a large room, perhaps forty feet long and almost as wide. Beneath a skylight that had been set into the sloping roof stood an easel and a huge worktable, its surface cluttered with pots of brushes and palette knives, tubes and jars of paint, unmounted rolls of canvas, an old cast-iron *cache-clou* holding nails and tacks of various sizes, and a dented brass ashtray brimming with cigar butts. Hanging straight down from the top of the easel like a rumpled suicide was a pair of faded blue, paint-stained overalls.

Beyond the work area, a couch and armchairs were grouped around a low table that held piles of books and newspapers, an untouched cup of coffee, and a brandy balloon. Paradou moved on, past a small dining table and into the narrow kitchen, which was separated from the rest of the room by a marble-topped counter. He examined the stove with a nod of approval. He liked gas. It had possibilities.

The bedroom and bathroom, off to one side down a short corridor, provided neither interest nor inspiration, and Paradou came back to the main room. He picked up the brandy glass, sniffed, took a sip; no bite, just the spreading warmth of very good, very old cognac.

He peered through a crack in the shutter at the courtyard below, a two-story drop. If one could ever arrange for three people to join hands and take a dive, it would do the job. Broken necks all around. Fat chance. He took another sip of cognac and started pacing out the distance from the kitchen to the middle of the room. Where would they stop, all together? His eye was caught by an old, cracked painting leaning against a leg of the worktable. Picking it up, he placed it on the empty easel, draping the overalls over most of it so that one corner of the canvas was left visible. Who could resist uncovering it?

It took him an hour to rig the studio, cursing at the lack of time. Given another twenty-four hours to get hold of the right detonators, he could have booby-trapped the whole place and been back in bed when the fireworks started. But dawn wasn't far away, and before long the building would start waking up. This would have to do. He checked the *plastique* again, one charge attached to the easel, another to the side of the stove, the wire connecting the two taped to the molding just above the floor or pushed into the cracks between the floorboards. He went back to the kitchen, turned the gas on low, and fixed the latch on the front door so that it could be opened with a twist of the handle. One final look around, and then he closed the door gently and went down the stairs.

They'd be arriving at ten, Holtz had said. He had just over four hours to kill, plenty of time to wait for a parking spot closer to the building. But first, coffee. He walked up to the Boulevard Saint-Germain as the night sky began to give way to the first gray signs of day.

————

Franzen sat on the edge of his bed. He had passed an uncomfortable and tiring night—fitful bouts of sleep interrupted by the recurring image of Holtz in the Ritz, squatting like a gargoyle over a suitcase filled with money, his finger beckoning. The little bastard didn't deserve the kind of work Franzen did for him. The Dutchman yawned and stretched, feeling the knots in his back. And then, rubbing the stubble on his chin, he smiled, suddenly in the best of moods. The one overwhelming consolation on this otherwise squalid and depressing morning was under the bed. He had the paintings.

He was whistling by the time he went downstairs to give in his key. The concierge, having exhausted the delights of his magazine, was staring out at the street with bored and bleary eyes.

"It was a night I shall always remember," said Franzen. "The welcome, the room, the service—exquisite, all of it."

The concierge lit a cigarette, not visibly moved by the compliments. "Did you take a shower?"

"There weren't any towels."

"I have towels. Twenty francs."

"If only I'd known," said Franzen. With his overnight bag in one hand and sixty million dollars in the other, he walked around the corner to the Gare de Lyon, breakfast, and an assessment of his immediate future.

17

FRANZEN sat in the café on the main concourse of the Gare de Lyon and contemplated his croissant, golden in the middle and darker brown at each tip, the way he liked them. He dipped one end in his coffee, bit it off, and chewed thoughtfully. It was surprisingly good for a station croissant, still with its early morning freshness, and the coffee was hot, strong, and restorative. The inner Franzen began to feel slightly more human. The outer man, he noticed as he looked down at his wrinkled shirt and the traces of gravy on his tie, needed some attention. A shave, a shower, a clean shirt—then he would be ready to attack the day. As soon as he finished breakfast, he would find a proper hotel.

The thought of hotels took his mind to the Ritz and, inevitably, to the prospect of seeing Rudolph Holtz again. It had never been something that Franzen enjoyed, and now, after being evicted from his apartment, the Dutchman felt resentment boiling up in him like heartburn. When they had spoken on the phone, Holtz had treated him as though he were

nothing more than a lackey; in fact, their relationship, as he looked back on it, had never been much
different. Holtz had the jobs, Holtz had the money,
and Holtz took pleasure in making people jump. It
was in his nature.

Franzen brushed the crumbs carefully from his
mustache, and as he did so he found himself smiling.
This time, it could be different. He glanced down at
the case that was wedged beneath the table. He had
the paintings, and while he had those he held the
advantage. He was, despite his shady occupation, a
man of some integrity and would never consider trying to extort more than the agreed fee. But there had
to be a little give-and-take. He wasn't Holtz's exclu-
sive property. It was only right that he should have
the freedom to make an honest living, to forge for
others when the opportunity arose. And just such an
opportunity was on his doorstep, or would be in a
matter of hours, when Pine and his friends arrived at
the apartment.

Franzen fished through his pockets and took out
Pine's card. He looked at his watch: still too early for
a civilized man to be awake. He had plenty of time
to find a hotel and call from there. Cheered by his
decision, he gathered up his bags and went out of the
station into the thin sunlight of a new and, he felt
sure, better day.

Bruno Paradou sat in his car, watching the Rue des Saints-Pères come to life. A door opened, and a middle-aged, bespectacled man appeared—a pessimist, wearing a raincoat and carrying an umbrella in defiance of the settled, cloudless blue of the morning sky. The man looked up, glanced at his watch, set off at a purposeful walk toward the boulevard: a subway man, of no use to Paradou.

It was half an hour before he saw what he had been waiting for. A woman crossed the narrow street to unlock a car almost opposite Franzen's building. Paradou pulled out and moved down, blocking access to the parking spot. The woman settled into her seat and embarked on a line-by-line review of her makeup in the mirror before taking a brush from her bag to arrange her already carefully arranged hair. Behind Paradou, a waiting driver sounded his horn. Paradou put his arm out of the window and made the time-honored gesture, then sounded his own horn. The woman turned to look at him, her face a study in scorn. With exaggerated deliberation, she took out a pair of dark glasses, put them on, and eased away from the curb.

Bon. Paradou parked, cut the engine, and spread a copy of *Soldier of Fortune,* the magazine of the well-read mercenary, across the steering wheel. Not having more than a few words of English, and those mostly the scrapings of the language picked up in bars, he missed the subtleties of the editorial content.

But he loved the pictures and the advertising. As a diligent investor might pore over the *Wall Street Journal,* so he pored over the announcements—fascinating if only partly understood—of new and improved tools of destruction. Today, his eye was first caught by the new Glock 26, photographed nestling in the palm of a manly hand. Nine-millimeter caliber, ten-shot magazine, weight 560 grams, the kind of gun you could tuck in your double-knit, combat-tested Swiss army sock. Leafing through the pages, he paused at other advertisements: a knife that could sever a three-inch free-hanging manila rope, an enticing subscription offer from *Machine Gun News,* deerskin gloves with lead knuckles, night vision equipment of all sizes, a sniper training course, bulletproof vests. What a wonderful country America was, he thought, studying a picture of a blonde wearing an ammunition belt, an automatic weapon, and nothing else. From time to time, he looked up to check the street, but for the moment there was nothing to do except think of ways he might spend his fee. Seventy-five thousand dollars would go a long way, even with Uzis the outrageous price they were.

———

As it often does, jet lag proved to be more of a stimulus than any alarm clock. That, and Lucy's excitement at the thought of seeing more of Paris, led her and Andre down to breakfast at the Montalembert just after seven. They found Cyrus already there, pink-cheeked and smelling faintly of bay rum, looking through the *Herald Tribune.*

"Good morning, my dears," he said. "I didn't expect to see you this early. What ever happened to breakfast in bed? A romantic boiled egg overlooking the rooftops of Paris, a splash of champagne in the orange juice . . ."

Lucy bent down to kiss him on the cheek. "I think it's time we found you a girlfriend."

"Yes, please." Cyrus took off his reading glasses to look around the room. "Do you see anything here that might suit? A wealthy widow with an angelic disposition, a firm and opulent bosom, and an apartment on the Ile Saint-Louis. Ability to cook preferred but not essential; must have a sense of humor."

"Have you tried room service?" asked Andre.

As the pots of coffee came and the room began to fill, they discussed what is surely one of the most pleasant dilemmas in the world: what to do on a fine day in Paris. There was, of course, the ten o'clock appointment, with the possibility of lunch with Franzen if all went well. But the afternoon was theirs, and Lucy was bombarded with well-meaning but infinitely confusing suggestions from Cyrus and

Andre: the Musée d'Orsay had to be seen, the view from the top of the Arc de Triomphe, Sacré-Coeur, a *bateau mouche,* the café La Palette, where Andre had spent most of his university career, the pyramid of the Louvre, the final resting place of Oscar Wilde, Willi's Wine Bar, and on and on. At last they stopped, giving Lucy a chance to speak.

What she would like, she told them—what she would really like, corny as it might be—was to be a typical tourist, just for one day. The Champs Elysées, the Eiffel Tower, the Seine. And what would make her the happiest tourist in Paris would be for Andre to take photographs of her to send home to Grandma Walcott, who had never been further from Barbados than Port of Spain, when her nephew married a Trinidadian girl twenty years before. Was that too terrible, she asked, looking anxiously at the two men.

"How I long to see the Eiffel Tower again," said Cyrus. "Don't you, dear boy?"

Andre was silent, watching Lucy's face. She wasn't sure whether Cyrus was serious or making fun of her, and there was a sweet solemnity to her expression. "You're not kidding?" she said.

"I never kid this early in the morning. Now, what shall we do first, before we see Franzen? The river or the tower?"

The river won. They left the hotel shortly after

eight—only a few unfortunate minutes before a phone call came through for Monsieur Pine, suggesting some changes to the arrangements for the morning. The bellboy ran up to the boulevard in the hope of delivering the message, but he was too late. There was no sign of Pine among the figures hurrying to work.

As it happened, they had gone the other way, taking the backstreets to reach one of Andre's favorite corners of Paris, the area around the Rue de Buci, where every day seems to be market day.

The atmosphere here is more like that of a busy country town than a capital city. Stalls spill into the street; market dogs dispute among each other for scraps under the trestle tables; greetings, insults, solicitous inquiries after health in general and the condition of the liver in particular pass between stallholders and their regular clients. There is a great feeling of appetite in the air, with a spectacular abundance of cheeses, breads, and sausages; and vegetables of every shape and color, from the squat potatoes called *rats* to haricot beans little thicker than a match, so fresh they snap. There are permanent shops behind the stalls, many of them *traiteurs* with their galantines and terrines and tarts and tiny, delicious birds arranged and presented in the windows like the works of art they are. On one corner, while the season lasts, there are barrels of oysters and a man with leather hands who shucks them and puts them on beds of crushed ice. And always flowers—flowers in extraordinary profusion, offering a variety of pleasures to the passing nose: the heady scent of freesias, the moisture of petals, the fine green smell of ferns.

Lucy stopped at one of the stalls and made her first Parisian purchase: two tiny roses of the darkest red, *boutonnières,* which she put in the lapels of the men's jackets. "There," she said. "Now you're ready to have your pictures taken." They set off down the Rue Dauphine for the river and Paris's oldest bridge, named, naturally enough, the Pont Neuf.

An hour passed, a slightly silly hour of posing for Grandma Walcott against a selection of backgrounds chosen by Lucy and photographed in turn by Cyrus and Andre. When not behind the camera, each man took the part of an extra or a human prop—Andre on one knee in front of Lucy, Cyrus leering from behind a lamppost—until finally Andre was able to persuade a gendarme to take a picture of the three of them on the bridge, arms linked, the Ile de la Cité in the background. And when the gendarme agreed to have his picture taken with her, Lucy was sure it would be the talk of Barbados.

"It's funny," she said as they were walking back to their appointment in the Rue des Saints-Pères. "All you ever hear is how snotty Parisians are. You know? Difficult, rude, arrogant. But can you imagine getting a cop in New York to take your picture?"

"What you have to remember," said Andre, "is that they're French first and cops second. And a proper Frenchman will always make an effort for a pretty face."

"Quite right, too." Cyrus looked at his watch, quickening his pace. "Is it far? I don't want to be late."

———

As they were turning off the quay to go up the Rue des Saints-Pères, Paradou flicked the last of a chain of cigarette butts out of the car window, put away his magazine—several pages turned down at the corners for future reference—and concentrated on the street, looking for figures that matched the descriptions given to him by Holtz: a tall silver-haired man, well dressed; a younger man, dark, possibly with a camera; a slim, good-looking black girl. Not a difficult trio to spot. Paradou took the detonating device from the bag next to him on the passenger seat. Five to ten. Any minute now.

He saw them hurrying down from the direction of the Boulevard Saint-Germain, their faces animated and laughing, the girl almost having to run to keep up with the two men. He watched them dispassionately, seeing them not as people but as seventy-five thousand dollars on the hoof, his mind taken up with timing. Five minutes after going through the courtyard door, maybe a little more if the old one was slow up the stairs. And then, *paf!*

They stopped outside the door as Cyrus took a scrap of paper from his pocket, checking the code Franzen had given him before tapping it into the key pad. He stood aside to let the other two pass through, straightening his bow tie, a half-smile on his face. Paradou watched the door close behind them and checked his watch. He had decided to give them seven minutes.

———

They made their way across the courtyard and were looking for a buzzer to push by the front door, when it opened and a man came out wheeling a bicycle, a cellular phone to his ear. He brushed past them with hardly a glance, and they went through to the hallway. Cyrus consulted his scrap of paper again: top floor, right-hand door. They began to climb the stone staircase. Out on the street, Paradou's eyes never left his watch, impatient fingers tapping the steering wheel.

"Well," said Cyrus, a little breathless as they reached the top of the stairs, "living up here would keep you fit." Andre knocked twice; the deep note of the old brass knocker echoed against the walls; the door yielded to his touch on the handle and hung ajar. They waited, undecided.

"He must have left it open for us," said Andre. "Come on." He pushed open the door. "Nico! Good morning. We're here."

They had stopped on the threshold, noses wrinkled against the pervasive smell of gas and feeling a little like trespassers, when there was the shuffle of slippered feet behind them in the hallway.

"*Il est parti.*" The voice, thin and suspicious, came from an elderly woman who had emerged from the neighboring apartment. She wiped her hands on a faded apron, bright old eyes flicking from Cyrus to Lucy to Andre. "*Parti,*" she said again.

"But he was expecting us," said Andre.

The old woman shrugged. That was of course possible, she said, but artists were irregular and not to be relied upon. Last night, there had been comings and goings. She—being a light sleeper, you understand, not from any vulgar curiosity, although one had a duty toward one's neighbor—she had heard noises. Evidently, the sounds of departure. And, she said, sniffing the air, it was clear that someone had left the gas on. She shook her head at such careless and clandestine behavior. "*Ils sont comme ça, les artistes. Un peu dingues.*"

Paradou saw the second hand of his watch mark the end of seven minutes, and he hit the button.

The double blast ripped through the apartment like a thunderclap, destroying the kitchen, one end of the studio, the skylight, the windows, and a good part of the roof. The force of the explosion, amplified by gas, blew the front door from its hinges, picked up the group on the landing, and threw all four of them against the wall. Then there was silence, except for the thud of a falling piece of masonry and the soft rain of settling debris.

And then, from the old woman, came a torrent of abuse as she struggled to push a dazed Cyrus from his reclining position across her chest. Andre shook his head against the painful ringing in his ears, felt the touch of Lucy's hand on his shoulder. They both spoke at once: "Are you OK?" Two relieved nods.

"Cyrus? How about you?"

"Fine. I think." He moved an arm gingerly, provoking another squawk from the old woman. "I'm sorry, madame. I beg your pardon. Andre, do tell her it wasn't intentional."

Slowly, they disentangled themselves. Andre helped the old woman stand up. "We must call the *pompiers,*" he said to her. "May we use your phone?"

The old woman nodded, her hands instinctively smoothing the front of her apron. "Wipe your feet before you come in."

———

Even filtered by distance and muffled by walls, the roar of the explosion had sounded reassuringly loud. Paradou wondered how soon it would be before the police and the fire department arrived. And an ambulance. He needed to see the bodies. Already, three or four passersby had stopped in front of the building, staring at the closed double doors to the courtyard and telling each other that something very grave had undoubtedly taken place. It wouldn't be long before the street was sealed off and getting out would be impossible. Paradou decided to risk a ticket, leave his car on the Boulevard Saint-Germain, and come back on foot, just another ghoul attracted by someone else's disaster.

Preceded by the tinny bleat of klaxons, a fire truck turned into the street and came to a halt outside the building, followed by a police car, and then another. Within minutes, uniformed figures had taken over the area, throwing open the double doors, pushing aside the growing knot of spectators, diverting traffic, shouting instructions over the crackling hubbub of their walkie-talkies. Paradou put on dark glasses and attached himself to a small group of people on the sidewalk opposite the building.

The uniforms split up at the top of the stairs, a squad of *pompiers* moving cautiously through the ruins of Franzen's apartment, two police officers going next door to question the four survivors. The old woman was now sufficiently recovered from her shock to be indignant and was delivering a lecture to the senior police officer—a weary-looking man with an end-of-the-shift blue chin—on the scandalous irresponsibility of her neighbor. Even now one could smell the gas. They could all have been killed, *écrasés,* and she a woman of nervous disposition, alone except for her cat.

The police officer sighed and nodded with as much sympathy as he could muster. A *pompier* put his head around the door to report the absence of any bodies in the wreckage. The long process of taking names, addresses, and depositions began.

Paradou waited in vain for the hoped-for ambulance. As the minutes passed without any signs of further explosions, bloodshed, or corpses to divert them, the spectators were gradually drifting away, making his efforts to be unobtrusive more difficult. He looked up and down the street for a refuge, before ducking into an antiquarian bookstore, where he positioned himself near the window, camouflaged as a browser with a leather-bound volume of Racine.

———

The police officer referred back through the pages of his notebook and looked up, rubbing his eyes. "I don't think I need detain you any longer," he said to Andre. "One of my men will drive you all back to your hotel. I regret that you've had such an unfortunate experience in Paris." He turned to the old woman. "Thank you for your cooperation, madame."

"You will want me to come down to the station, I suppose." She sighed heavily, the dutiful citizen. "For more of your questions."

"No, madame. That won't be necessary."

"Oh." She stood in the doorway to watch them leave, mild disappointment on her face.

———

Paradou saw the three human targets, dusty but otherwise unharmed, come out of the building and get into the back of a police car, as a *pompier* ran out to move the fire truck that was blocking their way.

"*Merde!*" Tossing the book on a table, he dashed through the door and off to his car. The bookseller watched his departure with raised eyebrows. Racine was not to everyone's taste, as he knew, but such a vehement reaction to the great man's work was rare.

The police car drove fast through Saint-Germain, Paradou keeping up with some difficulty, swearing steadily. *Putain* police. They drove like lunatics. He shook his head and fumbled for a cigarette. How could they have walked away from a blast like that? He could see them now, all three in the back seat, the older man turning his head to say something to the girl beside him. Seventy-five thousand dollars was sitting there, not ten meters away. And now, as if he didn't have enough problems, he felt an insistent pressure on his bladder. Where the hell were they going?

With a squeal of tires, the police car turned right off the boulevard into the Rue du Bac and down the side street to stop at the Montalembert, leaving Paradou, in his mounting discomfort, to find somewhere, anywhere, to park his car.

"I don't know about you two," said Cyrus, "but I could do with a drink." As they were turning to go into the bar, the girl from the front desk ran across the lobby. "Monsieur Pine? This came just after you left. We tried to catch you"—she gave a charming shrug—"but you were too fast for us."

Cyrus thanked her and read aloud from the slip of paper: "*Regret change in plans. Please call me at the Relais Christine, 43.26.71.80. Franzen.*"

"Now he tells us," said Andre. "Do you think he knew?"

"We'll soon find out. Order me the biggest vodka they've got, would you? I'll be right back."

Andre and Lucy went into the bar, hardly noticing the burly man in dark glasses just ahead of them, somewhat agitated, who ordered a Ricard and asked the whereabouts of the men's room in the same breath. They sat down, and Andre brushed a smudge from Lucy's cheek.

"I'm sorry about all this, Lulu. Are you sure you're all right?"

She nodded. "We were lucky, weren't we? If that old lady hadn't come out . . ."

Andre took her hand, a cold, still-trembling hand, in both of his. "Rum?"

She grinned. "Double. No ice."

Paradou returned to the bar, taking a seat as far away as possible from Andre and Lucy. He hid behind a newspaper, nursing his frustration. The only success in an otherwise dismal morning's work was that he knew where they were staying. But for how long? While they remained inside the hotel, there was no chance of his arranging an accident. Holtz had said he would be in Paris by this evening. Maybe he would be able to suggest something. Meanwhile, there was nothing to be done except stay close to them. He signaled for another Ricard, watching over the top of his newspaper as the older man joined the other two.

Cyrus took a deep pull at his vodka and leaned forward, his expression serious, his voice low. "I'm afraid that didn't get us very far," he said. "Franzen was horrified when I told him about the explosion— sounded very shocked, asked if you were both OK— and he still wants to meet us. But not in Paris."

"Why not?"

"Says it's too dangerous. He's got the wind up about something—or someone. But he wouldn't say what or who. Just that Paris was unhealthy for all of us."

Andre felt Lucy's hand creep into his. "Well, he's been right so far today. Where does he want us to meet him?"

Cyrus stared into his drink, shaking his head. "He said he'd let us know, but he's leaving Paris now. We've just got to sit tight until he calls—oh, and another thing: He said we might be followed."

Instinctively, they looked around the room, seeing nothing but normality. Couples and groups were at several of the tables—smiling, talking, ordering lunch. A gaunt, pale girl alone at a table for two glanced at her watch in between looking out at the lobby. A man in the far corner was reading a newspaper. The thought of danger in such a pleasant setting, among relaxed, ordinary people, was ridiculous.

"Tell me, Cyrus," said Andre. "Did you believe him? Why should anyone want to follow us?"

"Here's what I feel." Cyrus finished his vodka. "First, as I said, he sounded quite genuine. And quite scared. Second, it doesn't take a genius to work out that this has something to do with the painting. And third"—turning to Lucy—"I think it would be better if you went back to New York. You, too, Andre. I'm the one who wants to do a deal. You don't need to get involved."

They looked at one another without speaking, the murmur of conversation suddenly louder and more distinct. ". . . and so I told him," said an American voice, "if the divorce isn't through next month, I'm out of here, promises or no promises, and screw the love nest. Jesus, these French guys. What do you think? The salmon looks good."

Lucy giggled. "Come on, Cyrus, loosen up. It was an accident. You smelled the gas. Or maybe it was someone with a grudge against Franzen. Anyway, I'm staying." She looked at Andre. "We're staying, right?"

Andre smiled at the determined, almost pugnacious set of her jaw. "I think Lulu's right. You're stuck with us, Cyrus."

"I couldn't be more pleased," said Cyrus, and indeed they could see the pleasure on his face, the return of a twinkle in his eye as he took a deep, decisive breath. "I seem to remember there's a very nice little place around here called the Cherche-Midi, and there's nothing like a good explosion to give a man an appetite. Shall we?"

———

Paradou gave them time to cross the lobby and go through the door before following. The pastis had made him hungry, and when, ten minutes later, he watched them go into the little restaurant, he felt hungrier still. After waiting until he was sure that they had been given a table, he went off in search of a sandwich.

18

FRANZEN joined the traffic on the *périphérique,* relieved to be getting away from Paris and Holtz and murderous psychotics with bombs. He suspected—no, he was almost convinced of it—that Holtz was behind the explosion, only giving him warning to protect the paintings. God bless those paintings, thought Franzen; a portable life insurance policy. What he needed now was a safe haven, time to think, time to decide. And there was, he knew, a fundamental decision to be made: Holtz or Pine. It had to be one or the other.

Without conscious thought, he found himself following the signs leading south, on the A6 that cuts down through Burgundy to Lyon. The south held good memories for him, and one of them in particular just might—with the right mixture of apology, flattery, invention, obvious desperation, and winning charm—provide the answer to his immediate problem. His mind drifted back to Les Crottins, the tiny village lost in the countryside between Aix and the mountains, and the tumbledown house with its view of Mont Sainte-Victoire. And Anouk.

He and Anouk were together—off and on, it had to be said, because of Anouk's highly volatile temperament—for six years. She was in every way an imposing woman: her voice, her height, her opinions, her mane of hair, her presence, her generous contours. Critics might have called her overupholstered. Rubens would not, nor would Franzen. On the whole, those years together had been good years, and seemed even better with the rosy tint that time imparts to these things.

The break had come eighteen months before, over what Franzen considered a trifling artistic misunderstanding. One afternoon, Anouk had returned to the house unexpectedly, to find Franzen adjusting the slender limbs of a village girl who had agreed to pose for him. All would have been well if the girl had been wearing anything more than a garland of flowers in her hair (it was for a painting in the romantic style), or if she had been reclining in a more decorous manner, or indeed if Franzen had been wearing his trousers. As it was, Anouk had jumped to conclusions and had thrown them both out. Attempts to clear up the misunderstanding had failed, and Franzen had retreated to Paris with his tail between his legs.

But time was the great healer, he told himself as the sprawl of Paris gave way to open countryside, and despite her volatile disposition she was a good-hearted woman. He would call her tonight and throw himself on her mercy, a man on the run. With the reconciliation already accomplished in his mind, his thoughts turned to more mundane matters, prompted by a capacious stomach that had been given nothing since the early morning and that was making audible complaints.

After the squalor of the previous night and the tragedy of a missed lunch, Franzen felt he deserved the consolation of an excellent dinner and a clean bed, and a sign for Mâcon and Lyon triggered his memory. Somewhere between the two, off to the west, lay the town of Roanne. He and Anouk in their early days had once stopped there for a lunch at Troisgros that came back to him now, a lunch with many chilled pewter jugs of the house Fleurie and seven exquisite courses, a lunch that left them so overcome that they could barely cross the street to the small hotel opposite the restaurant. What fugitive could ask for more? As if confirming the wisdom of the decision, Franzen's foot pressed harder on the accelerator.

———

Paradou's afternoon was doing nothing to improve his mood. He had taken the chance of going to fetch his car and had sat in it for two hours outside the

Cherche-Midi. When at last Andre and the others had left the restaurant, he had followed their taxi to the Eiffel Tower, for another interminable wait. Now they were on the top of the Arc de Triomphe, and Paradou had run out of cigarettes. He used his cell phone to call his wife and see if there were any messages. She asked him if he would be home for dinner. How in God's name did he know? The worst of it was that he knew there was no chance of doing the job on them in such public places, but at least he would be able to tell Holtz where they had been. It was almost five o'clock. How much longer would they want to stare down at the *putain* Champs Elysées?

———

"There's one more sight you should see today," Cyrus said to Lucy as they stood at the bottom of the Arc de Triomphe, the spokes of the great avenues radiating out around them. "Every girl on her first trip to Paris should have a drink at the Ritz, and I can show you the *cinq à sept.*"

Andre grinned. "You're a wicked man, Cyrus."

"I'm ready for something wicked at the Ritz," said Lucy. "But what is it?"

"It's an old tradition," said Cyrus, giving his bow tie a tweak. "The two hours between five and seven are when Parisian gentlemen entertain their mistresses before going home to their wives. Very discreet, very romantic."

"Romantic?" Lucy stiffened; if she hadn't liked Cyrus so much, she would probably have bristled. "That's *terrible*. That's the most chauvinistic thing I ever heard."

Cyrus beamed at her. "Absolutely," he said, his eyebrows going up. "But then Chauvin was a Frenchman, although better known for patriotism than for sex."

Lucy shook her head. "You're a piece of work, Cyrus. This is the French happy hour, right? Do I have to do anything special?"

"Indeed you do, my dear. Look beautiful, cross your legs, and drink champagne."

Lucy considered for a moment. She inclined her head. "I like it."

Andre had other plans. "There's a little errand I have to do," he said, "and I'm not dressed for the Ritz. Lulu, if you hitch that skirt up a couple of inches, they'll give you extra peanuts."

She stuck her tongue out at him and tucked her hand under Cyrus's arm. "I won't even ask where you're going."

"A surprise," said Andre. "I'll see you back at the hotel."

———

Paradou scowled as he watched the group split up to go in different directions, the older man and the girl to look for a taxi, the young man to the Métro station on the Avenue Kléber. That decided it. He couldn't leave the car here, and he couldn't take it down there. He would keep an eye on the other two.

———

Lucy and Cyrus were still in the thick of the Champs Elysées rush hour when Andre came up from the subway at Saint-Germain and made for the antique shop in the Rue Jacob. It was, like many similar establishments in the neighborhood, presented in a way calculated to lure the tourist off the street—an artful, seemingly random clutter of objects, most of them dusty, none of them priced. Porcelain bowls, bundles of cutlery tied with string, brass hatracks, mirrors showing the bloom of age, mustache cups, ebony and silver button hooks, vintage corkscrews with brushes in their handles, goblets and cordial glasses, tiny footstools, snuffboxes, pillboxes, crystal inkwells—all of them were thrown together in a haphazard, apparently careless fashion. Innocent window-shoppers could be forgiven for thinking that they had stumbled upon the last surviving outpost of that modern rarity, the bargain. Andre, having been a friend of the owner since his student days, knew the truth: the prices were extortionate, and the best stuff was always in the back.

He pushed open the door and stepped over the supine body of the stuffed cat that never failed to deceive the unsuspecting visitor. "Hubert! Wake up! It's your first customer of the day."

A grunt from behind a lacquered screen was followed by the appearance of the proprietor, a tall man—exceptionally tall for a Frenchman—with curly brown hair, eyes half closed against the smoke of the cigar between his lips. He was wearing a collarless white shirt and ancient pinstripe trousers held up by an equally ancient silk tie in colors that identified him as a member of the Marylebone Cricket Club.

He removed his cigar, craning his head forward as he walked from the gloom to the front of the shop. "Is this who I think it is? The modern Lartigue? Tomorrow's Cartier-Bresson? Or is it you, Andre, you *salaud*? What are you doing here?"

Andre was given a Havana-scented hug before the big man held him at arm's length and inspected him. "You're too thin. But I forget—you live in New York, where there is nothing for a civilized man to eat. How are you?"

"I'm well, Hubert. And you?"

"Oh, scratching a living from the parched earth. Hand to mouth, as always."

"Still got the racehorse?"

Hubert winked. "Three, but don't tell Karine."

The two men compared recent histories, falling into the easy way of old friends: well-worn jokes, affectionate insults, gossip about shared acquaintances, speculation about their wives. It was half an hour before they got down to the purpose of Andre's visit.

Hubert listened attentively as Andre explained what he was looking for; then he nodded. "You've come to the right place, my friend." He led Andre over to an old partners desk. "Here—have a look at these." He pulled open the wide middle drawer and took out a large tray covered in moth-eaten velvet. With the smooth flourish of a conjuror producing a particularly noble white rabbit, he whisked away the covering. *"Voilà.* The best selection in Paris, although I say it myself."

Andre looked down through the haze of cigar smoke and whistled. "Where did you steal all those?"

Hubert shrugged. "See anything there you like?"

Andre looked more closely at the rows of small silver photograph frames, all in the Art Nouveau style, the fluid, beautifully worked curves smooth and gleaming and soft. Hubert had put sepia photographs in each of them—Dietrich, Garbo, Piaf, Jeanne Moreau, Bardot—and there, given pride of place in the center of the tray, was exactly what he wanted. A little bigger than the rest, it was a perfect reproduction of the iron signs above every Métro station. Set into the design was one word in simple capital letters: PARIS. And smiling out of the frame, her spit curl making a black crescent on her forehead, was Josephine Baker. Andre picked it up, feeling the heaviness of the silver and the silky nap of the backing. "I like this," he said.

Instantly, Hubert the friend was replaced by Hubert the professional antique dealer, preparing his customer for the shock of the price. "Ah, yes. What an eye you have, Andre. Very few of those were made—I've only seen two in the past five years, and you hardly ever find them in such perfect condition. It's all original, even the glass." The big man nodded, putting his arm around Andre's shoulder and squeezing. "And for you, I throw in the photograph for nothing."

The price—Hubert mentioned it sorrowfully, as though it had been imposed against his will by a higher authority—was all that Andre had expected and took all the money that he had with him. The frame was gift-wrapped in a page torn from that day's edition of *Le Monde,* and, business concluded, Andre borrowed a hundred francs from his friend and went to celebrate his purchase with a glass of wine in the Café Flore.

The frame heavy in the pocket of his jacket, he sat watching the evening parade on the boulevard, looking forward to the sight of Lulu's face when he gave it to her. He smiled at the thought, feeling a surge of happiness. It was wonderful to watch her fall in love with Paris.

———

"Is the traffic always like this?" Lucy and Cyrus were inching their way down the Rue Saint-Honoré in a taxi, the driver's irritated monotone providing a commentary on the stupidity of other drivers, on the gendarmes who only added to the congestion, on the impossibility of earning a living under such conditions. They didn't need to understand the words; it was the cabdriver's lament, an international hymn of woe, the same in every big city in the world.

Cyrus paid him off at the corner of the Rue Royale, leaving him like a cork in a bottle as they finished the rest of the journey on foot. A hundred yards behind them, Paradou got out of his car and saw them turn left into the Place Vendôme. Unable to move, unable to leave, he got back in the car and banged the horn in frustration.

"Now, my dear," said Cyrus, as they walked toward the great column commemorating Napoleon's military triumphs, "I'm not going to take you anywhere near Armani, and it's for your own good. See his shop over there? The ruin of many a credit rating. I'm always astonished by—"

"Cyrus, wait." Lucy took his arm, pulling him into

a doorway. She nodded in the direction of the main entrance to the Ritz, where a black Mercedes had stopped at the bottom of the steps. A man and a woman wearing dark glasses stood by the open trunk, watching the luggage being unloaded, the woman a head taller than her companion. "I know her," said Lucy. "That's the woman who runs the magazine, Camilla."

Cyrus looked intently at the couple. "Well, I'll be damned," he said. "I know the man with her. That's Rudolph Holtz." Rubbing his jaw and frowning, he watched them go up the steps and into the hotel. "Would you be very disappointed if we gave the Ritz a miss? I think we'd better go back to the hotel and find Andre. Come on—I'll tell you about Holtz on the way."

Paradou drove twice around the Place Vendôme, parked, and walked around again before accepting the fact that he'd lost them. He stopped in front of the Ritz and looked at his watch. Unless Holtz had been delayed, he would be there by now. He and his seventy-five thousand. *Merde,* what a day! Squaring his shoulders and cursing his bladder, he ran up the steps and into the hotel.

———

Camilla was making the two calls she made by habit as soon as she arrived in any hotel: champagne from room service, and a dear little person from housekeeping to take away all her important clothes for a quick sponge and press. She was feeling more like her old self now, after a journey during which Holtz's mood had improved greatly, as it always did when things were going his way. And although he hadn't gone into any of the details, it was clear that he anticipated good news. One could tell from the fact that he tipped the hotel staff instead of pretending they weren't there. He was on the phone now, chattering away in that marvelous French of his, as the champagne arrived. Putting a glass in front of him on the table, Camilla glanced out of the window at one of her favorite views; the Armani boutique here was such a joy. She'd pop across tomorrow morning while Rudi was having his massage.

He finished his conversation and was reaching for his glass when the phone rang. "Yes," he said. "Send him up."

"Now, sweetie," said Camilla, "where would you like to eat tonight?"

Holtz picked up his glass and brought it to his nose. "Oh, somewhere simple. Taillevent or the Grand Véfour. You choose. The concierge will get us in." The first sip of champagne was still prickling against his tongue when there was a knock on the door of the suite.

Camilla opened it, and Paradou came in like a

sheepish crab, barely nodding in greeting before he asked to use the bathroom.

Camilla waited until the bathroom door was closed. "Who on earth is he? Does he always walk like that?"

"He's been doing a little job for me." Holtz saw no reason to tell Camilla about it; the fewer who knew, the better. He smiled apologetically. "I'm afraid he doesn't speak English, my dear, so you'll find our meeting very dull."

"I can take a hint, sweetie. I'll pop downstairs and sort things out with the concierge." She looked askance at the emerging Paradou, zipping up his fly, gave him a polite smile, and closed the door quietly behind her.

"Well, Paradou." Holtz settled back in his chair. "Help yourself to a drink and give me the good news."

Paradou drank an entire glass of champagne before speaking. When he did speak, it was in the clipped, unemotional style that was customary in the Legion, whether reporting victory or defeat. Times, details, circumstances, everything in chronological order; no opinions, many facts. As he spoke, he saw Holtz's expression change from benign anticipation to stony displeasure. When he finished, there was a long, heavy silence.

"So," said Holtz eventually, "we know where they're staying. Can anything be arranged there?"

Paradou shook his head. "Impossible."

"Impossible." Holtz sighed. "Would a hundred thousand dollars overcome the difficulties?"

"Monsieur Holtz, one can always kill people if one doesn't mind getting caught. Fanatics do it all the time. Yes—of course I could shoot them as they came out of the hotel. Killing is easy. Getting away, that's different. With the Algerians carrying on like they are, the police are all over Paris." He clasped his hands across his stomach. He had nothing more to say.

Holtz got to his feet and began to pace the room. It was a setback, a serious setback, but nothing irretrievable. The explosion was no more than an accident, one of hundreds that take place in Paris every day. There were no links with Rudolph Holtz. He would have to fabricate some plausible story for Franzen when he called in, but that would be simple. Pine and his friends, however . . . they were altogether too close. One way or another, they would have to disappear. In the meantime, they would have to be watched.

Holtz stood by the window, arms folded, staring out at the lights of the Place Vendôme. "I want you to keep them under surveillance. Sooner or later, you'll get your chance. But remember, you must deal with all of them. We don't want a survivor running around telling tales." He turned to look at Paradou. "Is that understood?"

"Round the clock?" Paradou shifted in his chair, feeling the weariness in his back. "I'll have to get someone else to work with me. But the new fee will cover that."

Holtz blinked rapidly, as though he had been slapped. And then, with visible reluctance, he nodded. "All of them," he repeated.

Paradou smiled. "A hundred thousand, *d'accord*?" He prepared to leave, feeling that the day hadn't been entirely wasted. "I'll be in touch."

———

Andre came into the lobby of the Montalembert, whistling, and turned in to the bar. To his surprise, Lucy and Cyrus, their heads together, were already there. "What happened to you two?" He bent to kiss Lucy before sitting down. "Did they run out of champagne?"

"Developments, dear boy. Very curious developments." Cyrus waited for Andre to order. "Your friend Camilla has just checked into the Ritz, and she was with a poisonous little man named Holtz. A dealer. I met him once." He sniffed. "Which was quite enough."

Andre leaned forward. "Did they see you?"

Cyrus shook his head. "Luckily, Lucy saw them first. Now, I have to tell you that Holtz has a reputation in the business for doing big deals, some of the biggest. He handled a forty-million-dollar Picasso, for instance. But there's something else. . . . Only rumor, nothing proved —but word has it that he fences on the side." Cyrus paused as the waiter came with Andre's wine. "As I said, nothing's ever stuck, but I can quite believe it. He's an unscrupulous little brute; quite a few people in the business have been burned."

"What's he doing with Camilla?" Andre had never seen his editor socially and knew nothing of her private life. Nobody at *DQ* did, not even Noel. It was a source of great speculation at the magazine, some of it quite scurrilous. Her hairdresser at Bergdorf's, her personal trainer, the younger Garabedian, and a variety of interior decorators had been mentioned as possible admirers. Never anyone named Holtz.

"The big question," said Cyrus, "is what are they doing in Paris? I may be getting suspicious in my declining years, but I have a feeling there may be a connection. It can't be coincidence."

Andre couldn't help smiling. Cyrus looked like a terrier on the scent, alert, eyebrows twitching, his fingers drumming on the table, eager to go down the nearest burrow. "Let's assume you're right," said Andre. "The one who can probably tell us for sure is Franzen. Did he leave a message?"

The fingers stopped tapping. "No, not yet. I have

every hope, though. Whether he's involved with Holtz or not, forgers never like to turn down a job, and he thinks we've got one for him. He'll call." Cyrus nodded to reassure himself. "I know he'll call." He looked at the empty glass in front of him with his usual air of faint surprise, and then at his watch. "There's nothing we can do but wait. How does a shower and a modest little dinner sound?"

———

Lucy came out of the bathroom in a white robe three sizes too big, toweling her hair. "Do you know something? I think Cyrus is getting a kick out of all this. He's definitely wired."

Andre slipped out of his jacket and reached in the pocket for the frame. "How about you?"

Lucy shook her hair and came toward him, a smile on legs. "You don't have to ask, do you?" She draped the towel around her neck and looked down at the package that Andre was holding out. "What's this?"

"A souvenir, Lulu. Somewhere to put that picture of you and your gendarme boyfriend."

She held it flat in her hands, feeling the shape under the paper, her expression suddenly serious.

"Sorry about the wrapping. Go ahead; open it."

She tore off the paper and stood transfixed, staring at the frame, stroking it. "Oh, God. It's beautiful, Andre. Thank you." When she looked up at him, her eyes were wet.

"You don't have to put a picture of the gendarme in it. You know, Grandma Walcott, Cyrus swinging from a lamppost—" The sentence never finished, interrupted by a mouthful of warm, damp, sweetsmelling girl.

Later, standing in the shower, the water beating on the back of his neck, he heard Lucy call out: "Where are we going tonight? I'm trying to work out what to wear."

"Something tight would be nice, Lulu."

In the bedroom, she stood in front of the mirror, holding up all ten ounces of the Tocca dress she had bought months before, in case the right moment came along, and called out again. "Dangerously tight?"

———

Franzen settled down at his table for one, tucking the napkin into his shirt collar, feeling that the world was not such a bad place after all. Anouk had been predictably surprised by his call, but not altogether unsympathetic. An optimist—and Franzen certainly qualified, both by nature and from circumstance— might have described her as warm; guarded, but warm. Or at least not frigid. He would bring her something delicious in aspic from Troisgros, and some flowers. All would be well. He allowed himself to think of the long Provençal summer that was just beginning, those months of sunshine and pink wine, *aioli,* the succulence of fresh peaches, the light. Welcoming the waiter with a smile of supreme contentment, he addressed himself to the menu. Tomorrow morning, he would attend to business. Tomorrow morning, he would call Cyrus Pine.

The decision to abandon Holtz had almost made itself. Personal feelings aside, there was the question of the shattered apartment, which was almost certainly Holtz's doing. That would have to be taken into account before the paintings were returned. And who could tell what this new commission would lead to? Several hundred thousand francs, and that might be only the beginning. Yes, first thing in the morning, he would call Pine.

19

PARADOU had arrived outside the Montalembert shortly after seven to take over from Charnier,
who stood on the sidewalk next to the car, stretching
gratefully as he briefed his boss between yawns.

There was precious little to tell. Charnier had seen
them return to the hotel around midnight, and then
everything had been quiet; not a peep until the fresh
bread and *pâtisserie* were delivered just before six. A
couple of guests with early flights to catch had left
half an hour later. Apart from that, nothing. A quiet
shift, no need to budge, easy money. He wished they
were all like that.

Charnier turned up his coat collar against the chill
of the morning air as he moved off. "It's all yours,
chef. I'll call in this afternoon."

Paradou got into the car, opening the window to
let out the reek of stale tobacco smoke and garlic. A
good, steady man, Charnier, but he would bring that
damned *andouillette* to eat in the car, always leaving
the greasy, malodorous wrapper under the seat.
Paradou tossed it in the gutter and arranged his

things around him: cigarettes and cell phone on the dashboard, the nylon bag with its assorted armaments on the passenger seat, and a five-liter plastic jerrican with a screw top on the floor. After yesterday's two panics, he had no desire to be caught short again. It was one of the worst occupational hazards of long-term street surveillance; that and boredom. But after a good night's sleep, and with the prospect of a six-figure fee at the end of the job, he could put up with a little boredom.

The street was still wet from the cleaning trucks, the air fresh, the sun doing its best to break through gauzy layers of gray cloud. One of the boys from the hotel was sweeping the sidewalk in front of the entrance, while another watered the clipped evergreens that bordered the terrace. Paradou's eyes moved from them to the building next door. It was evidently unoccupied, its windows blind and dirty, a heavy chain looped across the entrance, its shabbiness accentuated by its immaculate neighbor. It might be possible to break into the empty building, Paradou thought, and then pierce the wall through to the hotel . . . and then what? No. Too noisy, too complicated. He needed to get them all together, off the street, away from the crowds, somewhere like the Bois de Boulogne. Why didn't they go there to jog? All Americans jogged.

———

Cyrus was shaving, negotiating the tricky planes and crevices just beneath the nose, when the phone rang.

"Good morning, my friend. It's Nico Franzen. I hope you're well?" He sounded cheerful and confident, very different from the worried Franzen who had last spoken to him.

"Delighted to hear from you, Nico. Where are you?"

"Well away from Saint-Germain, thank God. Now listen: I'm on my way to stay with a friend near Aix. Could we meet there? It's easy from Paris. The TGV will get you down to Avignon in four hours, and you can rent a car at the station."

Cyrus wiped shaving cream from the phone and reached for a notepad and pencil. "We'll be there. Where do you want to meet?"

"I'll give you the number where I'll be. Call me when you get to Aix. We have a lot to talk about." A brief pause, and then: "Cyrus, you didn't notice anything yesterday? You weren't being followed?"

Cyrus thought for a moment. If he mentioned seeing Holtz, there was a chance that he might spook the Dutchman. That could wait until they met. "No, old boy. Nothing."

"Good, good. Do you have a pencil?" Franzen read out Anouk's number and listened as Cyrus repeated it. "Tell me something." There was a note of concern in his voice that made Cyrus frown. "Where did you eat last night?"

"Brasserie Lipp."

"*Choucroute?*"

"Of course."

"Excellent. Well then, *à bientôt.*"

Cyrus called Andre and Lucy, finished shaving, packed, and was down having coffee in half an hour. They joined him a few minutes later, flushed and slightly tousled and eager for news.

"I told you he'd call," said Cyrus, the pink of his early morning complexion heightened by excitement. "Now we're getting somewhere. I'm only sorry that we're dragging young Lucy away from Paris." His eyebrows twitched in apology. "But they tell me that Provence isn't a bad spot. Never been to Aix myself. Have you, Andre?"

"Prettiest girls in the world. University students. Maybe even one or two rich widows. And you'll like it, Lulu. It's a beautiful town."

Lucy employed the pout that she had been practicing after observing Parisian women: lower lip thrust out, mouth turned down, the full oral shrug. "Beautiful girls?" she said. "Sounds like a nightmare. Couldn't we meet him somewhere else? What's the French equivalent of Hoboken? There I'd be comfortable."

———

By the time they had finished breakfast and settled the hotel bill, Paradou was on his fifth cigarette and wishing he had brought his magazine. When he saw them and their luggage come through the door, his heart sank. They were going to the airport. They were going home. With his hundred thousand dollars. *Merde.* As a taxi pulled to a stop outside the hotel, he turned on the engine, instinctively checking the fuel gauge.

The taxi crossed the river but, instead of continuing northeast in the direction of Roissy, turned sharp right. Paradou flicked his indicator, much relieved; they had to be going to one of the stations, Austerlitz or Lyon. After another five minutes, it was clear that they were going to the Gare de Lyon. Which meant he would have to leave the car in a tow-away zone. To hell with it. What was a fine compared to a hundred grand? With his free hand, he took the phone from the dashboard and stuffed it in his pocket, while he followed the taxi down to the entrance reserved for TGV passengers. If they already had tickets, it was going to be a scramble to keep up with them. Leaving the car with two wheels cocked on the curb, he took his bag and ran into the concourse.

And skidded to a stop, almost bumping into the girl as she stood looking at magazines on the newsstand. Then he saw the other two. They had joined one of the lines—the long, slow-moving, and, to

Paradou, infinitely welcome lines—waiting to buy tickets. He picked up a newspaper and, averting his head, joined the line next to them.

He reached his window just before they reached theirs. The sales clerk stared at him, surly and impatient. *"Alors, monsieur?"*

Metz? Strasbourg? Marseille? With a muttered excuse, Paradou moved aside and pretended to look for something in his bag, keeping his back to the line next to him, straining his ears.

He very nearly missed it, expecting to hear an American accent instead of Andre's Parisian French asking for three seats to Avignon. But then, in English: "Cyrus? The next one leaves in ten minutes."

So it was Avignon. Paradou shouldered his way back into the line, glaring down complaints from a woman and her yapping dog, pushing money through the *guichet.* He had a few minutes before the train left. No point in calling Holtz yet. He would wait until he was sure all three of them were on board.

———

Camilla was doing her very best to be bright and cheerful, but it was frightfully hard going. Rudi's good mood of the previous day had vanished—

ruined, she was sure, by that dreadful, uncouth man who had left the lavatory seat up, one of Camilla's pet peeves. Dinner at Taillevent, in spite of the heavenly food, had been less than sparkling. And all morning, Rudi had done nothing but growl: hardly touched his breakfast, didn't want his massage, and was really very coarse when she had suggested lunch with Jean-Paul and Philippe, who were such a fun couple. All in all, she was beginning to wish she hadn't come. Look at him now, sitting by the phone like a man in a trance. But it was time to make an effort, even if one would rather be spared the sordid details.

"Would it help to talk about it, sweetie?"

Holtz didn't take his eyes from the phone. "I doubt it."

Camilla lit a cigarette, puffing smoke in his direction with a toss of her head. "Rudi, there are times when I find your boyish charm quite resistible. I'm only trying to help. What is it? That Dutch person?"

Of course it was that Dutch person, wandering around Paris with a thirty-million-dollar Cézanne. The same Dutch person who was supposed to have called to say where he was. Until he called, until Paradou called, Holtz could do nothing except sit by the phone, a prisoner in the Ritz. He looked up at Camilla. "You don't really want to know, do you?"

Camilla ducked her head, unable to resist admiring the effect of her two-tone Chanel shoes against the muted pinks and greens of the Aubusson.

"Frankly, sweetie," she said, "no. No, I don't. I think I might pop out for a stroll."

Holtz grunted.

———

The train crept out of the station as the last passengers to board moved through the compartments in search of their seats. Diligent executives took off their jackets and snapped open their laptops, mothers with young children searched in their baggage for toys and distractions, holidaymakers opened their magazines and guidebooks, hardly noticing the train pick up speed—a smooth, gradual acceleration that would take them south at more than a hundred miles an hour.

Paradou had bought a second-class ticket and was making his way up from the rear of the train to the first-class compartments, his eyes behind dark glasses flicking from side to side as he looked for Lucy's distinctive mop of curly hair. The anxiety he had felt at the station had gone. He had watched them get on, and he knew where they were getting off. All he had to do before reporting back to Holtz was to check that they hadn't met anyone on the train. Then he could take it easy for a few hours.

He saw them halfway up the front compartment, sitting in one of the four-seat sections with a table. The fourth seat was empty. Reaching in his pocket for his cell phone, he ducked through the door marked W.C. at the end of the compartment, made himself as comfortable as the seat would allow, and tapped in the number for the Ritz.

It was an extended call, partly because Holtz took advantage of it to bring up something that had been nagging away at his mind all morning. Suppose Franzen was playing games? He should have called the Ritz by now; he hadn't. Why not? Either because he wanted to hold out for more money or because he had decided to ignore warnings, common sense, and his enormous moral obligation to Holtz in order to work with Cyrus Pine. Holtz began to describe the Dutchman.

Paradou stopped him. "It may well be that he is a greedy, ungrateful Dutch *putz*—whatever that is— Monsieur Holtz, but it doesn't help me to identify him. What does he look like, and what do you want me to do if I find him?"

Holtz collected himself and confined his remarks to Franzen's physical appearance, making Paradou repeat the description. He was less precise about further instructions, if only because he didn't know what to suggest. Eliminating Franzen—Paradou's first choice; he could see the fee escalating—was out of the question . . . at least until the paintings had been recovered. "Just let me know as soon as you see him," said Holtz, "and then I'll decide. And let me have the number of your cell phone."

Lucy came back from the bar car with three cups of coffee and a puzzled expression. "Now I've heard everything. Do guys go to the bathroom in twos over here? Is it a French thing?"

Andre looked up, smiling. "Never used to be, Lulu. Why?"

"When I came past just now, I could hear someone talking in there." She nodded in the direction of the toilet as she sat down. "You know, a real conversation." She shook her head. France really was different.

The train continued south, the rhythm of its wheels regular, gentle, and soporific. Lyon came and went, and the countryside changed from the spring—green curves of Burgundy to the more jagged scenery of the Midi, with vineyards clinging to steep hillsides and a perceptibly deeper blueness in the sky. While Cyrus snored softly, Andre told Lucy what he knew about Provence: a different country, with its own language and its own impenetrable way of speaking French; the personality of the people, hot and quick-tempered and Mediterranean; the perception of time, marked by seasons instead of clocks, with punctuality dismissed as a curious northern obsession; the empty beauty of the backcountry, the crowded good humor of markets; the flamingos and cowboys of the Camargue; and the food—the *tapenade* and *estouffade,* truffles and figs, goat's cheeses, olive oil, herb-flavored lamb from Sisteron, the diamond-shaped almond *calissons* of Aix.

Lucy put a finger over Andre's mouth. "You sound like a one-man tourist office. And you're making me very hungry."

The announcement came over the loudspeaker in French and English, advising passengers that Avignon was the next stop and that they would have two minutes precisely to disembark. Cyrus opened his eyes and shook his head. "Very nearly dropped off," he said. "Are we there?"

Avignon station is not the place one would choose as an introduction to Provence. It is in a permanent state of waiting to be cleaned up and waiting to be organized, with temperamental escalators and long flights of steps to make the carrying of heavy bags as awkward as possible, and an area in front of the station that seems to have been designed by a particularly malevolent urban planner with a hatred for cars. Chaos reigns. Voices are frequently raised, and from time to time the hands and arms of blocked, frustrated drivers are brandished in emphatic and vulgar salutes.

Paradou watched the three of them go through the door of the car rental office before he got into the back of a taxi. The driver turned to look at him, crooking an eyebrow.

"Wait for a moment," said Paradou. "I want you to follow a car."

The driver waved his hand at the parking area. "Plenty of choice, monsieur. Any particular color?"

A comedian. Paradou kept his eyes on the rental office door. "I'll tell you when I see it."

The driver shrugged. "It's your money." He turned on his meter and went back to his newspaper.

Ten minutes later, a blue Renault with Andre at the wheel came cautiously out of the rental parking lot. "That's the one," said Paradou. "*Allez.* Don't lose him."

The two cars turned under the railroad bridge and into the stream of traffic, following the signs to the A7 autoroute. In the Renault, Andre drove carefully as he accustomed himself to local driving techniques. As always when he first drove in France after an absence, he was uncomfortably aware of speed, of abrupt lane changes, and of the inevitable car that seemed to be attached to his exhaust pipe, waiting for a suitably dangerous moment to overtake him. It wasn't until they were past Avignon airport and had come onto the wider expanses of the autoroute that he felt the tension leave his shoulders.

Lucy and Cyrus had been silent, wincing at the near misses and the indignant blare of horns. "I don't understand these guys," said Lucy. "What's their rush? You told me it was nice and quiet and sleepy down here."

Andre braked as a baby Citroën cut sharply in front of him. "It's in the genes, Lulu. All Frenchmen are born with a heavy right foot. Enjoy the scenery. Try not to look at the cars."

They were still heading south, Paradou's taxi a comfortable distance behind them, the afternoon sun inching toward its gradual, spectacular dip into the Mediterranean. Even from the insulated cocoon of the car, they could sense the heat outside, the baked quality of the limestone hills, sharp against the dense blue of the sky. And then, approaching Aix, they saw the jagged mass of Sainte-Victoire, the mountain that held such fascination for Cézanne.

Andre opened his window as they eased into the Aix traffic, and they felt a touch of freshness in the air, a light breeze blowing spray from the grand and elaborate fountain at the bottom of the Cours Mirabeau. "There you are, ladies and gentlemen," he said, "the most beautiful street in France." They entered a long tunnel, green and cool and shady, formed by branches of the plane trees on either side of the Cours. "Now, it was a long time ago, but I seem to remember a hotel . . . yes, there. The Nègre-Coste. How about that?"

———

Paradou watched as they gave the car keys to the hotel doorman and took their bags inside. Giving them five minutes, to make sure they had rooms, he paid the cabdriver and found a bench almost opposite the hotel. He was wondering where he could rent a car, when there was the sound of ringing from his pocket.

"Paradou? Where are you?" Holtz's voice sounded thin and faint.

"Aix. They checked into a hotel five minutes ago."

"Have they met anybody?"

Paradou shook his head in exasperation. "I can't see through stone walls. Wait, they've come out again. Just the three of them." Silence while he watched them walk up the street. "OK. They're going into a café. I'll call you later." Paradou saw that the café was crowded. Service would be slow. He licked his lips at the sight of a waiter with a tray of cold golden beers and walked down the street in search of a car to rent.

———

While Cyrus went inside to call Franzen, Lucy and Andre examined the other customers on the Deux Garçons' terrace—tourists, local businessmen taking their ease after a hard day's work, and university students taking their ease after practically no work at all. Lucy was fascinated by the students, some of whom, as Andre had said, were remarkably good-looking: flirting, laughing, making great play with their dark glasses and their cigarettes, getting up frequently for their ritualistic embraces.

"Those aren't college kids," said Lucy. "They're serial kissers. Look at them."

"It's on the curriculum, Lulu. They major in osculation. What are you going to have?"

They ordered, and watched the slow-moving, ever-changing swell of humanity come and go on the sidewalk, stares from the passersby being met by stares from the café tables, an endless, leisurely exchange of idle curiosity. Andre smiled at Lucy; not wanting to miss anything, she moved her intent face from side to side like a radar scanner, sucking everything in. He took her chin between both hands and brought his face close to hers. "Remember me?" he said. "The one you came with?"

"Good grief," said Cyrus, standing over them as the waiter arrived. "It must be catching. There was a couple in the next phone booth absolutely *pasted* together. They're still there. Ah, youth." He sat down and picked up his glass. "Well, we're all set. We're meeting Nico at a restaurant called Le Fiacre in the country, about half an hour from here. He's bringing someone he calls his *petite amie*." He took a deep swallow of beer and smacked his lips with enjoyment. "Should be an interesting evening."

Lucy rolled her eyes. "Another babe. The place is crawling with them."

"I think we should just play it by ear," said Cyrus. "Don't you? But I'm inclined to tell him everything. I think we have to now."

They talked over the possibilities: whether Franzen had in fact painted the fake (more than likely); whether he and Holtz were firm partners (something Cyrus chose to doubt); whether Franzen knew Denoyer; whether he knew where the original painting had gone; a dozen questions and no answers. In the end, they were agreed that it was time, as Cyrus had said, to come clean.

The first faint violet tinge of dusk was turning the Cours Mirabeau into a luminous cavern. Students started leaving the café to pursue the educational opportunities of the evening. Strolling couples, arm in arm, stopped to look at the menus displayed outside restaurants. Paradou stood up, rubbed his aching buttocks, and left his bench to trail the three figures walking back to their hotel.

———

"You can see why the old boy painted it so often, can't you?" said Cyrus. "Look at that. Magic." They were heading east on the D17, Sainte-Victoire on their left, its peak catching the final afterglow of the sunset, its lower slopes already in deep shadow. And then, suddenly, darkness. Although they were only a few miles outside Aix, there were few signs of habitation apart from pinpricks of light from distant farmhouses. Traffic was sparse—the occasional unlit tractor wheezing home, the occasional hurtling car

going in the other direction. And one set of headlights well behind them, keeping an unusually con-
siderate distance for a French driver, hardly noticeable in the rearview mirror.

———

Paradou leaned back in his seat, bracing his arms
against the steering wheel. This was more like it. Out
here in the sticks, he would surely get his chance. He
was tempted to move up on them, run them off
the road, and finish the job with the gun that had
been burning a hole in his armpit since Paris; but
professional caution prevailed. Patience, Bruno,
patience. They weren't going far, or they would have
brought their luggage. When they stopped, that
would be the time.

———

"Are you sure this is right, Cyrus? It doesn't look
like a gastronomic wonderland out here, and I know
Nico likes his food." Andre slowed down to take a
sharp bend.

"He said it was marked by the side of the D17.
Look, what's that up there?"

It was a wooden post, supporting a sign with red,
white, and blue lettering: *FIACRE. Le patron mange*

ici. An arrow pointed up a side road little wider than a cart track. Cyrus let out a relieved sigh.

Andre followed the twists in the road for half a mile, and they came upon one of those delightful surprises that the French take for granted: a small, charming, and—from the look of the car park—popular restaurant in the middle of nowhere. Architecturally, it was modest, a plain, two-story building covered in the skin of pink *crépis* that often hides or holds together the stone of the original construction; modest perhaps, but well kept, with a vine trellis running the length of the facade, and a broad terrace with tables and chairs overlooking a floodlit garden planted with cypress trees, oleander bushes, and one wrinkled old olive tree.

"I'm sorry, Cyrus." Andre pulled into one of the few vacant parking places. "I take it all back. This looks serious."

A few heads turned as they walked across to the terrace, and there was Franzen, lost in conversation with a statuesque woman wearing a gray dress that set off her salt-and-pepper hair.

"Here we go," said Cyrus. "Fingers crossed."

———

Paradou came up the dark road on foot, carrying his bag, his car left by the side of the D17. Standing in the blackness at the edge of the garden, hidden behind a cypress tree, he was disappointed by what he saw. There were too many people, too many lights. But there was always the car. He walked softly around the gravel of the parking area until he came to the blue Renault.

20

A SHORT, round, smiling woman in blue jeans and white shirt met them at the edge of the terrace, using a rolled-up menu to protect them from the boisterous welcome of the restaurant dog, a terrier on spring-loaded legs.

"*Messieurs—dame, bonsoir, bonsoir.* You are the friends of Anouk?" She managed to swat the dog in midair. "*Hercule! Ça suffit!* Please—follow me." She led them through the tables with a rolling, nautical walk, the terrier capering beside her. As Franzen saw them, he got to his feet, smiling and nodding while he made the introductions to his companion.

Anouk was not conventionally beautiful but certainly handsome. Her profile, under the thick sweep of hair, would have looked quite at home on a coin, and she had the olive Mediterranean skin that seems to retain the glow of the sun. Her eyes were dark, her hands strong and capable; not a woman to be trifled with. Cyrus twinkled at her, instinctively adjusting his bow tie.

Franzen busied himself with a bottle of rosé, filling everyone's glass while he spoke: "Everything is good here, but the *pissaladière* is exceptional, and you won't find better lamb in Provence. Am I right, *chérie?*" He spoke to her in the solicitous tone of a man who was still on slightly shaky ground and treading carefully.

"Often not," said Anouk. "But in this case, yes." Her English was heavily accented but confident, her smile taking any sting out of her words. She watched Franzen with wary fondness, like a mother keeping her eye on a cumbersome, willful child.

The prelude to dinner—that most appetizing period of happy indecision and dither as menus are studied and dishes discussed—was allowed to run its unhurried course. It was some time after the first bottle had been emptied and reinforcements ordered that Cyrus felt that the subject of business could decently be raised. "Nico," he said, "we owe you an explanation."

Andre started, conscious of the close attention being paid to him by Anouk, her eyes never leaving his face, her expression impassive. Franzen, in contrast, reacted visibly to each development—Andre's visit to Denoyer and the theft of his equipment being greeted with very high eyebrows indeed. And then, before Cyrus had a chance to take over, the first courses arrived: open-face tarts of olives, onions, and anchovies; bowls of vegetable, bean, and pasta soup singing with basil and garlic; pots of *tapenade,* salt cod *brandade,* an unctuous, jammy *ratatouille*—the opening salvo of a Provençal meal, one of the most delicious conversation-stoppers known to man.

Between mouthfuls, Cyrus glanced at Franzen, trying to gauge the effect on him of what he had heard so far. But the Dutchman was intent on his food and Anouk, exchanging a sip of his soup for a taste of her *brandade,* as though this were just a normal, convivial gathering of friends. Cyrus hoped the mood would survive the next series of revelations.

On the other side of the table, Lucy was receiving some murmured and largely ignored hints from Andre on the importance of pacing and early restraint, bearing in mind the four courses still to come. But it was hard for her; she had a healthy young appetite, she had missed lunch, and these earthy, tangy flavors were unlike anything she had experienced before. She was eating as voraciously as a truckdriver on Sunday, and it was a joy to see.

With dishes and bowls wiped clean and cleared away, Cyrus took a deep breath and resumed the story where Andre had left off. When he came to the arrival of Holtz in Paris, there was a noticeable reaction—not from Franzen, who of course already knew and simply nodded, but from Anouk. Her face hardened, there was a contemptuous snort, and she picked up her glass and drank deeply, as though the wine could overcome an unpleasant taste in her mouth. Cyrus was encouraged by this to lay his final card on the table: He wanted to handle the sale of *Woman with Melons*. The original version.

The arrival of the lamb, rosy pink and aromatic, with flat, crisp cakes of sliced, roasted potato, allowed Franzen a moment to take in what he had heard. But only a moment. Anouk turned to prod him with a stern index finger. "*Alors,* Nico," she said. "You have heard from them. It's time they heard from you."

Franzen's account promised to take some time, with regular pauses while he dealt with his lamb. Yes, he said, he had done the fake, although he had never met Denoyer—Holtz had not thought it necessary. Again, at the mention of the name, a flicker of distaste went across Anouk's face; Cyrus marked her down as a potential ally. And then, Franzen said, something very curious happened: Holtz commissioned a second fake of the very same painting, something that the Dutchman, in many years of working with rogues, had never encountered before.

Cyrus, all innocence, might have been thinking out loud: "Extraordinary. I wonder who that could have been for?"

Franzen shrugged. "In my corner of the business, one doesn't ask. It was urgent, that's all I was told."

"Denoyer wouldn't be too pleased if he knew there was another one floating around while Holtz was trying to sell the original." Cyrus clicked his tongue in disapproval. "Most confusing—although it's quite possible that Holtz is planning to sell them both as originals." He noticed the puzzled looks around the table. "He'd need a couple of gloaters—two very discreet clients who didn't want any publicity—but there are plenty of those to be found. I know a few myself."

"And you're saying that each one would think he'd bought the original?" Andre shook his head. "Come on, Cyrus. It couldn't happen."

"Don't bet on it, dear boy. Some people—most people, probably—like to show off what they've got; but for others, it's enough just to possess great paintings, even if they're always hidden in a vault. In fact, I'm told that can actually add to the thrill." Cyrus sipped his wine, looking thoughtfully at Franzen. "You wouldn't happen to know where the original is, Nico?"

Franzen looked at Anouk. If he was hoping for guidance, none was forthcoming. Her face was expressionless, and Cyrus had his answer before the Dutchman spoke: "I have it," he said. "I have them both." He nodded, reaching for his glass. Anouk allowed herself the slightest hint of a smile.

Cyrus sat back, saying nothing as salad, a great *plateau de fromage,* and more wine were brought to the table. He watched the Dutchman, who was now taking Lucy through the mysteries of French cheeses: the goat, the cow, the sheep, and the pungent crock of *cachat,* laced with brandy and garlic.

Was it wishful thinking, or did Franzen seem to be relieved, like a man who had come to a decision? Cyrus gathered his thoughts and leaned forward.

"As I see it," he said, "there are two possibilities. We can join forces, go to Cap Ferrat, and sit down with Denoyer—tell him about the second fake, return the original, and hope that we can arrange something with him that would be profitable to all of us. From what Andre has told me, he appears to be a decent man. He's committed to a sale, which is something that I can handle. The commission will be substantial, and we can share it." Cyrus grinned. "That's if everything goes according to plan, of course. But I don't see why it shouldn't."

Franzen wiped his mouth and took some wine. "And the second possibility?"

"Ah, that," said Cyrus. "Not as much fun, I'm afraid. We can thank you for a splendid dinner, go back to New York, and leave you and Mr. Holtz to live happily ever after."

There was a thoughtful silence, during which a very sharp ear might have picked up the sound of a telephone coming from the darkness of the garden beyond the terrace.

———

Paradou retreated hastily from his vantage point behind the cypress tree until he was far enough away to speak. "They're in a restaurant outside Aix. They're with the Dutchman."

Holtz muttered something that sounded vicious in a language Paradou didn't understand. Then, collecting himself, Holtz said, "I'm coming down. Where's the nearest airport?"

"Marseille. I may have some good news by the time you get there. I've done some work on their car."

"I don't want anything to happen to the Dutchman. I'll call you from Marseille." The phone went dead. With a final wistful look at the lights of the restaurant—he felt as though he hadn't eaten a good meal for days—Paradou walked down the track to wait in his car.

———

The mood at the table had moved from discussion to celebration. Franzen, with some encouraging nods and nudges from Anouk, had taken the decision to throw in his lot with Cyrus. Tomorrow morning, they would meet at Anouk's house and go together to Cap Ferrat, where Denoyer, impressed by their honesty, grateful for their help, won over by their charm, and appalled by Holtz's underhanded behavior, would appoint Cyrus to handle the sale. Their good humor and optimism were not entirely due to clear thought and reasoned analysis. With coffee, Franzen had insisted on ordering glasses—or small tumblers, this being a generous restaurant—of the chef's private stock of *marc*. As an aid to digestion, the fierce distillation of pressed grape skins possessed certain benefits that even learned members of the French medical profession had been known to acknowledge. But coming on top of a long evening's wine, it was enough to soften the hardest of heads.

They parted company in the parking lot—Anouk and Franzen headed to their village, a mile up the road, the others in what they hoped was the general direction of Aix.

Andre kept his speed down, driving with the exaggerated care of a man still just sober enough to know that his reflexes have been thoroughly pickled. Lucy and Cyrus, after sporadic attempts at conversation, dozed. Opening the window and leaning over to take as much air in his face as possible, Andre drove on, paying no attention to the dimmed headlights well behind him as he peered into the night.

On unfamiliar, unmarked roads in the dark, filled with sudden forks and turnings, Andre felt the growing conviction through the muzziness in his head that he had lost his way. And then he was saved by a blessed blue and white sign for the A7. Once he was on the autoroute, it was only a few minutes to Aix.

He came down the access road, closing the window as he accelerated to keep up with the sparse traffic—mostly trucks on the night run to Paris with their cargoes of produce from the warm earth of the south. Anxious to be back in the hotel, and fighting off the heaviness in his eyelids, he blinked hard half a dozen times to help him focus, then pulled out to pass a double-length Spanish *frigorífico*.

It was late, and the driver of the truck was careless; he should have checked his mirror before beginning to change lanes. With the awful clarity that comes immediately before an accident, Andre saw the name on the back of the truck, the cluster of lights, the dusty mud flaps, the *Viva Real Madrid* sticker, the pattern on the tires—saw it all, saw it in the split second it took him to hit the brakes. And saw it all in extreme close-up when there was suddenly no resistance from the pedal as the brake cable gave way.

He wrenched the wheel to the left, taking the car over the grass strip and through the hedge of oleanders dividing the highway, across three lanes, through the barrier on the far side, and down the slope beyond, plowing through bushes and branches and rocks until, with a final screech of tortured metal and a crackle of breaking glass, the car came to rest against a pine tree. By some fluke, the engine was still running. Andre reached forward and turned it off with a hand that shook against the steering column.

———

It looked good, Paradou thought. It looked very good. It would have been perfect if they had hit an oncoming truck on their way across the road, but this would do. Now he would go and count the broken necks. He looked for the next exit so that he could make the turn back to the wrecked car.

———

There is nothing quite like a close brush with death to clear the head of alcohol, and three very shaken, suddenly sober figures clambered up the slope and onto the hard shoulder. "Can you make it across to the other side?" said Andre. "We'll hitch a lift into Aix." A gap in the traffic, a rush of adrenaline, a sprint across what felt like half a mile of highway, and they were on the opposite side, the nausea and shivering of reaction beginning to set in. Andre stood at the edge of the emergency lane, an unsteady but hopeful thumb extended toward an approaching truck. It passed without slowing down. So did the next one, and the half dozen after that.

"This isn't going to work," said Lucy. "You two get down there, out of sight. Come up when I whistle." With the two men waiting in the darkness at the foot of the slope, she undid the top buttons of her blouse, rolled up an already short skirt, and faced the oncoming headlights with a smile and an upraised hand. Almost at once, French gallantry came to the rescue with a great hissing of hydraulic brakes.

The driver of the truck opened the passenger door and looked down at Lucy with pursed lips and an appreciative gleam in his eye. She winked at him, adjusting the strap of her bra. "Aix?"

"Paris, si vous voulez, chérie."

"Great." Her whistle, and the instant appearance of Cyrus and Andre, happened too quickly for him to close the door. Some hundred-franc notes pressed into his hand helped him overcome his disappointment, and Andre's account of brake failure and the subsequent crash even produced a grudging sympathy—enough, at any rate, to make him leave the autoroute and drop them off near the center of town. They were back in their hotel while Paradou, gun in hand, was still beating the bushes around the wreckage of their car.

———

Holtz and Camilla sat together in hostile silence. The argument had started in the Ritz and continued in the car, and was now simmering in the back of the plane as the day's last flight headed south toward Marseille. She was livid with him for dragging her away from Paris simply—as she knew very well and he didn't bother to deny—to act as potential chauffeur and general dogsbody. It was too bad, and it was undoubtedly going to get worse, with the night spent in some ghastly little airport hotel with no facilities, Rudi in a foul mood, and absolutely nothing to wear tomorrow because they had left in such a rush.

The hotel was every bit as dreary as she had anticipated, and it wasn't improved by the sly, knowing expression on the desk clerk's face when they checked in with no luggage. He leered. He actually leered—as if any couple in their right minds would choose Marseille airport for a romantic assignation. The whole thing was too sordid for words.

Holtz made straight for the phone in their room and was having a long, obviously unsatisfactory conversation. At the sight of his scowling face, Camilla shut herself in the bathroom and ran the water for a bath—a long bath—hoping he would be asleep by the time she finished.

The mood of the following morning was still far from festive. They had made an early start, taking a taxi into Aix to meet Paradou, and the three of them were now in his car on the Cours Mirabeau, diagonally opposite the entrance of the Hotel Nègre-Coste.

"You're sure they're still there?"

Paradou turned a bleary eye on Holtz, who was sitting in the back seat with Camilla. "I checked at the desk last night. They came back, God knows how. I've been here ever since."

Silence returned to the car. The beauty of the shaded green street in the morning sun, the dappled light on café awnings, the delightful sights and sounds of a beautiful town coming to life—none of these did anything to improve Camilla's ragged temper, the nervous anxiety of Holtz, or the grinding frustration that Paradou was beginning to feel. How he longed for a few minutes of honest, conclusive violence and an end to the job. He fingered the crosshatching on the butt of the gun under his arm. Third time lucky, and this time he would do it at short range, so he could see them go down. He yawned and lit a cigarette.

Fifty yards away, an unusually subdued trio sat over coffee in the hotel. Shock and alcohol had given them a sound, almost drugged night's sleep, but the effects had worn off and they were coming to terms with the possibility that the crash might not have been an accident. Once again, Cyrus had suggested that he continue alone, and once again Andre and Lucy had brushed the suggestion aside. All they had to do, after all, was get to Cap Ferrat—but not in another rented car. They decided to take a taxi to the house in Les Crottins and go on together with Franzen.

And so, with the sun now well up, they left Aix behind them, their spirits beginning to lift in the serene and unthreatening normality of the back road that runs parallel with Sainte-Victoire. The mountain glowed with light from the east, no longer mysterious or sinister. Vans and tractors buzzed up dirt tracks between the fields of vines, magpies hopped and squabbled on the verge, a few high clouds tumbled across the great blue sweep of the morning sky: another ordinary, beautiful day.

The taxi came to a fork in the road and began the short, steep climb to Les Crottins, the driver cursing as two village dogs on their morning vigil darted out to snap at his tires.

"It's the house with blue shutters," said Andre. "There, at the end, with the Citroën outside."

There was another growl from the driver when he saw that Franzen's car gave him no room to turn and he would have to back down the street. These villages were built for donkeys. Somewhat pacified by his tip, he deigned to nod goodbye as his passengers got out, and put the taxi into reverse.

Franzen opened the door before they had a chance to knock. "*Salut, mes amis.* Come in, come in." Handshakes for the men, a whiskery kiss on each cheek for Lucy, and then he led them into a low-ceilinged room the width of the house, explaining that Anouk, a late riser, had wished them *bon voyage* and hoped to see them again soon. "But before we go," he said, "I thought it might amuse you to see these." He waved a casual hand toward the stone fireplace. "The light is unhelpful, I admit, but it would take a good eye to tell the difference, even side by side. Eh, Cyrus?"

On the stone mantel above the fireplace, Cézanne's *Woman with Melons* and her twin sister gazed out at them, placid, beautiful, and apparently identical. Cyrus went closer, shaking his head. "I do congratulate you, Nico. Quite, quite extraordinary. Tell me a trade secret: How long does it take you to—"

"Cyrus!" Andre, glancing through the window at the sound of an engine, saw a thickset, crew-cut man with dark glasses get out of a white Renault, his hand reaching inside his jacket as he came across the street to the house. "Someone's coming." And a moment later: "Jesus. He's got a gun."

They stood like four statues until a steady, insistent knocking jerked them back to life. "Through the kitchen," said Franzen. "There's a back door." Taking the paintings from the mantelpiece, he led the way out of the house and into a tiny, high-walled garden with a barred gate giving onto an alley. "My car's just around the corner."

"Yes," said Cyrus. "So is our friend with the gun."

"Just a minute." Andre pointed at the canvases under Franzen's arm. "That's what he's after. It has to be. Nico, give me one of those; the other one to Cyrus. Have your car keys ready. Lulu, you get behind me. Nico, behind Cyrus. Stay close, and we'll be fine. Nobody wants a Cézanne with bullet holes in it."

Paradou had stepped away from the door to look through the window, and it wasn't until he heard Holtz shout from the back of the car that he turned, to see two paintings walking around the corner of the house, each painting with four legs. Comedians: The world was full of them. He shook his head and raised his gun.

There was an anguished screech from Holtz, who by now had pushed his head and shoulders through the back window of the car. "No! No! For Christ's sake don't shoot! Franzen—Nico—we can do a deal. Listen to me. It was all a misunderstanding. I can explain. . . ."

Franzen, still shielded by Cyrus and the painting, opened the door of the Citroën and started the engine. Lucy and Andre slid into the back seat. Cyrus joined Franzen in the front, and the Citroën took off down the street, passing so close to Holtz that Andre could see the spittle on his lips and, behind him, the pale blur of Camilla's face.

"He has to back out," said Franzen. "We've got a couple of minutes' head start."

Andre looked through the rear window and saw Paradou getting into the Renault. "Go for the autoroute," he said. "There'll be more traffic. Where can we get on?"

"Not until Saint-Maximin." The big car lurched around a bend. "Do you think they'll follow us?"

Cyrus looked down at the painting on his lap.

"Thirty million dollars?" he said. "They'll follow us."

They were silent as Franzen reached the N7 and started pushing the car to the limit along a straight, flat stretch of road—so straight and so flat and so devoid of turnings and hiding places that he could do nothing but drive on the horn and hope for the best while Lucy and Andre kept a lookout through the rear window. Half an hour passed, as uneventful as any half hour can be at high speed on one of the most deadly roads in France, and the level of tension inside the Citroën dropped as they came off the N7 to join the access road to the autoroute.

Franzen pulled to a stop behind a line of cars waiting to go through the tollbooth, and all the air seemed to leave his body in one vast whoosh of relief. He turned to Cyrus with a grin. "I think I'll stick to forgery from now on. I wouldn't want to do that again. Is everyone all right? No heart attacks?"

"What I'd like to know," said Andre, "is who that guy was with—"

"Andre?" Lucy's voice was small and tight. "He's there."

Their eyes followed Lucy's nod. In the line next to theirs, easing forward to the tollbooth, was the white Renault. Paradou was staring back at them. He was smiling.

"Rudi, this is ridiculous." Camilla was feeling shattered, absolutely shattered, even though she had spent the last half hour with her eyes tightly closed. "It's just not on—I mean, guns and—"

"Shut up, woman. Paradou, what do you think?"

"The autoroute is not good for us, but they can't stay on the autoroute forever. We keep with them and wait."

Camilla tried again. "Suppose they go to the police?"

"They have a stolen painting and a forgery in the car," said Holtz. "I am trying to reclaim my property. I don't mind if they go to the police, but they won't. You're right, Paradou. Stay with them."

And stay with them he did, past Brignoles and Fréjus, past Cannes and Antibes, never more than two or three car lengths behind. Camilla huddled in the corner, wishing she were back in the tranquil safety of New York. Holtz reflected on the possibilities: If he were them, he'd head for Italy, cut up to Switzerland, and take the painting to the man in Zurich. Pine would know where to go. But that was a long way. They would have to stop for gasoline. Night would eventually fall. Paradou would get his chance. In a long and crooked career, Holtz had learned the value of patience. Sooner or later, everyone made a mistake.

———

There is a limit to the amount of nervous anxiety the human system can take before it adjusts, stops panicking, and reverts to some kind of logical thought. Over the course of two hours, the occupants of Franzen's Citroën had made that adjustment, but as Cap Ferrat grew closer, the white Renault was still with them, sometimes in one lane, sometimes in another, but always there in the rear-view mirror.

It was Andre who suggested a detour to Nice airport. "First, the place is always crawling with cars, so we might have a chance of losing them. And when they see us turn off, they'll think we're going to take a plane. We go into one of the parking areas, straight through the other side, and out." Franzen nodded, tightening his grip on the steering wheel.

———

"Goddamn it," said Holtz. "They're going to take a plane." Paradou did his best to stay within sight of the other car as it joined the melee of traffic fighting its way through the labyrinth of service roads that coiled around three sides of the main bank of buildings. He was foiled by a tourist bus pulling out in front of them, lost two precious minutes, and by the time the road cleared, the Citroën was gone.

"Go straight to the terminal," said Holtz.

But as they quickly discovered, Nice airport has two terminals, a considerable distance apart. Leaving Camilla and Holtz in the car outside one of them, Paradou ran up to the other and was rewarded by the sight of the back of Franzen's Citroën as it swerved out of the car park and took the exit road marked *Toutes Directions.*

Sweating, murderously angry, short of breath, he got back to the Renault, to find it surrounded by a knot of taxi drivers—voluble, gesticulating taxi drivers, who were shouting at the two figures cowering in the back to move their *putain* car from the rank where it was forbidden to stop, where it was trespassing on the taxi drivers' God-granted right to every parking space outside the terminal. He pushed through them, none too gently, and got into the car. "The bastards conned us," he said. "I saw them go."

———

Andre looked back at the traffic behind them on the Promenade des Anglais. Every other car seemed to be a white Renault. "I can't be sure," he said. "But I know they weren't behind us coming out of the airport. I think we're OK."

Franzen grunted. Cyrus stayed silent, going over in his mind what he would say to Denoyer. Andre and Lucy continued to keep watch through the rear window as the signs for Villefranche and Saint-

Jean came up and the Citroën turned down toward the sea.

———

Denoyer waved goodbye to his wife, pleased to have the afternoon to himself while she and Claude went into Nice. In previous years, he had always loved his first few days back on Cap Ferrat: the peace before the summer guests came, the garden with its pines and cypresses such a sculpted, orderly pleasure after the extravagant vegetation of the Bahamas, the different taste of the air, the comfort of his wine cellar and his library. There was much for a man to enjoy. But this year it wasn't quite the same. Try as he might to believe the reassuring words of Rudolph Holtz the last time they had spoken, the Cézanne was never far from his mind, and the lack of information over the past few days was disturbing. He would call Holtz again tomorrow—no, he would call him now. Surely there would be news.

He was halfway across the hall when he heard the sound of the buzzer.

"Monsieur Denoyer?" said an unknown voice over the intercom. "*Livraison.*"

Something else that Catherine had ordered. There was always a flurry of deliveries during their first days back. Denoyer pressed the button that opened the main gate and went to stand outside the front door.

———

The white Renault sat in the airport's short-term parking area, cooking in the sun, a situation that did nothing to improve the already overheated tempers inside the car. Camilla sulked, thoroughly bored with Rudi, Paradou, nasty little cars, France, and wild-goose chases. Her solution to the problem—to walk over to the terminal and take the first flight to Paris—had produced a predictably stinging response from Holtz. She now sat, lips firmly sealed, staring with distaste at the perspiration running down the back of Paradou's thick neck. Holtz was muttering to himself, thinking out loud.

"That might be it," he said finally. "They think they can sell independently; they might be going to do a deal. It's all we've got anyway. Paradou? Cap Ferrat, as fast as you can." Camilla recoiled as Holtz suddenly turned to her. "You can find Denoyer's house, can't you? You spent enough time there."

"What are you going to say to him?" But Holtz was already far away, his imagination hard at work on a story of Franzen's theft, double-crossing, duplicity, and his own hero's role as last-minute savior.

———

It had been a startling, almost shocking half hour for Denoyer as he tried to absorb the details that Cyrus and Andre took turns in describing. While they talked, his eye kept returning to the paintings propped up against a chair. Whatever else these people had done, he thought, they had at least brought back his Cézanne. And that indicated a certain honesty. Could he believe them? Could he trust them? Did he have to, with the painting back in his possession?

"It goes without saying," said Cyrus, "that you may not want to have anything more to do with us"—a doleful look—"but should you decide to go ahead with the sale, I think I can promise you the utmost discretion, and obviously I'll be happy to provide any references you may require."

Denoyer looked at the four attentive faces around him, looked again at the paintings—the forger had really done a formidable job—and shrugged. "You're not expecting an instant decision?"

Of course I am, thought Cyrus. "Of course not," he said.

The buzzer sounded out in the hall, and Denoyer excused himself. He was a puzzled man when he came back into the room. "Someone who says he's with Rudolph Holtz," he said. "I didn't open the gate."

Through the open window, they heard the popping sound of two gunshots in quick succession, then a third. "I think he's opening it himself," said Andre. "Is there another way out of here?"

Denoyer looked through the window. At the end of the drive, a figure was kicking at the bars of the gate. "Come with me." Scooping up the paintings, he led them through to the back of the house, out across a terrace, down into the tunnel to the dock. "I have to call the police," said Denoyer. "This is outrageous."

———

Camilla flinched as that dreadful man emptied a fresh clip of ammunition at the gate. She was on the verge of a serious migraine, she could tell. "Rudi! Rudi! Stop him! This is Cap Ferrat, for God's sake!"

Holtz ignored her, watching Paradou test the lock with another kick. The Frenchman shook his head. "Do you want to try ramming it with the car?"

Holtz chewed his lip, staring through the bars, trying to accept that it was too late. Denoyer was probably calling the police by now, and there was only one way out: the way they had come. It was time to leave; he couldn't risk getting trapped. And he realized he wasn't going to get hold of the painting—not here, at any rate. But Pine would go back to New York, and once he was in New York . . . A movement in the distance through the tops of the trees made Holtz squint into the sun. He saw a small shape move across the dark mirror of the sea, leaving a long white gash on the surface that led in a straight line from below the house. He stepped away from the gate. "Forget it," he said. "Take me to the airport."

———

None of them drew breath until the water-ski boat, low in the water with five on board, was two hundred yards offshore. Lucy relaxed her grip on Andre's hand. "I hate to tell you," she said, "but I get seasick unless I'm distracted."

Andre looked at her and smiled. He had never seen a less sickly-looking face in his life. "Would the thought of another week in Paris take your mind off it?"

"It would help." She reached up to wipe the spray from his face. "Two weeks would definitely do it."

Denoyer eased the throttle back to idling speed and turned to look at his house. "Outrageous," he said again. "Guns! Gangsters on Cap Ferrat! *Scandaleux.* I can tell you one thing, Monsieur Pine. We go straight to the police in Saint-Jean, and after this, there will be no further dealings with Holtz." He smiled at Cyrus, who was shielding both canvases with his jacket. "Naturally, I would be much happier if there were one less forgery in the world."

"Indeed," said Cyrus. "Absolutely. See your point entirely. Nico?"

The Dutchman sighed. He leaned over to Cyrus

and selected a canvas. He brought it close to his face, kissed it, and, with a backward jerk of his arm that threatened to capsize the boat, flung it over his shoulder. It landed flat and bobbed gently on the surface, the Woman with Melons staring up at the sky as water washed across her face.

"I hope to God that was the right one," said Cyrus. But he said it to himself.

Look for these and other Random House Large Print books at your local bookstore

Berendt, John, *Midnight in the Garden of Good and Evil*
Brinkley, David, *David Brinkley*
Brinkley, David, *Everyone Is Entitled to My Opinion*
Carter, Jimmy, *Living Faith*
Chopra, Deepak, *The Path to Love*
Crichton, Michael, *Airframe*
Cronkite, Walter, *A Reporter's Life*
Daly, Rosie, *In the Kitchen with Rosie*
Dexter, Colin, *Death Is Now My Neighbor*
Flagg, Fannie, *Daisy Fay and the Miracle Man*
Flagg, Fannie, *Fried Green Tomatoes at the
        Whistle Stop Cafe*
Gilman, Dorothy, *Mrs. Pollifax, Innocent Tourist*
Guest, Judith, *Errands*
Hailey, Arthur, *Detective*
Hepburn, Katharine, *Me*
Koontz, Dean, *Sole Survivor*
Koontz, Dean, *Ticktock*
Landers, Ann, *Wake Up and Smell the Coffee!*
le Carré, John, *The Tailor of Panama*
Lindbergh, Anne Morrow, *Gift from the Sea*
Mayle, Peter, *Chasing Cezanne*
Michael, Judith, *Acts of Love*
Patterson, Richard North, *Silent Witness*
Peck, M. Scott, M.D., *Denial of the Soul*
Phillips, Louis, editor, *The Random House Large Print
        Treasury of Best-Loved Poems*
Powell, Colin with Joseph E. Persico, *My American
        Journey*
Rampersad, Arnold, *Jackie Robinson*
Shaara, Jeff, *Gods and Generals*
Snead, Sam with Fran Pirozzolo, *The Game I Love*
Truman, Margaret, *Murder in the House*
Tyler, Anne, *Ladder of Years*
Updike, John, *Golf Dreams*
Whitney, Phyllis A., *Amethyst Dreams*